DAUGHTER OF WAR

SIOBHAN DAIKO

Boldwood

First published in 2015 as *The Orchid Tree*. This edition published in Great Britain in 2024 by Boldwood Books Ltd.

Copyright © Siobhan Daiko, 2015

Cover Design by JD Design Ltd.

Cover Images: Shutterstock

A CIP catalogue record for this book is available from the British Library.

Paperback ISBN 978-1-83633-132-2

Large Print ISBN 978-1-83633-133-9

Hardback ISBN 978-1-83633-131-5

Ebook ISBN 978-1-83633-134-6

Kindle ISBN 978-1-83633-135-3

Audio CD ISBN 978-1-83633-126-1

MP3 CD ISBN 978-1-83633-127-8

Digital audio download ISBN 978-1-83633-130-8

This book is printed on certified sustainable paper. Boldwood Books is dedicated to putting sustainability at the heart of our business. For more information please visit https://www.boldwoodbooks.com/about-us/sustainability/

Boldwood Books Ltd, 23 Bowerdean Street, London, SW6 3TN

www.boldwoodbooks.com

In memory of my parents and grandparents

AUTHOR NOTE

The characters in this story use language appropriate to the historical period, and are an accurate reflection of the era they are living in, which some readers may find upsetting. Thankfully, we now live in more enlightened times.

PROLOGUE
HONG KONG, DECEMBER 1948

Another deep blast reverberated from the ship's horn. The deck vibrated beneath my feet, my toes tingling as the engines grumbled to a stop. Hong Kong Island loomed, like an enormous whale rising into the morning mist. The salty tang of the sea filled my nostrils. Was I doing the right thing? On the water, the dark shapes had turned into ships, junks and sampans. I was home and there'd be no going back now.

My wrist touched the metal rail, cold as the Japanese executioner's sword, and my breath caught. A blade, glinting in the sun. A streak of silver. Shining. Silent. Deadly. Choking back a sob, I raked my nails across the scabs on my hands, scratching harder and harder until I could bear the pain no more.

The clatter of the anchor chain sounded, then the chug-chug of a motorboat. I leaned over the barrier. *Where is Papa?*

A young man in a navy-blue jacket strode up the gangway. 'Miss Wolseley?' He swept off his peaked cap. 'Lieutenant James Stevens,' he said, introducing himself. 'I'm here to take you ashore. Your father sent me.'

I forced a brief smile. Lieutenant Stevens was taller than me by a couple of inches, and his bronze-coloured hair had curled in the moisture-laden air; he was patting it down as if he wanted to draw attention to himself.

'There aren't any liners direct from Sydney. I'm sorry you had to come all the way out to the middle of the harbour,' I said.

'Not a problem. How long were you away?'

'Over three years. Since September 1945.'

'You were in Hong Kong during the occupation?'

'In the internment camp at Stanley.'

'I've heard about that place,' he said, frowning.

I flinched. I'd grown up in 'that place', behind barbed wire, suffering cruelty and starvation at the hands of the occupying Japanese, my heart frozen ever since.

So why come back?

PART I

1941–1945

1

HONG KONG, DECEMBER 1941

Kate

Bamboo by the side of the path rustles in the breeze, and a waterfall gurgles into a natural pond. My pony bends his head to crop the grass. I let go of the reins and slip off my riding hat. It's time for a rest now. Papa and I set out from the stables at Jardine's Lookout an hour ago and have ridden right round Happy Valley.

After dismounting, I run my hands over the smooth leather of my saddle. It's too small since my recent growth spurt; I'm such a beanpole.

I glance at my father. 'Papa, do you think I can have a new one for Christmas?' I give him my best smile.

'We'll see.' He winks and reaches into his pocket for his pipe. Papa is tall with wavy dark-brown hair, amber-coloured eyes and a high forehead. I adore him, of course, but hate taking after him. I wish I'd been born blonde and blue-eyed like my beautiful mama.

Rubbing Merry's dusty chestnut neck, I breathe in the sweet scent of equine sweat, one of my favourite smells. Of course, Papa will get me the saddle. Mama says I'm spoilt rotten and it's true. Only Papa does the spoiling, though...

'Come on, Kate,' he says. 'I need to change my breath.' Papa says that every week and it's become a joke between us. All he really wants is a change of scene. We remount and trot back to the stables, then stop off at the Yacht Club on the way home.

Papa goes to the bar, but I'm not allowed in there as I'm not sixteen yet. So I wait outside the clubhouse, soaking up the winter sunshine and watching the junks in the harbour, their sails open like giant butterfly wings. The creak of an oar echoes as the boat-woman selling orchids from her sampan sculls across the water. She ties up at the jetty and steps ashore with a bouquet in her hands. I smile at the baby, head lolling but fast asleep, in a sling on her back. Then I pay the woman and clutch the purple flowers. I'll give them to Mama, like I do every Sunday. And Mama will nod, smile, and hand them to one of the servants as usual. Far be it for her to put them in a vase herself.

The scrunch of foot falls on gravel come from the path behind, and Papa arrives. 'All the chaps have been called up for manoeuvres,' he says in a false jaunty tone. 'I was practically the only one in there.'

A prickle of anxiety creeps up my spine. With a sharp intake of breath, I grasp his hand.

'Nothing to worry about, dear girl.'

I relax my shoulders and walk with him towards the pier.

* * *

The next morning, air-raid sirens wail from Victoria City far below. I stifle a yawn, thinking it's only another drill. I pull at my maroon school jumper and lean back at the breakfast table opposite Mama and Papa. There's a geography test in this afternoon's class and I wonder if I've done enough revision.

A pang of disquiet disturbs my equilibrium. Something's different. The sirens are wailing longer than usual, and a droning sound echoes. The door bursts open and my amah erupts into the room.

I spot the chopping knife in my old nanny's hand. Ah Ho has been a constant presence for as long as I can remember, yet never have I seen her take a knife from the kitchen.

Rocking from one foot to the other, Ah Ho drops the blade onto the table and wraps her arms around her starched white tunic. 'Too much airplane,' she says in a shrill tone of voice. 'Too much airplane.'

Leaping up, I send my chair crashing to the floor. Hong Kong only has a few aeroplanes. Are these intruders American? Or even Chinese? Not Japanese, though. That would be unthinkable. Besides, everyone knows how hopeless their pilots are...

I rush through the wide doors and onto the veranda skirting the front of the house. Planes soar in a V-shaped formation above the harbour almost level with my eyes. Grey planes with a red sun under their wings. Something, I'm not sure what, spills from their bellies.

The echoes of explosions ricochet off the distant hills. Papa comes up and pulls me towards him. 'Bally hell!' His grip is so firm that it hurts.

My gut twists and the orange juice I drank at breakfast comes back up my throat, the sourness stinging my tongue. A flying boat is on fire. Coils of smoke rise from the airport. I clamp my hands to my ears, a sick feeling spreading through me.

Papa's hold tightens. I push my head into his shirt; I've recently turned fifteen and haven't done that for years. Then I lift my gaze.

One by one, the planes tilt their wings and peel off in the direction of China. 'Is it over?' I manage to ask.

Papa shields his eyes with a hand, his knuckles white. 'I hope so.' He leads me back into the house.

In the dining room, I run to Mama. She stands at the picture window, her lower lip trembling. I squeeze her icy fingers. 'They've gone.'

Mama blinks, takes her hands away and shakes her bobbed hair. 'Why on earth did you run outside?'

'I don't know. I just had to see. Where's Ah Ho?'

'She went to find Jimmy.'

He's Ah Ho's son, one year older than me and a close friend. Breathing in short, sharp bursts, I run after my amah.

Pray God Jimmy hasn't left for school yet!

* * *

The planes come back again and again.

I bite my nails. This can't be happening. Things like this don't happen. Yet, it *is* happening, and nothing will ever be the same again. I should be at school, not crouching in the sitting room with Jimmy, Ah Ho and my parents, in near darkness, as Papa has ordered the typhoon shutters to be put up on all the windows.

I can't stop thinking about the people I know who might be caught in the bombing: the flower seller at the Yacht Club; the grizzly old newspaper vendor on the ferry concourse.

Are they still alive? My heart thuds against my ribs. Are we all going to die?

'I'm frightened,' I whisper.

Ah Ho strokes my hair like she used to when I was little. 'Everything be all right.'

Jimmy pulls a pack of cards from his pocket. 'Let's have a game of Canasta to keep our minds off things.' He smiles his crooked-toothed grin. It's too dark to see, though, and impossible to concentrate. Jimmy puts the cards away and we sit in silence, arms drooping.

Every now and then, Papa turns on the radio. The same announcement is repeated each time. There haven't been any sightings of the Japanese Navy steaming towards Hong Kong. 'The raids are probably just a show of force,' Papa says.

Towards evening, the all-clear is sounded. But the typhoon shutters stay up.

* * *

That night, I toss about in bed, the sheets wrapping themselves around my body. I can't rid the image of the bombs dropping from my mind. If the planes come back tomorrow there won't be anything left of Hong Kong.

The sound of a radio wakes me; it must be morning. I pad across the corridor and push open the door to my parents' room. My feet sink into the deep pile carpet as I stare at the untouched tea tray on Mama's bedside table. My gaze passes to Papa. Why is he still in his dressing gown?

'The Japanese have bombed Singapore and the American base at Pearl Harbor in Hawaii,' Papa says in a shocked tone. 'And their bally troops marched across our border last night. Not to worry, dear girl, our chaps will soon see them off. But in the meantime, we have to be brave.'

I sit down heavily on my parents' bed. I will be brave. Of course I will. Just like the Hong Kong Volunteers and the garrison soldiers are being brave. They'll defeat the enemy and life will return to normal, won't it? The alternative doesn't bear thinking about.

2

CHARLES

Charles Pearce is helping his father load up their old Austin, standing on the front drive of a large house overlooking the Jockey Club in Happy Valley. He spent the whole of yesterday crouched with Ma and his little sister under the dining room table, ears ringing with the boom of explosions, the crash of falling masonry and glass. His stomach twisted into knots from the terror... the indescribable terror. Either the Japanese pilots thought the racecourse was a strategic target or they were useless at aiming for the oil tanks at North Point. This morning there's a lull in the bombing, thank God, and Pa has decided it's time for them to leave.

Charles turns round for one last look at his home, perched on the side of the hill with a gap next to it like a missing tooth. His neighbours' mansion has been reduced to a pile of rubble, the fate of its occupants unknown.

Hope we'll find shelter on the other side of the island...

After checking his shortwave radio is carefully stowed, Charles lifts his knapsack onto his shoulder and piles into the car with his little sister. Ruth's light brown curls are tied in bunches, the red ribbons unravelling, and fear is in her eyes. He gives her a hug. 'We'll be safe now.'

Pa gets behind the wheel and pushes back his thatch of white-blond hair. Ma sits next to him, dressed as ever in a cheongsam, her delicate face pinched with worry.

They take the road that cuts through the hills and leads to the south. Cresting the rise, they come to a roadblock. A European soldier points his rifle at the car and Pa winds down the window. 'Let us pass! We're British!'

'Japs are on the island. Didn't you know?'

Pa jerks his head back so fast his glasses fly off the end of his nose.

'We'll stop them here,' the soldier says as Pa contorts downwards to retrieve his specs.

Charles slumps in his seat. No point in worrying Ma and Ruth, but he thinks that the European was being a tad optimistic, given the fact that the British couldn't halt the Japanese advance on the mainland. *How wrong of them to have expected that an attack, if it had to happen, would have come from the sea...*

The road levels out by the Repulse Bay, and Pa says they should wait in the car while he goes and sees if they can stay here. The hotel faces the beach, its main section and two right-angled wings coming forward towards the ocean and forming three sides of a square, with the road, sands, and South China Sea making up the fourth side. Behind are steep slopes covered with trees and scrub undergrowth where Japanese soldiers might well be hiding.

Charles puts his arm around his sister again. He tells himself he mustn't let her see he's scared. She's only eight and a half and he's twice her age.

Pa emerges from the front of the hotel. 'There's lots of food, apparently. But not many staff. Just a group of Naval Volunteer officers and a few British families. I think this'll make a good bolthole. The senior pageboy is doubling up as receptionist and he's sorting out a couple of rooms for us.'

Moments later, Charles finds himself steering Ruth across the lobby behind his parents. The scent of polish from the parquet floor mixes with the aroma of freshly baked scones. It's just like he remembers from his last visit. It's hard to believe there's a war on.

A British woman, slumped in a rattan chair at the far end of the room, suddenly calls out in a braying voice, 'What're those Chinese doing? They've got no right to be here.'

Ma rolls her eyes and keeps walking. Charles swallows the bitterness in his throat. He carries both suitcases and shields Ruth from the woman's stare. Luckily Pa is half-deaf as well as being short-sighted, otherwise there'd be hell to pay. It's obvious that his father is English, just as it's obvious that Ruth and he don't look anything like the locals. Ma is Chinese, but she has finer features than the Cantonese, because she's from the north. Charles mutters to himself. *Shame they couldn't find refuge with their family in Macau...*

* * *

The following morning, he finds a seat by the open French windows in his bedroom. Ma has gone with Pa and Ruth to the lobby, saying they need to establish themselves.

Fat chance of that!

Charles picks up the Steinbeck novel someone has left on the desk. Sunlight filters through the window and he catches movement outside on the road.

He shades his eyes and discerns short, stocky men with black hair, fully armed and camouflaged with bits of leaf and grass, slouching in front of a garage.

Charles takes off his shoes, lets himself out onto the veranda, then down to a small lawn. *Better find out who they are.* He crawls for a short distance, rough prickly grass scratching his stomach, then freezes. *Damn!* The men are wearing peaked caps with red bands. *Japanese uniforms.*

He hides behind a low wall, his palms sweaty, and peers over the top. An enemy soldier is pointing a bayonet at six British men dressed in uniform. Another man, obviously an officer as he's wearing a sword, has started yelling and repeatedly slapping one of the Europeans on the face.

Heart pounding, Charles wriggles his way back across the lawn then runs to the dining room, where the British commander is taking tea with his men.

'There're Japs. On the main road,' Charles yells. 'They've got some of our chaps. I think they're going to kill them.'

'Stay here,' a Volunteer shouts, grabbing his rifle and charging off down the corridor.

Charles sneaks back to the veranda and flattens himself against the wall. On the other side of the lawn, the Japanese officer is still slapping the British soldier. The man stands taking the blows and doesn't even seem to notice them.

The Volunteer takes aim. Cold sweat spreads over Charles's body. He holds his breath. Bullets catch the Japanese officer on the side of his face and neck, spinning him around. His body crumples to the ground. Charles has never seen anyone killed before and nausea swells his chest. He retches, and half-digested porridge spews down his chin.

The rest of the Volunteers have apparently formed a cohort at the windows above. They open fire, aiming wide of the British. The unarmed prisoners scramble headlong into the garage with the enemy behind them, colliding and tripping each other up. Five of the Japanese fall in twisted heaps.

The surviving Japanese soldiers now poke their rifles out of the garage. Charles hides behind a pillar. A bullet whizzes past his left ear and his bowels become water. Shaking like a dog with distemper, he runs back to the lobby.

* * *

Three days later, he's sitting on a brick in a drainage tunnel behind the hotel, hiding with the rest of the civilians to avoid catching a stray bullet from the continuing battle. The chill seeps into his bones and the stench of rotting vegetation comes through the dank walls.

Ruth pulls at his trousers with one hand and points with the other towards the shadows, her eyes enormous. A huge rat is watching them, whiskers twitching.

'You're being so brave,' Charles whispers to her. The rodent scuttles away as he touches Ruth's arm. He regards the collection of people around them... English men and women, for the most part, and a handful of children.

'The Volunteers have decided to leave tonight,' one of the men murmurs. 'They're heading for Stanley Fort.'

Charles's stomach clenches. The soldiers are abandoning them; they probably realise this is a lost cause. Or maybe they think by staying they're putting the civilians in more danger.

With a crash, the trapdoor springs open. Charles jumps, but it's only the junior pageboy. The boy drops down, balancing a tray with water, coffee and food. *How has he managed to avoid getting shot?* Shrugging, Charles reaches for a sandwich and passes it to his sister.

They munch in silence. It has been easy to keep quiet for the twelve hours a day they've been hiding in the darkness. The periodic sound of gunfire above their heads would quieten anyone.

Unless help comes soon, however, capture is certain. Fear gnaws at Charles and grows stronger by the minute.

Night comes; it's too dark for the snipers to see their mark. He creeps back into the hotel with the others. They wait in tense silence on the first-floor corridor; anything could happen at any moment...

The senior pageboy and his assistant arrive with trays of supper. A sudden glow flickers on the windowpanes. Lights are flashing in the north wing. Charles can hardly breathe. Japanese voices and footsteps echo. A patrol is going from room to room. The enemy forces are battle-stained and most likely battle-maddened; they'll shoot everyone on sight, Charles realises. *Best to let them know that only civilians remain.*

He leaps up and calls out, 'There aren't any soldiers here!'

The door crashes open. Two Japanese men come in and point their bayonets directly at him. Everyone puts their hands up. The women let out muffled sobs. Charles stands still.

Keep calm! Don't let the side down!

The soldiers glare at him, then spin on their heels. There's a stunned hush.

Within minutes, the heavy tread of more soldiers comes from the other side of the door. The senior pageboy, eyes wide and jaw set, steps forwards to bar their entrance.

Pa rushes to stop him. Too late. An enemy soldier knocks the pageboy back against the wall. With a flash of steel, his commanding officer makes a jabbing motion and sticks a bayonet into the pageboy's chest. Blood spurts, the pageboy twitches and his eyes glaze over.

Charles glances at Ruth. She's still asleep on her mattress, thank God. But how will he ever forget what he's just witnessed?

There's no time even to think about it; the officer is barking orders to the civilians to line up. 'You must get ready. Tomorrow very early you go North Point.'

Charles gives his sister a gentle shake.

* * *

After packing what bags they can carry and snatching a few hours' sleep, Charles and his family troop outside with the other prisoners. He blinks in the early morning sunlight. A foul stench hits the back of his throat, like nothing he's ever smelt before: much worse than the stink of the drainage tunnel or even the raw liver their cook had once forgotten to put in the fridge. It fills the air, lodging in Charles's mouth, clinging to his taste buds and coating his tongue. He gags. The smell is coming from something or someone who's died, and he shouldn't look. A force beyond him, an intense curiosity, turns his head with an invisible hand.

He eyes the building opposite. Eucliffe mansion, property of a Chinese millionaire. Piles of bodies lie by the balustrade overlooking the sea. British prisoners. Tied together. Shot and left to rot. Ma snatches a couple of handkerchiefs from her bag. 'Cover your nose!'

During the long, dreary trudge up the hill, they pass the bodies of numerous soldiers, left unburied by the side of the road. Each time, Charles places himself between Ruth and the dead men. Each time, his stomach lurches. Each time, his anxiety grows.

At the top of the hill, he sets off with Pa and the other men; they'll march the rest of the way. Except, a Japanese soldier points his rifle and indicates his place is with the women and children in some lorries that will take them down to Happy Valley.

Charles frowns. *How old do they think I am? I'm in my second to last year at school, for God's sake...*

The roads are empty, but the sound of mortar-bombing reverberates in the distance. Hong Kong hasn't surrendered yet.

At an abandoned factory, the Japanese herd the prisoners into a wide ground-floor storage area lined with cans of paint. They give them water and sugar, the only food they've had all day.

'I'm hungry,' Ruth whines.

'Hush.' Ma opens her bag and rummages around. 'I wish we'd thought to pack something to eat.'

Pa and the rest of the men arrive. 'Let's spread our overcoats on the floor and make ourselves a den,' Pa says.

Even sitting on his coat, the concrete chills Charles's bones. 'It's Christmas Eve. Why don't we sing some carols?' he suggests. Tentatively, he starts on the first verse of 'O Come All Ye Faithful'.

A middle-aged couple, who've copied them and are sitting on their jackets, put their thumbs up and add their voices. 'Sing choirs of angels.'

The groups of internees around them join in, one after the other. 'O Come let us adore Him.'

Charles progresses to 'Hark the Herald Angels Sing' and they all chorus, 'Peace on earth and mercy mild, God and sinners reconciled.'

The Japanese soldiers start to shout and wave their rifles. The singing stops. *Have they understood the words?* With the carols, unity of a sort has developed among the prisoners; more likely, their captors simply wanted to spoil it, Charles thinks.

* * *

The next night, he sits with Ma, Pa and Ruth, clumped on the damp deck of an old ferry. *God only knows where the Japanese are taking them...*

The skyline is dark, yet Charles can make out the stately old colonial buildings lining the waterfront. He tucks his hands under his armpits to warm them. Waves slap against the side of the boat and the breeze feels as if it will pass straight through him.

At Kowloon pier, the gangplanks wobble under his feet as he takes Ruth's hand. Ma and Pa line up next to him on the concourse. Japanese soldiers wave their bayonets threateningly and then they march Charles and the others in the direction of Nathan Road.

Ruth nudges him and makes a face. 'I hope they give us something proper to eat. I didn't like that nasty cold rice and those turnips this morning.'

'I hope so too,' Charles says, smiling at his sister.

The streets, normally bustling with people, cars and rickshaws, are quiet. In five minutes they arrive at the back of the Peninsula Hotel, and a soldier ushers them into a hostel. On the fifth floor they're given a pokey room with only one bed, which they'll have to share with another family.

'This isn't the worst of it,' Pa says, his mouth twisting. 'I've just heard that the governor has surrendered to the Japanese.' He pauses. 'Happy Christmas!'

Charles lets out a hollow laugh. 'A *very* Happy Christmas.'

3

KATE

I turn the last page of *Rebecca*. Maxim de Winter is so romantic, even if he has committed murder. How odd that his second wife doesn't have a name. And Mrs Danvers! Altogether too creepy for words...

My parents and I have been confined to our house on the Peak since the surrender. Thank God I'm an avid reader, and Mama has said I can read my way through her collection of books, otherwise I'd be terribly bored. We've been waiting for the Americans to come and liberate Hong Kong for ever, it seems.

Papa's pipe smoke wafts across the room, making me sneeze. Then, out of the blue, I catch the sound of gravel crunching in the front courtyard, followed by footsteps scuffling in the hall. Strange at this time of the day, I think, given that it's nearly lunchtime.

My pulse suddenly hammers. A Japanese officer is standing in the doorway.

Mama's face has frozen... eyes wide, lips pressed together, cheeks colourless. This is our first encounter with the enemy face to face and certainly not unexpected, yet it's terrifying all the same.

Papa puts down his pipe, gets up from his armchair, and glares at the officer. 'What can I do for you?'

'You go Stanley Internment Camp tomorrow,' the Japanese man says, saliva spraying from his mouth as his tongue trips over the English words. 'All things will be good. Plenty food.' He fingers the sword hanging from his hip and smirks, his thin lips curling but his eyes expressionless.

I gape at him, trying to take in what he's just said. Stanley is a prison on the other side of the island where they usually send murderers. Why are they putting us there?

The officer puffs himself up, thrusts his chest forward, and points at Papa. 'Bow!'

Papa stands immobile and fixes his gaze on the opposite wall. Should I go up to him and whisper that he must bow if he doesn't want to get into trouble? But my feet are rooted to the floor. The second hand on the grandfather clock ticks through half a minute, and I hold my breath.

The officer shrugs, marches up to Papa, and slaps his face with a front-hand-back-hand motion. Slap. Slap. Slap. The sound plays in my head again and again like a stuck gramophone record. A trickle of urine wets my knickers; I put a hand to my mouth, my cheeks burning.

I shake myself. Finally, my legs obey me and I run to Papa. He wipes his moustache, grimaces and bows his head to waist-level. His eyes hold mine and he mouths the words, 'Steady, dear girl!'

The officer struts out through the open door, his long sword trailing behind him. Gravel crunches outside again and an engine races. Then silence. Even Mama, normally unafraid to have an opinion on everything, has been struck speechless.

I hug my father. 'Poor Papa. Look what he's done to you.'

'Stings a bit, but not to worry. I'll be all right,' he says, although a red blotch has formed on his cheek.

Mama moves from the sofa, as if in a trance, and dabs at his cut with her handkerchief. 'Did he say there'll be lots of food in Stanley? We've almost run out here.'

'We've run out of more than food.' Papa's voice is quiet. 'Japs have locked up practically all the British. They only let us stay up here on the Peak this past month while they sorted out where to put us all.' He shakes his head. 'I suppose we'd better start packing.' He turns to the crystal decanters on the mahogany sideboard, pours himself a large whisky, and swallows it in one gulp.

I don't want to pack; I don't want to leave my home and go to a prison. Yet there's no getting out of it. I walk from the room, my feet dragging. 'I'm going to see Ah Ho.'

After changing my underwear, I cross the small courtyard dividing the staff quarters from our two-storey house. My mouth trembles, but I clamp my jaw firm. It's the way things are done in our family.

Mama and Papa are keeping calm, so I'll do the same and not think about what might happen.

I run up the steps and pull open the door to Ah Ho's room, breathing in the comforting scent of camphor from the White Flower Oil she rubs into her knees to ease their stiffness. 'Where will you go after we've gone?'

'Back to China,' Jimmy says from his chair by the window.

'But the war's there too, isn't it?' I tug at my hair and tuck it behind my ears.

'Our village won't interest the *Law Pak Tau*.'

'What?'

'Turnip heads.' Jimmy giggles. 'That's what we call the Japanese because they're always eating turnips.'

I pick up a handful of rice from the sack in the corner and let the starchy grains trickle like tiny pebbles through my fingers. 'Where will you live?'

Jimmy sits forward and places his elbows on his knees. 'Uncle will take us in.'

Ah Ho has perched dejectedly on a stool; she must be dreading going back to the subsistence life of a peasant in the old country.

I take the seat opposite Jimmy. 'Will you be able to go to school?' Papa has paid for Jimmy to attend an English-speaking school in Hong Kong since he turned six.

'I'll need to work in the fields with my cousins.'

A picture comes into my mind of farmers in the New Territories, near the border with China, planting rice in the paddy fields, their wide-brimmed straw hats shaped like giant toadstools, backs bent double as they push the seedlings one after the other into the water-sodden soil. I make fists of my hands. Jimmy is a brilliant student; he shouldn't have to give up his studies.

'It won't be for long, you know.' I try to inject a note of optimism into my voice. 'The Americans will rescue us.'

Jimmy's lips have formed a straight line; it's clear he doesn't believe me.

'I heard my parents talking about it,' I say. 'Papa said the American Air Force is the best in the world and they'll help us. Once they've recovered from Pearl Harbor, of course.'

Ah Ho has got up from her stool and is pulling a metal comb through her long, thin, black hair before fastening it in a bun. She strikes a match and lights a joss stick. The fragrance is so familiar that my breathing slows. If only I could stay here with the people I love, where I've grown up, where I feel safe.

I get to my feet and face the small statue of the Bodhisattva of Compassion by the door, running my palms up and down the smooth white soapstone. *The Japanese will be defeated quickly. They have to be.*

Ah Ho puts her hands together and bows three times. With a sigh, she reaches under her bed for a battered leather suitcase.

'Let's go out to the garden,' I say to Jimmy. 'Some fresh air will cheer us up.'

On the other side of the terrace, Papa and Ah Woo, the houseman, are digging a large hole. 'What are you doing?' I go and ask them.

'Burying the family silver. We can't let the Japs get their hands on it.'

'We're just heading down there.' I point to the path leading to the tennis courts.

The oleander bushes sway in the breeze, and a gecko scuttles back into its hole in the hedge. I pluck a heart-shaped leaf from the orchid tree and crush it between my fingers; the dried-pea scent teases my nostrils and the garden walls enclose me as if I were already imprisoned.

'Jimmy, let's have one last walk around the Peak.' I pull him gently towards the front gate and meet with little resistance. He probably wants to escape for a while as well. I look behind to check we haven't been seen. Papa would have my guts for garters if he knew I was leaving the compound. 'Why are the Japanese going to lock us up?' I ask Jimmy. 'We could stay up here and not be any trouble.'

'They won't allow white people to look down on them.'

His dark eyes briefly meet mine before he glances away. I throw my arms around him, but he's so unyielding I might as well be hugging a rock.

I let him go, and he follows me along the pathway circling the summit of the Peak. The pungent sweaty socks smell of the subtropical forest wafts into my nose. Brushing past a plant with leaves as large as elephants' ears, I peer through dense clumps of vegetation hanging like interwoven ropes.

The houses, apartments and office blocks below are so small they could be mistaken for children's toys. Where are the junks and sampans usually clogging the harbour? Only Japanese ships have anchored in its depths. Kowloon Peninsula, a narrow piece of flat land, juts out into the deep blue-green water. Bare hills, with ridges like dragons' backs, form a framework to the scene. When will I see it again?

I spot a British anti-aircraft gun battery nestling halfway down the western flank of the Peak. I grab Jimmy's wrist. 'Come on. There's no one about. Let's see if we can find any mementos.'

Slabs of concrete and metal bolts stick up from the ground, and there are gaping holes blasted through the thick walls of the brown and green camouflage-striped buildings. Shards of broken glass shimmer in the sunlight. I pick up a spent bullet. A cold gust comes from nowhere and I shiver. Someone or something is moving in the azalea bushes below...

'A soldier died when this place came under heavy artillery fire,' Jimmy says, glancing from left to right. 'He's probably a ghost now.'

My scalp prickles. A spirit is definitely lurking in the untamed vegetation, ready to cause chaos. We'd better get out of here...

'Come on!' Jimmy breaks into a run and heads back up the hill.

I follow his zigzag footsteps. The soldier's ghost will be hungry for revenge, but Jimmy once told me that spirits can only travel in straight lines. Jimmy and I will be safe enough.

Our feet pound the dusty track, and scores of butterflies rise from the feathery fronds of the wild banana trees. We sprint past the high broken-glass-topped walls of the mansions of the wealthy, and into our own open gateway at number eight. We barge through the front door, still uselessly guarded by stone lions, then turn right into the kitchen.

Ah Ho looks up from chopping vegetables. 'Wah! Missy angry no can find you.'

'Sorry, Ah Ho.' I peck my amah on the cheek.

Jimmy goes to his room, and I head for the sitting room, sliding across the polished parquet floor to where my mother sits at her antique rosewood desk.

I shift my weight from one foot to the other. 'What are you doing, Mama?'

'Making lists of the items we won't be taking into the camp. So we can check they're still here when this nightmare is over.' She puts her pen down. 'Where have you been?'

'Jimmy and I went for a walk.'

'What were you thinking of?' Mama's voice is sharp. 'Don't you realise how dangerous that was? I've just heard from Ah Ho that Jap soldiers have been doing unspeakable things to women, and even girls of your age. Jimmy wouldn't have been able to protect you.'

'I'm sorry. I didn't think.' And it's true; I never thought for a moment I might be in danger.

'Well, you'd better start thinking. Do something useful and take the silver-framed photos to the garden!'

Outside, the trench full of silver opens up like a grave and I stare at the cup I won last year in a show-jumping competition. My eyes sting. It's been fifty days since I've seen Merry. Fifty days since the enemy came across the border. Fifty days waiting to be rescued.

I wince, no longer able to keep what Mama said about the Japanese out of my mind. I can guess the unspeakable things they are doing to women. A shiver of fear rips through me. Will they do unspeakable things to women and girls like me in Stanley?

4

KATE

I'm standing in the doorway of Ah Ho and Jimmy's room. It's the morning after the Japanese officer's visit, and my voice, clogged with emotion, sounds almost strangled to my ears as I tell them I've come to say goodbye. I stare through the window at a bank of fog obscuring the view of the garden. Chilly, damp and miserable, it fits my mood.

Ah Ho perches on her stool, her bottom spilling over the edges. 'You sit down.' She pats the seat of the rattan chair next to her.

I lower myself and give Jimmy a half smile. 'All packed?'

He nods and hands me a small package. I tear it open to reveal a jade bangle. 'To bring you luck,' he says.

I slip it onto my wrist, the emerald-green stone cool against my skin. 'It's beautiful. Thank you. I've got this for you.' My words are even more choked now. I give him my treasured copy of *Murder on the Orient Express*. 'My mother will give you some of her jewellery, too.' I squeeze Jimmy's hand. 'You can sell it.'

Ah Ho sobs, open-mouthed, and enfolds me in a warm embrace. I rub my cheek against the starched white tunic. My throat tight, I swallow hard. I won't let myself cry. Instead, I give my amah a hug and say, in my brightest voice, 'I expect we'll be together again before too long.'

An hour later, I stand on the forecourt with my parents and Ah Ho. The houseboys are loading up an open-topped lorry: mattresses, an electric hot plate, three suitcases full of clothes, my mother's jewellery, and a large hat box. The Japanese officer ordered Papa to arrange our own transport to the camp.

Mama, dressed in her mink coat, hands Ah Ho a gold necklace. 'To be sold. Divide the money between you.'

I fling myself into my amah's arms. 'I'll miss you,' I sob. The tears run freely; I can't stop them.

Ah Ho kisses me noisily on the cheek. 'I come back by and by.'

My lower lip wobbles, but I stiffen it.

* * *

Heading south, the lorry trundles its way around the craters and potholes left by the shelling. Soon we reach the Repulse Bay Hotel, where I would have Earl Grey tea and cake as a special treat with Mama before the war came. The fountain at the front of the building is dry and the palm trees gracing the gardens have a downhearted look, as if they've seen things they'd rather forget. At the checkpoint further up the road, a Japanese soldier barks questions to our driver. My heartbeat races, but the soldier waves us on.

We pass the resort where I used to spend lazy summer days swimming and paddling a canoe from the rocks with my best friend Mary. Mama and Papa would play bridge with Mary's parents and drink gin slings in their beach hut, only occasionally venturing into the warm waters of the South China Sea. Mary left for Australia with her mother last year. We've been writing to each other faithfully. How will I keep in touch with her now?

There's the lido! It's boarded up. What did I expect? Hardly likely the Japanese would keep it open for Sunday afternoon tea dances...

Gears grinding, the lorry climbs the headland then follows the road down to Stanley Village. Fishing boats line the beach like deckchairs. Old men sit in doorways smoking their long pipes; dogs and children play in the dust; washing hangs from bamboo poles.

Such a different world to the Peak...

On the other side of the police station, we cross a short strip of land leading to a small peninsula. Barbed wire blocks the road. Japanese guards verify our names and let us through.

'Out you hop,' Papa says in a false bright voice. 'I'll go and find out where we're to be billeted.'

A cold wind whips my coat. I shiver and stare at a queue of people waiting by a building. Papa returns with a short bald man. 'This is Mr Davies from the Housing Committee.' His voice is still chirpy. 'We're in the Indian Quarters.'

'What are the Indian Quarters?'

'Where the Indian prison wardens used to live. The Japs have kept some of them on as guards, but they're living in the village now.' He smiles briefly. 'I don't think it's going to be too bad here, after all. The camp is governed by the internees. Housing, food distribution and medical care are all run by our chaps. Apparently, the Japanese just oversee things and send in supplies.'

Papa folds his gangly frame into the lorry. I heave myself back into the cab with Mama and the bald man, all squashed in together. We pass a school and stop by a block of garages. The last two hundred yards we struggle on foot, carrying our luggage down a few steps, past a small mosque, and along a stony path. Piles of rubble greet us.

'How can you put us here?' Mama drops her hatbox. 'These buildings have been bombed to bits.'

'Not all. Follow me!' Mr Davies leads us up a narrow stairwell. 'I've managed to get you a room to yourselves.'

'A room?' Mama echoes.

We enter a two-storey block facing the sea and climb the stairs to the first floor. 'Our youngest amah has a room bigger than this. And she has the room all to herself.' Mama places her hands on her hips and, with a shudder, eyes the grubby grey walls. Her face looks as if she's swallowed a mouthful of sour milk. 'Is there a bathroom?'

'A washroom with a tap,' Mr Davies says apologetically.

I glance at the lavatory. We have similar loos at home for the staff, and Jimmy calls them 'crouchers' on account of having to squat over a hole. If Jimmy can manage, I'll manage too. But Mama must be beside herself with disgust.

Mr Davies waves his arm to the left. 'There's a sort of kitchen as well.' A single tap graces a small annex; it's like no kitchen I've ever seen. Filthy stone benches line the sides; there's neither a stove nor any cooking utensils. A balcony runs along the front of the flat, and an open passage through the back.

I peer into the adjacent room. 'Who lives there?'

'The Chambers and the Morrises. They seem to be out at the moment.'

'Two couples sharing?' Papa stands on the tiny floor space next to the mattresses, our suitcases piled on top. He frowns. 'For God's sake, my dear chap. That's a bit poor.'

'This is the best I can do for you. You've no idea what things have been like. In other parts of the camp, where the rooms are bigger, we've had to pack even more people in. Some of the apartments and bungalows have between thirty-five and forty-five souls with only one bathroom.' Mr Davies sighs. 'There's no water for the toilets either, so they're overflowing with sewage. And there aren't any beds. People have been reduced to sleeping on the floors. No provision has been made whatsoever. It seems the Japs had no idea there'd be so many of us to deal with.'

'We should've been rescued before now,' Mama says, opening a suitcase. 'What *are* the Americans doing?'

'We've discussed this, Flora.' Papa puts his arm around her. 'They've got other fish to fry. I shouldn't think it will take them too long to defeat the Japs, though. We must have faith, that's all.' He turns to me. 'Stay and help your mother unpack, dear girl, and I'll go back up the hill with Mr Davies to fetch our other stuff.'

Papa returns momentarily, and I hover by the cases. This room is far too small. How will we cope all cooped up together? I've never spent more than an hour a day in both my parents' company before now.

'Thank God we've brought a few basics.' Papa takes a hot plate into the so-called kitchen. 'I presume the electricity is working.'

'It's the only thing that does,' Mr Davies says.

Mama trips over one of the mattresses and falls against me. 'Must you get underfoot, Kate?'

I step out of the way. 'Can I go and explore outside?'

'If you're careful,' Papa says. 'But don't go near any Japanese!'

* * *

I stroll along a narrow trail leading away from our quarters and around the headland. Waves smash against the shingle below and the scent of the sea fills the air. Sunlight sends a gleam of gold across the turquoise swell of the ocean. I contemplate the stark beauty of the hills on the other side of the bay; the vegetation slopes down like the wing of a bird to rocks hugging the shore. A long coil of barbed wire hangs halfway down the cliff like a hedge of thorns. Despondency washes over me. I'm imprisoned, and no amount of beautiful scenery will compensate for my loss of freedom.

I walk until I reach an asphalt road. White-washed prison ramparts rise up, cut by massive black gates. There's a glint of steel. A Japanese sentry is standing straight-backed, his rifle pointing skywards. Heart thudding, I duck from view.

A path edges the jail gardens and I follow it, the grass soft and springy under my shoes. I climb through a thicket of conifers. A clearing opens up ahead, dotted with old tombs spread out as if they were on a plate of enormous Swiss rolls and up-ended biscuits. I sit on one and recover my breath. Twiddling my plaits, I take in my surroundings. Then I stop and listen. Someone's coming up the hill, swinging his arms and heading straight for me...

I scramble down from the tomb, crouch behind it, and peer over the top. A tall boy, dressed in a light blue jersey and beige slacks. He's definitely not a Japanese soldier; he's wearing civilian clothing. Getting to my feet, I study his dark brown hair and European features. The boy has oriental eyes, though, and they widen with surprise as he catches sight of me.

'Oh! You made me jump,' he says. 'What are you doing here all by yourself?'

'Exploring. I'm Kate Wolseley. Who are you?'

'Charles Pearce. You're a bit young to be wandering around on your own, aren't you?'

'No, I'm not. I'm fifteen,' I say, indignant. 'How old are you?'

'Seventeen. I'm sorry. You look younger.'

Heat whooshes up to my face. If only I'd worn my hair loose

around my shoulders, instead of tied up in the schoolgirl plaits that make me appear like a twelve-year-old child...

Charles sits cross-legged beneath a tree and I lower myself down next to him, the ground hard and dry. I gaze in silence at a junk tacking its way across the bay, sails flapping, then take a quick peek at him. He's terribly good-looking, like a young Clark Gable minus the moustache. I smile, but he only gives me a brief glance before looking away again.

He seems a bit standoffish.

'How long have you been in Stanley?' I ask. *Might as well be friendly.*

'Three weeks. We were interned in a hotel before that. Where were you?'

'The Peak. We only got here an hour or so ago.' I stare at the crumbling tombs. 'How old is this cemetery, do you think?'

Charles hugs his knees. 'I went to St Stephen's, the school here,' he says in a proud tone. 'So I know the history. It's where they buried the soldiers killed by pirates, or those who died of typhoid fever and malaria in the last century.' A spark of warmth flashes in his eyes. 'I'll show you around the camp if you like.' He pushes himself to his feet. 'It won't take long and you'll be able to get your bearings.'

I follow him down the hill, past a mound of freshly dug earth. 'What's that?'

'A communal grave, I'm afraid.'

I let out a gasp. 'What happened?'

'St Stephen's became a hospital towards the end of the battle. Stanley held out until Christmas morning, you know, shortly before the Governor surrendered.' Charles falls silent; he seems to be considering what to say next. 'Some drunken Japanese soldiers went on a rampage and did terrible things... and afterwards the survivors buried the dead here in this cemetery.'

A chill slices through me. 'Have the Japanese killed anyone else since you arrived?'

'No, we've been left alone and the Camp Commandant isn't even Japanese. He's Chinese.'

'I thought Japan was at war with China.'

'My father said a group of Chinese spies had wanted to get the British out of Hong Kong and they're in the pay of the Japs. It's one of the reasons they defeated us so quickly.'

'Oh.' *How strange! I've always thought of China and the colony as separate entities, not part of the same country at all.*

We pass the building where I saw people queuing earlier. 'This used to be the Prison Officers' Club,' Charles says. 'Now it's a canteen where you can buy expensive groceries. Problem is, there isn't much available.' He pauses. 'I say, would you like to meet my parents and sister?'

Without waiting for a reply, he sets off towards the sinister-looking gates of the prison, then down a short road on the left, and I practically have to run to keep up with him. 'They call these the Married Quarters.' He indicates with his hand. 'It's where the married British prison warders used to live. Our "mess" is very over-crowded, unfortunately, and we're sharing with another family.'

In the front room of the first-floor flat, a European man sits on a camp-bed and squints at me through the thick lenses of his glasses. 'Hello,' he says, running a hand through his hair. 'Welcome to Stanley! Have you just got here?'

'We were allowed to stay on the Peak for the past month. But now we're in the Indian Quarters.'

A petite Chinese woman with porcelain skin and a chignon appears at my elbow. 'I'm Charles's mother. So sorry they've put you in those awful flats. They seem to have reserved the worst billets for people from the Peak.'

A girl, sitting with a book in her hands, looks up from a camp-bed. Her curls are tied in neat bunches, and her eyes tilt attractively in her oval face.

'This is my sister, Ruth,' Charles says.

I smile at the girl then gaze around the room. On the far side, an Englishman, a Chinese woman, and three children of junior school age sit despondently on camp-beds pushed against each other on the bare parquet floor. 'This place is bigger than ours. But at least we've got ours to ourselves,' I risk saying.

'Well, that's a blessing.' Mrs Pearce lets out a short laugh. 'Please can you ask your mother if she has any clothes to spare? The nights are freezing and we can't get warm, although we all huddle together. We weren't able to bring much with us.'

'Yes, of course.' Mrs Pearce's dress is hanging off her, and her husband's face has a sunken look. 'I'd better be off. I'll see what my mother can find.'

Charles is sitting with his sister on the camp-bed and isn't looking in my direction. What to make of him? He was pleasant enough while showing me around the camp, but now I feel like a stray puppy he's found and handed over to his parents. Picking my way between the beds, I head out of the door. I've been exploring for at least an hour and my parents are probably worried.

I stroll along the path overlooking the shore. A Sikh guard stands with a rifle in his hands, ignoring me as I edge past him. Below, the sea has turned choppy in the breeze. I knuckle the hot tears from my cheeks; I've held them back all day. Now I'm alone, I let them flow.

I'm so afraid.

'But I will be brave,' I repeat like a mantra all the way back to the Indian Quarters.

5

SOFIA

Sofia Rodrigues gazes out of the back window of her father's limousine at the people on the pavement. There are so many more beggars out on the streets of Macau since Hong Kong surrendered to the Japanese. She reaches into her pocket for a coin. It's the last of her pocket money, but she doesn't mind. Father will give her more when she asks for it. The car slows at the pedestrian crossing, and she tosses the money into the tin held out by a thin Chinese man dressed in filthy grey rags.

With a sigh, Sofia eyes Natalia, sitting next to her, and smiles to herself. Her governess isn't what you'd consider a beauty, with her beaky nose and cropped grey hair. No man would have wanted to take Natalia for a concubine, like Father took Mother a year before Sofia was born. A lump of regret swells in her throat. Poor Mother. If only she'd had the chance to know her. But then she wouldn't have Natalia, would she?

Sofia grasps her governess's hand. 'I can't wait to get to Uncle's. He promised he'll take me out on his biggest junk.' Uncle's junk-master taught her how to handle the sails on her own last autumn, the day after she turned thirteen. She hugs herself, excitement sparking in her chest. That sense of freedom she gets when the boat runs before the wind is so intoxicating...

Natalia squeezes her fingers. 'You worked hard on your studies this morning, my Sofichka. I hope you enjoy the sail.'

Sofia smiles. 'French verbs, English translations, algebra. I feel as if my head is about to explode. I need some fresh air.'

The car pulls up in front of Uncle's mansion, a two-storey structure with a balcony running along the side. She's seen pictures of the buildings in Portugal, and Uncle's house wouldn't look out of place there.

Sofia shrugs. She's never been to Portugal; she's only ever visited China, Hong Kong and the Philippines. The British colony is her favourite. She can speak perfect English, albeit with a slight Russian accent, thanks to Natalia, and she loves to go to the cinema in Hong Kong to watch British and American films. She and Natalia always stay in the Peninsula Hotel. Unfortunately, they won't be able to do that any more.

Sofia huffs to herself. *I wish the Japanese hadn't come and spoilt everything.*

The Japanese seem to be everywhere, despite Macau, like Portugal, being neutral in this war. She's seen Japanese soldiers and the *Kempeitai*, their secret police, parading openly in the streets. Sofia doesn't know any Japanese and she doesn't want to, either; she's heard stories about what they've done to people in China...

She clambers out of the car. Natalia has some errands to run in the old town, where she'll stock up on necessities before the shops sell out of everything. 'See you later, darlink,' her governess says.

Uncle's houseman opens the front door, and Sofia strides across the marble-tiled hall to the sitting room. She stops dead.

Why is Uncle still in his long robe? He should be in the trousers and jacket he normally wears sailing.

'Ah, my child,' Uncle says in the Chiu Chow dialect he has taught her to speak with him. He pushes up his sleeves, his fat cheeks wobbling. 'I tried to telephone earlier, but the lines are down. I'm afraid we can't set out for the open sea. Those turnip heads have put a blockade around Macau and it's too dangerous to try and slip through in broad daylight.'

'I was really looking forward to our sail.' Sofia tries to keep her voice from sounding sulky. She can't stand sulkiness; she stopped being friends with Jennifer Kwok last year because the girl was so moody. 'What can we do instead?' Sofia asks.

'Well, I can take you to lunch at the Solmar, if you like.'

Sofia claps her hands. 'My favourite restaurant.'

Uncle is good to her, but then, most people are. There're only a couple of people she can think of who aren't, and one of those is Leo, her half-brother. She can guess why that is, and there's nothing she can do about it.

* * *

She gets home early to the white villa overlooking the old town of Macau. The afternoon stretches before her with no lessons and the prospect of boredom. Sofia hates being bored almost as much as she despises moodiness. She decides to go and find Father.

The walls of his study are panelled in teak, and a Tientsin carpet, decorated with a floral medallion surrounded by blue and purple birds and animals, covers the centre of the room. She feels the thickness of the pile through the thin soles of her house shoes and inhales the scent of beeswax. Father is sitting at his mahogany desk. She crosses the room, and he looks up from his papers.

'*Querida!*' Father likes to use the Portuguese term for 'beloved', although they usually speak Macanese with each other. 'You're back early.'

'Uncle says sailing is too dangerous because of the Japanese. I wish they'd just go and leave us alone.'

'Not much chance of that, I'm afraid. Your uncle is quite right not to put you in danger and I'm glad you're back in time. We have visitors this evening. Japanese visitors.'

'Father! How can you invite the enemy here? We should have nothing to do with them.'

'Hush, *querida*. All is not as it seems. We must be polite to them, that's all. They've children of thirteen and twenty like you and your brother. In import-export, like we are. Be nice to them!'

'All right.' Sofia gives a sigh. 'But what about Leo?'

'Oh, he's very enthusiastic. He's been telling me we should side with the Japanese. He says European civilisation has come to an end and it's the turn of the East now.'

'Typical of Leo to say that.'

'Now, now, I want you two to get along this evening for once.'

'I'll try.' And she will. She always tries to get along with Leo...

'Is your wife going to be there?'

'I wish you'd call her Mother.'

'Siu Yin isn't my real mother.' Sofia moves to stand by Father's side. 'My real mother wouldn't look down her nose at me all the time.'

Father puts his arm around Sofia's shoulder. 'Just ignore her. She's quite harmless, really.'

Sofia wriggles out of his embrace. She won't tell him of the snide remarks about her illegitimacy, or the surreptitious pinches that really hurt. She hates tale-tale-tits even more than she despises moodiness and boredom.

'Shall we have a game of chess before getting ready for dinner?' She tilts her head.

'And have you thrash the living daylights out of me?' Father says in an indulgent tone. 'Why the devil not?'

* * *

A large rosewood table dominates the centre of the dining room. Sofia shoots a glance at Leo, placed opposite, and eyes his tall muscular frame. He has the physique of a grown man and appears far more Portuguese than Eurasian. A throw-back, everyone says, despite Siu Yin being half English on her father's side and Chinese on her mother's.

Chinese blood. That's what links them. But they're a hotch-potch, really. Sofia has the light skin and dark brown hair Father inherited from his Dutch great-grandmother. Would she like to be just one nationality? No. That would be so boring...

Leo's voice cuts into her thoughts. He's preaching about Asian nations achieving independence from the Western powers – one of his favourite topics. There's an arrogance to Leo's nature that simmers beneath the surface. Being the legitimate son of the head of the Macau Consortium must give him a sense of power in the territory. She's seen how he behaves towards others – lording it over them like a big-headed prince – but she's also seen a side to him that few have.

When she was small, he used to carry her around on his shoulders, and he taught her how to swim almost before she could walk. Yet something happened as she grew older, and it turned him against her. Shrugging to herself, Sofia gives her attention to the Japanese girl on her left. Her name is Michiko, and she's delicate-looking, with an oval face, straight nose, and bow-shaped mouth. 'What a pretty Kimono,' Sofia says in English. She doesn't speak Japanese, and neither do Father, Siu Yin nor Leo. That doesn't matter – the Kimuras speak fluent

American English. Apparently, they used to live in San Francisco...

Michiko thanks Sofia politely, then remains silent. Sofia gives up trying to draw the girl out and, suppressing a yawn, studies the boy opposite her. Supposedly her age, he's shorter than she is and uglier than his sister, who's actually quite pretty. The boy is shovelling rice into his mouth as if he hasn't had a square meal in weeks. But from his general chubbiness, it's probably only been a couple of hours...

Sofia fidgets and turns her gaze towards the mother. Mrs Kimura is an adult version of her daughter, and Father is having more success at drawing her out than Sofia is with Michiko. The older woman giggles at something Father has said and hides her mouth behind her hand.

Siu Yin's chatter drifts across the table, and Sofia peers at her stepmother. Siu Yin sits at the far end between Mr Kimura and Leo, tossing her glossy black hair and pouting her lips like some Hollywood actress. They're discussing pearls, of all things. *Pearls!* Father's business is in gold. Sofia glances back at the Japanese woman. Mrs Kimura is wearing a long string of the largest pearls she's ever seen. Could that be the import-export business Father was talking about? Why else would he invite a Japanese family to dinner?

Sofia picks at the grouper fish on the plate in front of her; she's not hungry. One large meal a day is enough, and she ate more than enough at lunch with Uncle. Boredom nudges at her. Threading her fingers through the lace at the edge of the table-cloth, she lets her mind wander.

Father said all was not as it seemed. What if Mr Kimura wasn't really a businessman? She's been reading about spies in the Helen MacInnes novel *Natalia* got for her to improve her English. It would be fascinating if Mr Kimura was a spy. Natalia said Macau is full of Japanese spies...

6

KATE

An acrid stench of overflowing latrines hangs in the air, contrasting with the loveliness of sunbeams dappling the leaves on the orchid trees beside the main road as I stroll towards the canteen. We were cramped in our shabby room, and Mama has all but pushed me outdoors this morning.

We've been in Stanley for over a week now, and I've already found out that the few classmates I had are here too. Classmates, not friends. My friends left Hong Kong at the same time as Mary.

My step lightens as I spot Ruth and Charles, who are crouching behind a shrub up ahead. They're staring at a group of European men loading tins onto trucks, parked by warehouses everyone calls 'godowns'. Japanese and Indian guards sit on the side, smoking.

'What's in those cans?' I whisper to Charles.

'Food.'

'If they've got all that food, why can't we have some?'

'It's *our* food. The government stashed it here before the invasion, so we'd have enough to last through a blockade. The Japs've stolen it just like they've stolen Hong Kong.'

I shade my eyes. Each time a guard happens to look the other way, I notice that one or other of the European men manages to drop a couple of tins into a ditch. A man with sandy coloured hair has even tied his trousers at the ankles and is filling the improvised bags with sugar from some torn sacks. The man motions to the guards, goes behind a bush not far away (probably pretending to go for a wee), and empties the sugar into a sack he must have hidden there earlier.

Moments later, the working party moves off and Charles beckons.

I scramble down to the trench after him and collect as many cans as I can squirrel up my jumper: a jar of strawberry jam, a tin of potatoes, and a can of bully beef.

Charles does the same, and Ruth shoves a packet of biscuits into her pocket.

I follow them up to the road, but suddenly a blond boy jumps out from behind the godowns and blocks my way. 'Hand that over,' he barks.

I stand firm. 'Finders keepers!'

'Those men are in the Hong Kong police,' the boy says with a sneer. 'You've pinched some of their loot.'

'Rubbish!' Charles glares at him and plants his feet wide apart. 'It's the police who've done the stealing. By rights they should share everything. Anyway, there's plenty left down there. We've only helped ourselves to what we can carry.'

The boy raises his fist and aims a punch at Charles. Before the blow can land, Charles moves to the side and leaps into the air, floating for an instant. His whole body twists and he kicks the boy's fist away.

My mouth opens like a goldfish at feeding time. I've heard about Chinese fighting skills, but I've never seen them in action before now.

'I'll get you later,' the boy shouts, backing away. He scrambles down the bank towards the gully and disappears behind the warehouses.

Charles stares after him. 'I've seen him hanging around with some rough-looking boys. I wonder who he is?'

I shrug. Charles looks at me and shrugs back. He turns and I fall into step beside him, eager to take my pickings back to the Indian Quarters.

* * *

The chill of winter has given way to the mugginess of spring. I stretch as early morning sunshine slants through the curtain-less windows and moisture fills the air. Running my tongue over the beads of perspiration on my upper lip, I taste the salt. It's late May now, and in a fortnight or so the heat and humidity will be ten times worse.

If only I could be back in my comfortable room at home where I used to sleep under a ceiling fan, its whirring lulling me on hot summer nights. Beneath my mosquito net, I'd imagine I'd been cast adrift on the ocean under a transparent sail. In Stanley, though, I'll soon be melting in a pool of sweat and covered in mosquito bites. I give a shudder; those mosquitoes might carry malaria.

Rolling over, I feel my bones rubbing the stone floor through my lumpy mattress. I was dreaming of breakfast: bacon and eggs, toast and marmalade and a cup of steaming hot tea. I'm fed up with the congee we have here; I always gobble the rice and water porridge too quickly and am left desperate for more. The last time I had an egg was at Easter, when the guards gave us one duck egg each. Far from doing unspeakable things, the Japanese officers keep their distance and, when we first arrived, the guards even gave us kids sweets from time to time.

That was ages ago, though, and now they don't give us anything. Hunger knots my belly and I glance at my parents snoring on their mattresses. They've both lost so much weight; their bodies have shrunk inside their clothes.

I creep out of bed and pull on a cotton dress. It hangs off my skinny shoulders but feels cool and comfortable. Outside, the early morning queues for hot water have already formed, and the blond boy from the godown raid has staked a place at the front of the line. Yesterday I discovered his name, Derek Higgins, when a teacher called it out. There are lots of teachers among the internees, and the adults said we children were running wild, so, a week ago, a group of parents decided to organise classes. A good thing too, otherwise I'd be terribly bored.

Derek is fluent in Chinese, and I've seen him spending his time with the Eurasian boys whose mothers married English policemen. He shuffles up to me barefoot now. Like most of the kids, I discarded my shoes weeks ago. I rub my feet on the gravely soil; they've grown as tough as leather.

Derek approaches, runs his hand through his wispy blond hair and glowers at me. 'Where're you going?'

'None of your business!'

I turn on my heel and head up to the cemetery, where I sit behind a headstone and think about Charles. I've got into the habit of standing close to him in the supper queues, yet he hardly talks to me and I'm too shy to start a conversation. Whenever I see him, my heart rate flutters, and I want him to like me as much as I like him.

My experience with boys has been limited to those spotty English youths who fumbled the odd kiss at school dances, and

Jimmy, of course. He used to call me his *mui mui* – 'little sister'. I didn't mind Jimmy thinking of me like that; he was like a brother to me. But I want Charles to think of me differently. How differently? Not like a sister, that's for sure…

I peer around the gravestone. Derek Higgins is coming up the hill, looking from left to right. What's he up to? *Ha!* If he thinks he'll find me, he's got no chance. I gather up my dress and prepare to run. The chorus of birds in the thicket abruptly falls silent and the hairs on the back of my legs tingle. There's a presence behind me. A ghost? The cemetery is probably full of them…

I spin around and give a gasp. A huge cat is crouching in the undergrowth, two eyes burning bright in a striped face, enormous whiskers quivering.

Oh my God! It's about to spring.

I leap to my feet, yelling, 'Tiger! Tiger!'

'Don't be stupid,' Derek shouts, chasing after me. 'There aren't any tigers in Hong Kong.'

I reach the main road. Charles is carrying a pail of water in my path, and I run full pelt into him.

'Steady.' He drops the bucket. 'This is hot.'

I suppress a smile as Derek runs off.

Charles rubs his hands on his shorts. 'Why was he chasing you?'

'I told him I saw a tiger and he didn't believe me.'

'Are you sure the light wasn't playing tricks with your imagination?'

'I saw a real tiger. I'm positive.'

'Right.' He picks up the bucket and, balancing his weight carefully, looks at me. Our eyes meet, and my heart beats so loudly I'm sure he can hear it.

I wave Charles off just before a shout echoes. Papa arrives, his lips pinched together. He wipes his forehead and puffs. 'Where have you been? I've just found out one of the guards has been mauled by a tiger.'

Should I run after Charles and warn him? But Papa grabs my hand and leads me away.

7

KATE

I scoop the last of the watery rice from my breakfast bowl, then push myself to my feet. The sooner I get my chores done, the sooner I'll get away from the claustrophobia of this room.

I pick up my parents' bowls and take them through to the kitchen. Papa has bought lye soap from an enterprising man in the flat below. It's made of wood-ash and lard. Problem is, the man used too much wood-ash in the recipe. The soap is caustic and irritates my skin, but it's all that's available to clean my teeth, wash my body and do the dishes.

I pour the water I queued for at daybreak into a pan and scrape off a few flakes of soap with a knife. After immersing the breakfast bowls in the suds, I rub them with a threadbare cloth, then take them back to the room. The soapy water will be used to flush the stinking toilet later.

'A rumour's going round some people have managed to escape,' Papa says, wiping his moustache and looking up at me.

'I thought Stanley was escape-proof?' Mama mutters from her mattress. 'I mean, we're surrounded by barbed wire and sea on three sides. And the road to the village is always guarded.'

'It appears two or maybe even three groups of people have managed to sneak out, my dear. They're going to find it difficult, for it's a long way to unoccupied China.'

'The Japanese would be punishing the rest of us if it were true. Just like they made those policemen they caught after the godown raid march up and down the main road for hours.'

'Not necessarily. They can't be seen to lose face.'

'I'm surprised no one's formed an escape committee.'

'We've enough wretched committees in this place, Flora,' Papa retorts with a huff.

'Has anyone formed a committee to catch the tiger?' I ask. I haven't told my parents about how near I came to ending up as the animal's supper.

'No, and you're not to go anywhere near the thickets, Kate,' Papa says.

* * *

A week later, I find myself strolling along the path leading to the old football field in front of the Indian Quarters. The village green, as everyone calls it, bears little resemblance to those traditional village greens in my childhood picture books. A scrappy piece of land, parched and forlorn in the dry weather when we first arrived, is now a soggy mess in the wet of summer. But at least it's somewhere for the children to play.

I've been cooped up with my parents all morning. They've been bickering over which piece of Mama's jewellery they'll sell next to buy some food. I press my lips together. What does the jewellery matter if we starve to death? All we get at every meal are a few tiny pieces of bad fish or a couple of teaspoons of stringy, watered-down buffalo stew. And the rice is contaminated with particles of grit, cockroach droppings and the occasional weevil. *Disgusting!*

I give a sudden start. A ginger-haired man is approaching from the opposite direction. The sun has turned his skin a fierce shade of pink and his legs, poking out of his baggy shorts, remind me of a couple of raw sausages.

'*Aalreet*, little lass?'

'Sorry?'

'Forgetting me manners,' he says in a thick accent. 'Name's Bob.'

'I'm Kate. How do you do?' I offer my hand.

'Well as can be expected,' he says, smiling.

'Where are you from in England?'

'Newcastle. What are you up to?'

'Nothing much. In fact, I'm terribly bored.'

'You don't need to be bored. I'll show you a game I used to play when I was a lad. We called it "cannon".'

Bob takes an empty can from his pocket. There's a picture of pears on the label and I deduce he must have been involved in the police raid on the godowns. After setting the can down in the middle of the field, he scrabbles around for a couple of sticks. Then he takes a tennis ball from his other pocket. 'It's a competition, you see,' he says. 'The person who throws the ball and knocks the tin and the sticks over with the fewest tries is the winner.'

I have three turns before I manage it, then I give the ball back to Bob. 'Your go.'

But a sudden shout rings from the entrance to the Indian Quarters. 'Kate, come back this instant!'

'Sorry. I've got to rush. Can we play again another time?'

'Aye, whenever you like, pet.'

At the bottom of the staircase, Mama grabs me by the arm and marches me inside. 'Stay away from him! He's not our sort of person.'

My jaw drops. 'What do you mean?'

'He's one of those rough northern policemen.'

'I thought he had a different accent. I couldn't understand him at first.'

'I don't want you mixing with the likes of him. Why they had to move those policemen over here from the college buildings is beyond me.'

'They repaired those blocks on the other side of the village green, and I expect they were very crowded in St Stephen's.'

'The committee could have installed families. That would have been much more suitable.'

'I think you should be glad the policemen have moved here.'

'Really? And why's that, young lady?'

'Well, they've taken over all the heavy jobs for a start.'

Mama watches me with raised eyebrows, but I carry on. 'Everything's much better organised. We don't have such long queues for food.'

Mama sniffs.

'And they've pasted V for Victory signs on the glass doors,' I say. 'I think we should be grateful to them.'

'Are you answering me back, Kate?' Mama taps a foot. 'Because if you are, I want you to stop right away.'

'Well, I think you're being a snob.'

Before she can respond, I run from the room. On the stairwell I career into Papa, nearly knocking him over. I don't stop to apologise. Glancing at him, I find I have nothing to say. If I told him about Bob, he'd back Mama up. He gives in to her more than ever these days.

I stomp along the pathway that edges the coastline, then slow down and listen to the sound of the sea. Shutting my eyes, I imagine the waves washing through me, rinsing away the squalor of Stanley, and carrying me back home to the Peak and my memories of life before the Japanese arrived.

* * *

Two nights before the bombs started falling, Papa and Mama went out to what was called the 'tin hat ball' at the Peninsula Hotel, organised to raise money to buy a bomber for Britain. Freed from my mother's strict rules about what I could and couldn't eat, I squatted at the staff table for some *chow fan*.

Whenever Papa and Mama went out to socialise, which happened often, I would have supper with the servants and my parents never found out. They didn't like Chinese food, but I loved it.

I picked up a piece of crunchy pak choi with my chopsticks from the communal dish. The oyster sauce dribbled down my chin and I put the bowl to my teeth and shovelled the steamed rice in, coolie style, letting out a burp like the locals to show how much I'd enjoyed my food. (Only once did I ever make the mistake of belching in front of Mama – a topic of scorn for days.)

Ah Ho was sitting on a low stool. Her bottom, as ever, overflowed the edges. She smiled and her gold teeth shone in the low light. '*Bo*,' she said as she always did. *Full up*.

I listened to the staff gossiping about the other families on the Peak. I wanted to join in but would have needed to sing different tones in their tricky language, which changed the meaning of words, and I usually sang them wrong – even though I understood most of them.

Anyway, Papa and Mama didn't like me to speak Cantonese. *Not the done thing*, they said, which was one of their favourite expressions. And Jimmy always laughed when I made mistakes; his command of my own language was perfect.

Later on, upstairs, I slipped into my mother's dressing room, I remember. The wardrobe overflowed with the latest fashions, copied from *Vogue* by expert tailors. I tried on one of Mama's ball gowns and sprayed behind my ears with Chanel No. 5. Preening in front of the mirror, I smoothed the silk against my skin then smeared my lips with a bright red lipstick. But Ah Ho came through the door, scolded me, and sent me to bed. I smile to myself now as I recall bridling and thinking that Ah Ho still treated me like a child.

* * *

I'd give anything to be treated like a child by my amah now. I stare towards the horizon. Where is Ah Ho? Have she and Jimmy managed to get to their family in China? There's no way of knowing. I've visited that huge country beyond the Kowloon hills only once. When I was nine, my parents took me with them on a trip to Shanghai. It was a cultured vibrant city in comparison with sleepy provincial Hong Kong. After I returned to the colony, though, I was relieved to get back to my routine of school from Mondays to Fridays and weekends at the riding school.

Thinking about my favourite pony, I twirl my jade bangle and taste the salt of my tears. Did Merry survive the bombing? Who's looking after him now? Sniffing, I brush my cheeks with my hands and make my way down the path. Crying for my old life is a sign of weakness I won't allow myself to feel.

Back at the Indian Quarters, Papa gets me to clean out the foul-smelling lavatory as a punishment for being rude to my mother. The smell of the backed-up sewage makes me retch, and I must force down the usual revolting lunch.

I set off for school in the afternoon. On the village green, my foot knocks against a pebble. Only it isn't a pebble; it's a boiled sweet. Sneakily, I take off the cellophane wrapper and pop it into my mouth.

The sugar has an immediate effect, making me quicken my step and run up the road. By the time I arrive at the school hall, my energy has gone and guilt has taken its place. It was selfish of me to keep the sweet for myself instead of sharing it; I'll never be able to admit what I've done.

Later, after Professor Morris has set our Latin homework, I go to sit next to Charles. He'll probably ignore me as usual. But I'm surprised when he smiles and says, 'I'm sorry I didn't believe you about that tiger. It's just that normally we don't have them roaming the countryside.'

'That's all right. I wouldn't have believed it either if I hadn't seen it.' His eyes meet mine and a thrill of pleasure courses through me. 'This morning,' I continue, 'I met one of those policemen who've moved into the block next door to ours. He was showing me how to play a game called "cannon". Only my mother won't let me talk to him again.'

'Well, that's easily fixed.' Charles appears thoughtful for a moment before smiling his lovely smile, the smile that makes my heart rate flutter. 'I'll ask him to teach me the game and show it to the rest of the children. If everyone's out there playing with this man, your mother won't have a leg to stand on, will she?'

'Mama never does anything but complain and get my father to run around after her. She's impossible.'

'I suppose she's finding it hard to get used to how things are here.'

'I suppose.' I giggle, grab his hand, and pull him to his feet. 'Come on! School's finished. Let's take Ruth along to find Bob and we can put your plan into action!'

8

KATE

'They've caught that tiger,' Papa says at supper three days later. 'An Indian guard shot it.'

I put down my spoonful of cold gritty rice. *Thank God.* 'Do you know where it came from?'

'Apparently, it escaped from a circus. A fellow who used to be a butcher at the Dairy Farm will skin it. I wonder what tiger meat tastes like? No doubt only the Japanese will get any.'

Papa said the Japanese rations were almost as poor as ours; of course they'll get first sniff of the tiger meat. Mama must be shuddering on her mattress at the very thought of being interned with a butcher. In Hong Kong society she wouldn't have dreamt of mixing with a tradesman.

'How many of us are here in this camp, do you reckon?' I ask my father.

'At the latest count, two and a half thousand British, sixty Dutch and nearly four hundred Americans, but the Yanks are due to be repatriated any day now.'

'Lucky them.'

'They're about to be exchanged with some Japanese nationals

in the United States.' Papa stands and makes a move to gather our empty plates, then quickly sits down again. 'Bugger! All the strength's gone in my legs.'

'It must be the bad diet,' Mama says from the other side of the mattress. 'Too much polished rice and no greens. The hot weather doesn't help.'

'We'll be able to cool down a bit this morning.' I deliberately insert cheerfulness into my voice. 'Don't forget we've been given permission to swim!'

Papa's mouth twists grimly. 'You go with the young ones, dear girl. It's too much of an effort for your mother and me.'

* * *

After doing the washing up, I line up with the rest of the children. Two guards march us down a path edging the bleak white walls of the prison. Dense scrub hides the beach from sight until we walk through a clearing in the canopy.

'Last one in's a rotten tomato,' I call out, the sand hot between my toes.

I pull off my shorts, and wade into the ocean in my knickers and a thin cotton vest. Charles and Ruth come up behind me, laughing and splashing. Treading water warm as a bath, I gaze at starfish splayed on the sandy seabed. 'Why don't we swim over to those rocks and look for sea urchins? My father told me we can eat them.'

Charles sets off at a crawl and I follow, swimming at a slower pace. Light-headed from the exercise, I clamber onto the sun-warmed rocks, then stretch out and half-close my eyes.

Low clouds of humidity cover the tops of the distant islands. The sun beats down through the haze and dries me in minutes. The pungent smell of seaweed, left by the retreating tide, tickles the back of my throat. The gentle waves make a sucking sound as they slosh against the barnacles. I brush salt from my arms and stare out to sea, picking at the mosquito bites on my legs. 'I wish we could swim like fish and get away.'

'My mother saw four of the men who'd escaped. They've been caught.' Charles squints in the sunshine. 'They were in an open lorry being driven into the prison. We have a good view from our balcony and Ma hardly recognised them. She said they were like walking skeletons.'

'How terrible!'

'Ma was angry. She thought the men had been starved.'

There's the sound of splashing echoes, and Derek Higgins swims towards us with two of his friends.

Charles pushes himself to his feet. 'Go away! We were here first.'

Derek heaves himself onto the rocks. 'We've got as much right to be here as you.'

He leers at me and I look down. My tiny breasts are visible through my damp vest. How humiliating! Derek speaks in Cantonese to the other boys; they snigger and make a lewd remark about my nipples.

Charles lets fly a stream of Chinese insults, calling them stupid pigs. My cheeks burn as he turns to me. 'I'll race you back to the beach,' he says quickly. 'It's too late to look for sea urchins. I can see the guards waving their rifles. They want us to go.'

On our way back up the hill, I keep my arms folded in front of me. I should have packed a swimming costume when we left the Peak. But I never thought I'd need one; the Japanese were supposed to have been defeated before now. Worst of all, Charles must have seen me semi-naked and realised what a kid I am...

* * *

After school, I hurry home, finish my Latin translation, and queue for supper. The adults have organised a concert on the lawn in front of the canteen. Everyone says it's a sham. A team of Japanese press and cameramen are making a propaganda film about the supposedly cheerful, contented detainees enjoying their treats.

I sit next to Ruth on the grass in the front row. Charles is on the other side of his sister. Best to ignore him; I'm still too mortified about what happened earlier. Frogs croak and crickets screech in the thickets that separate the canteen from the Indian Quarters, almost drowning out the crash of waves on the rocks below. There's a tang of fresh vegetation in the air. Rain in the early evening threatened to cancel the performance and the ground is still moist. The new moon cuts a thin sliver of silver in a sky that billows with stars.

Leaning back on my arms, I watch the show. The Japanese have commandeered a floodlight from somewhere to illuminate the stage and mosquitoes and moths flutter in the beam. A group of internees are singing and dancing to music performed by the orchestra, a collection of people who've managed to bring their instruments into the camp. They play discordantly, but no matter; the tunes distract us from the filming.

'This is stupid,' I mutter. 'How can those cameramen and journalists think we're happy to be locked up here?'

'Let's show them!' Charles says, giving the V for Victory signal.

'Yes,' Ruth joins in.

Impossible to ignore Charles now. I giggle and make the sign with my fingers. The other children swiftly catch on, even Derek Higgins. Seconds later, most of the adults lift their hands in the air as well.

The photographers stop filming and Yamashita, the newly arrived Japanese Commandant, jumps up from his seat. 'No more entertainment for one month,' he spits, hopping from one foot to the other and reminding me of a manic tap dancer.

A heavy crunch of boots comes from the path behind, and I twist around. Where's Charles? I hold back a scream. A squat Japanese guard is pointing his bayonet straight at him. 'You! Boy! Very bad!'

9

KATE

It's late August, and waking up after a hot, mosquito-infested night, I think about Charles with a heavy heart. Something changed in him when he spent twenty-four hours in the prison. He's been avoiding me, and he doesn't even come swimming these days.

I crawl off my mattress and stare at a small black speck, marooned in the middle of my sheet. 'What's that?' I point it out to Papa.

'A bed bug, I think.' He comes and squashes the insect between his thumb and forefinger. 'What a stink!'

I wrinkle my nose and inhale a whiff of bitter almonds. 'Yuk!'

Papa fetches a knife from the kitchen, turns the mattress over and cuts a hole. Thousands of slimy, shiny, black bugs squirm about as if irritated at being disturbed.

I back away, revolted. Then I stare at the spots on my legs and my stomach heaves. 'I thought these were mosquito bites. Do you think they're in your beds as well?'

'More than likely,' Papa says.

Mama pulls up her nightdress and examines the angry, red

wheals on her thighs. Her face blanches. 'I can't take any more,' she sobs.

'There, there.' Papa pats Mama on the back. 'I'll find something to get rid of them and, in future, we'll make sure we do spot checks.'

I clutch my sides as hysteria builds up. 'Ha, ha, ha spot checks!'

'Be quiet, you silly girl!' Mama slaps me on the arm. 'We can't let the neighbours know we've got bed bugs. Whatever will they think?'

'If we've got them they've probably got them too. Stay here with your mother, Kate, while I look for a container.'

He manages to find an old kerosene tin, which he trundles over to the Police Block. I strip the beds as my mother looks on helplessly.

Half an hour later, Papa returns with Bob.

'Aalreet, pet?' Bob says, before pouring carbolic acid from the tin into our only pan. Then he mixes it with the water I collected in a bucket from yesterday's rainfall. 'This is how we deal with the little beasties.' He chuckles, setting the pan on their hotplate.

The water boils, and Papa soaks all three mattresses with the liquid. Afterwards, Bob and I haul everything over to the balcony. Mama stands to the side and fixes the policeman with a frosty stare.

'I'll be off now,' Bob says. 'Got to get back to me rice-cooking shift. Did you hear the good news?' He smiles. 'There's been a delivery of pork today. Disease has struck a pig farm in the New Territories and they've killed the whole herd. We'll have some meat with our dinners for once.'

Papa shakes Bob's hand and thanks him for his help. I go with my friend to the bottom of the stairwell and watch him saunter across the village green. He stops and throws a 'cannon ball' with a group of children. *Such a nice man.*

Back indoors, I help Papa scrub our sheets in lye soap, wishing my mother had shown more gratitude to Bob.

'How low we've sunk that we can even contemplate eating diseased pig,' she says.

Papa heaves a sigh. 'I'm sure the colonial vet will check to make sure it's safe.'

Mama glowers at him. 'We'd have been able to buy more bully beef from the canteen if you hadn't used up our spare cash for your wretched tobacco.'

'There hasn't been any tinned meat available for ages, my dear. Do you think I'd put my pipe before your needs?'

'I can't understand why you still insist on smoking it when it's so difficult to get hold of tobacco. I've managed to give up my cigarettes. You should give up your pipe too.'

'Having a smoke clears my airways. You don't want me catching TB again, do you?'

Papa's TB was the reason my mother and I were still in Hong Kong when the Japanese came. Most of the British women and children, including Mary and my other school friends, had been evacuated eighteen months before then, as the authorities must have thought war was on the cards. If it weren't for that TB scare, Mama wouldn't have had the excuse to stay and nurse him back to health.

Papa never believed the Japanese would attack, so he was happy for her to remain, and I didn't want to go without her. Mama fed him huge amounts of protein and moved his bed onto the veranda so that he could breathe plenty of fresh air. When fog came to the Peak, she bundled him into the car and drove him to Repulse Bay with the window down. Gradually he recovered, but his poor health kept him out of the Volunteers.

Thank God for that. If he'd survived the battle he'd be in the POW camp in Kowloon instead of with the civilians in Stanley.

I put the sheets in the sun. The mattresses are still airing on the balcony, so I sit on the concrete floor. A sudden rumble of thunder echoes, and I run outside. Rain is peeling across the village green and people are scurrying for cover. 'Everything is soaked,' I mutter.

Mama bursts into tears. 'I can't bear it.'

'Maybe tonight we'll sleep in soggy sheets stinking of carbolic acid,' I say. 'But it's better than being eaten alive by bed bugs, don't you think?'

'Cheer up!' Papa puts his arm around Mama and gives me a disapproving look.

'I'm sorry,' I stutter. 'I didn't mean to be rude.'

* * *

From then onwards, Papa's pipe makes rare appearances. Often, I see him stooping and picking up cigarette butts discarded on the roadside. He retrieves the small amount of tobacco then mixes it with dried sweet potato leaves and toilet paper, which is really just a piece cut up from *The Hong Kong News*.

Our neighbours soon give every indication that they're struggling with the over-crowded conditions as well. They've divided their room in two by hanging a curtain made from old sheets stitched together. It's difficult sharing the kitchen and bathroom with the Chambers and the Morrises. Squabbles often break out between us about who's responsible for cleaning the communal areas.

I remember the first time I met the two couples last February. After an awful meal on our first night, I stood with my parents at the door dividing our rooms. A grey-haired man staggered to his feet. 'Professor Stuart Morris, Hong Kong University,' he said, introducing himself.

A mousy-looking woman got up from her camp bed. 'And I'm his wife, Diana.'

I spotted another woman, fast asleep under a large, brown overcoat. A tousle of wavy red hair spread over the pillow.

'You'll excuse my wife if she doesn't get up?' A burly man with a dark beard stepped forward. 'She's suffering from a nasty cold. Bloody freezing here at night. We're the Chamberses, by the way. Tony and Jessica. Welcome to Stanley!'

'We've met before, haven't we?' Mama held out her hand. 'Weren't you at the Boxing Day Meet last year?'

'Of course. How could I forget?' Tony Chambers clapped his hand to his forehead.

His brown eyes smiled at me. 'You're something of a horse-woman, young lady, aren't you?'

'I can't stand the creatures myself,' my mother chipped in. 'They make me sneeze. Well, we'd better get on. Things to do. No doubt we'll meet again.' She laughed in an almost hysterical way and I followed her through the door, wishing I could have shrunk to a speck of dust on the floor. I was so embarrassed.

Since then, I've seen a lot of Professor Morris at school as he's my Latin teacher, and his wife helps out with French. But the Chambers keep themselves to themselves.

* * *

After the discovery of the bed bugs, Mama has become obsessed with getting me to do the cleaning. She makes me scrub our room from wall to wall every day then wash the clothes. I rub them with lye soap until my hands bleed.

'Off you go,' Mama says to me one morning after I've done my chores. 'I can't be doing with you getting in my way any longer.'

'I haven't been getting in the way. I've been slaving over a scrubbing board. Why can't you do more of the work?'

Mama lifts her hand. I duck, and before my mother's palm can reach its target, Jessica Chambers pokes her head around the door. 'Your daughter has stolen my lipstick.'

Mama's eyes widen. 'I beg your pardon?'

'Well, who else? The children are out of control, thieving left, right and centre.'

Mama gives me a stern look. 'Did you take Mrs Chambers' lipstick?'

I cross my fingers behind my back. 'Of course not.'

'Let this be a warning to you, Little Miss Butter-Wouldn't-Melt-In-Her-Mouth,' Jessica spits. 'If ever I catch you in our room, you'll receive the severest of punishments.'

'Please don't threaten my daughter!' Mama holds up her hands. 'I know my Kate's mixing with all *sorts* of people in this place, but she wouldn't steal.'

I slip out of the room, pretending that I'm leaving. But I hide behind the door instead, peer through a crack, and listen.

'Perhaps it wasn't her. The lipstick went missing yesterday. Not the first thing that's been taken,' Jessica says, the colour rising in her cheeks.

Jessica Chambers has red hair. Not auburn, but deep red. Bob's hair is distinctly carroty by comparison. Jessica is probably only in her mid-twenties, no more than a decade older than me, yet despite the months of living in close proximity, Jessica hasn't spoken a word to me until this morning, which makes her fair game. Jessica left the lipstick in the kitchen, so what did she expect? She should have looked after it. I turn around and march out of the flat.

On my way down the stairs, guilt ties my stomach up in knots. Maybe Mama is right and Stanley is changing me? I wouldn't have dreamt of stealing anything when I lived on the Peak. I put my hand into the pocket of the shorts I stitched together from an old rice sack and clasp the tube. I'd wanted to make myself look pretty for Charles. Now I'll have to bury the lipstick on the hillside behind the cemetery, so no one will discover I took it.

I reach the village green and stop dead in my tracks as I notice Derek Higgins bent double, surrounded by a circle of European men, his white buttocks bared and receiving six of the best from a thin bamboo cane.

The cane comes down with a thwack, and I wince. Thwack, thwack, thwack. I screw my eyes shut. *Poor Derek!*

Finally, the men leave and Derek comes up to me. 'Why were you watching? I suppose it seemed funny to you.'

'No, it didn't. Not at all. I just wanted to make sure you're all right. Who were they and why were they beating you?'

'They're from the camp tribunal. They caught me with some cans of bully beef I took from the canteen a few weeks ago. I only took them because my dad is sick.'

'Gosh! I wouldn't like that to happen to me. Do you think they'd beat girls as well?'

'More than likely. Better than the Japanese gendarmerie, I suppose. Well, I'd better get back to my parents. Dad's ill with beriberi because he's not getting enough vitamins. That's why I took the cans.'

'Oh. I'm sorry. Did you know the Red Cross are sending comfort parcels? Hopefully they'll arrive soon and we'll have some extra food.'

I say goodbye to Derek and go up to the cemetery. Burying the lipstick, I promise myself I won't take anything that belongs to someone else ever again. What was I thinking of?

* * *

Three weeks before my sixteenth birthday, in early September, Papa rushes into the flat and exclaims with a wide grin, 'The parcels are here. Come on, we're to line up at the canteen.'

We wait for an hour in the queue, Mama complaining all the while that she has things to do. What these things might be, I can't imagine. After all, I'm the one doing all the washing and cleaning.

'Flora, my dear, you don't want to be shut up indoors on such a lovely morning,' Papa says, laughing. 'It'll do you good to get some fresh air.'

I look up at the sky, so blue and cloudless it seems to go on forever. For once, the high hills separating Stanley from the other side of the island are clearly visible, not hidden by warm mist.

Finally the Red Cross representative hands us two packages each. Back in the Indian Quarters, Mama says we don't have enough storage containers so we can indulge in an instant feast. I open my parcel. *Chocolate tablets, biscuits and packets of sugar!* I tear the wrapping off a Dairy Milk bar and stuff every morsel into my mouth, savouring the sticky sweetness. A sensation of fullness settles in my belly, which lasts the rest of the day. For the first time in months I go to bed without feeling hungry.

* * *

The sound of screaming wakes me, and I blink in the morning sunshine. What's wrong with Mama?

'There are ants crawling on everything,' she wails.

'I'll boil up some water and pour it over them,' Papa says in his 'keep calm' voice.

After he's done so, Mama eyes the soaked sugar. 'All ruined now. What a mess!'

I help Papa scoop up the soggy packets then glance at my mother. *Oh, no!* Her face has a yellowish tinge.

* * *

That night, a moan comes from Mama's mattress. 'I feel terrible. I've got the shakes and my head is killing me.'

Papa grabs a thermometer and takes her temperature. 'Good God! It's one hundred and three,' he says, shaking the glass tube. 'I'll fetch some water, my dear.'

I hold Mama's hand as she groans and thrashes about, then I help Papa sponge her down. Finally, Mama slips into a fitful sleep, but neither Papa nor I can bear to leave her side.

'I'll take your mother to the camp hospital,' he says at daylight. 'They'll be able to help her. She's probably got malaria and they must have some quinine.'

Regret surges through me as I remember my harsh words to my mother. I stay in and do my chores. How long has Mama had malaria? No wonder she's been even more standoffish than usual these past weeks. I scrub the toilet. How to make sense of things? Mama doesn't resent me. She's just ill, that's all...

Papa returns at lunchtime. 'They'll keep her under observation for a few days,' he says, his expression grim. 'Your mother would like you to visit.'

I follow the path around the headland to arrive at a three-storey red-brick building. Mama is in a ward on the second floor with four women and their new-born babies. I perch beside her on the bed.

'Oh, darling,' she says. 'It's dreadful. I can't sleep with all the noise. Can you read to me, please? I need distracting.'

There's a bookshelf in the corner of the room where I find a well-thumbed copy of *Gone with the Wind*. I read aloud as my mother dozes.

'"Let's don't be too hot-headed and let's don't have any war. Most of the misery of the world has been caused by wars. And when the wars were over, no one ever knew what they were all about."'

Then, later: "'Hunger gnawed at her empty stomach again and she said aloud: As God is my witness, and God is my witness, the Yankees aren't going to lick me. I'm going to live through this, and when it's over, I'm never going to be hungry again. No, nor any of my folks. If I have to steal or kill – as God is my witness, I'm never going to be hungry again."'

I put the book down and wipe Mama's forehead with a damp cloth. She has to survive this. She has to...

At the end of the week, Mama is released from the hospital. Her fever peaks and troughs, but Papa says she's out of danger. Even so, my chest aches with worry.

I hope he's right; he has a tendency to be over-optimistic.

* * *

On the morning of my birthday, I roll out of bed onto Mama's mattress. She pulls an item from under her pillow. 'I made it myself.' Two of Papa's silk handkerchiefs have been stitched together to make a halter-neck top. 'I hope you like it.'

I take the gift and hold it against my chest. With joyful tears, I hug her and receive a peck on the cheek in return.

'And I've got this for you.' Papa hands me a bar of chocolate. 'It's the last one from my comfort parcel. I managed to save it from the ants.'

If anyone had told me a year ago that I'd be happy to receive such gifts, I'd have thought they were mad. My usual presents are cashmere cardigans, Yardley's toiletries, riding accessories and books. When the war is over and life returns to normal, I'll appreciate every single thing I used to take for granted. It's a firm promise I make to myself.

Once dressed, I go to queue for hot water. I took over the duty months ago, supposedly to give Papa some respite. But, actually, it's a way for me to see Charles, even though he usually ignores me. This morning, though, he waves and I go up to him.

'Happy Birthday,' he says, touching my arm.

My heart dances. I've known him for about eight months now, but I never tire of looking at him. I've such a crush. If only I were more gown-up and knew what to do where boys were concerned...

How can I tell if he likes me as much as I like him?

* * *

On 30 October, I'm at an informal celebration for Charles's eighteenth birthday on the village green. Even though the weather is still hot, the air has turned dry and we no longer drip with sweat. Mrs Pearce has saved her flour rations and has baked a sponge cake in one of the communal ovens. I've contributed the few biscuits I kept from my comfort parcel.

The Red Cross deliveries indeed included some desperately needed medicines. Only a small amount of quinine, though, which has to be shared among countless others. Mama sits on the edge of the group, sipping watered-down tea. She's receiving Malaria treatment, but she's still weak.

I bite into the unaccustomed floury texture of the cake and lick my fingers. There were tears as I struggled to find something pretty to wear. In the end, I put on one of Mama's blouses. It's too big for me, though, and looks funny worn over my shorts.

I giggle at Charles; he's doing an impression of Professor Morris and has got his 'now for your Latin homework' saying spot-on. Out of the blue, a loud drumming noise echoes. I lift my eyes. A flock of silver planes is soaring above. I can just make out the stars of the US Air Force under their wings. 'Look! They've come to rescue us!' I squeal.

'They're probably headed towards Canton,' Charles says calmly.

Gunshots ring through the air. The Japanese soldiers at the fort on the other side of the camp have started firing at the planes, even though they're a mile high. 'Ha,' Charles laughs. 'They'll never hit them.'

'Come indoors,' Mama says briskly. 'We don't want to catch a stray bullet.'

In our tiny room I huddle with my parents, Charles and his family. Explosions boom in the distance and, through the window, a cloud of black smoke rises behind the mountains.

'They're bombing the airport,' Papa says in a loud voice.

Charles leaps up. 'It's begun.'

'At last,' Mama murmurs.

'The Americans are going to set us free,' I shriek, excitement making me dizzy.

* * *

The next afternoon, I set off for school as usual. There hasn't been a repeat of the bombing raid. Surely there'll be another one soon? Then the Japanese will be so badly hit they won't be able to do anything but surrender Hong Kong.

I sit on a mat spread on the floor. Charles lowers himself next to me, and I give him a surprised glance before going back to the algebra problem scribbled on the back of an old piece of card. There aren't any exercise books available for school. I chew the end of my pencil; I haven't got the faintest idea how to do the sum.

'Here, let me help you.' Charles talks me through the working-out step by step.

'I've think I've got it.'

'Are you sure?'

'No. Not really. I hate maths. I'm much better at geography.'

'Then, when we do geography, you can help me.'

I'm sure he's good at geography too, but the lie doesn't matter. He fixes his gaze on me and our eyes lock. I glance away then back again, not knowing what to say. *Idiot! Ask him something about himself!* 'Is it strange for you to be in your old school?'

'A bit. I keep expecting to bump into one of my old teachers. Which school did you go to?'

There's only one school considered suitable for expatriates. 'The Central British School in Kowloon,' I say. 'It took me ages to get there and back every day. I would have gone to boarding school if it hadn't been for the war.'

'I'm hoping to go to university in London. When the war ends.'

'I sometimes wish my mother and I had been evacuated. Papa was ill so we stayed on. My parents never believed the Japanese would dare attack.'

'My mother tried to get us evacuated, you know.'

'Did she?'

'She thought we'd be eligible as we've got British passports. She was told by the authorities they didn't know what to do with the likes of us.'

'That's terrible,' I say, shocked.

A shuffling sound comes from behind, and Derek Higgins mutters, 'Stop talking or I'll tell the teacher.'

'Don't be a snitch!' Charles glowers at him before giving me a smile that makes my heart miss a beat.

After class, he walks me back to the Indian Quarters. At the bottom of the stairwell, he turns to me as if about to say something. Then he takes my hand and gives it a brief squeeze. 'See you tomorrow.'

Smiling, I run up the stairs and into our room. Papa is sitting on his own. 'Thank God you're back, Kate. I've just taken your mother to the hospital. The fever's returned and her temperature is sky high.'

* * *

Mama is in a side room, apparently fast asleep. A nurse leads Papa and me to one side. 'Mrs Wolseley has slipped into a coma,' she says. 'There's very little we can do, I'm afraid.'

'No!' All the saliva drains from my mouth. 'She can't die.'

Papa grabs me to him and whispers, 'Be brave, my dear girl. Your mother might be able to hear and you wouldn't want to upset her.'

I pull out a chair for him, and we sit in silence, giving each other worried glances until the nurse makes signs that visiting hour is over. For the next three days we visit and watch helplessly as Mama slips away. Each day, I feel it's like being in a living nightmare. Each day, the sense of unreality grows. Each day I ask myself, *How can my beautiful vibrant Mama have been reduced to this inert creature lying wraith-like on a bed?*

10

SOFIA

Sofia stands at her bedroom window peering at two coolies pulling a cart up the road. *It's laden with dead bodies!* She shudders. People have literally been freezing to death on the streets. A year has passed now since the fall of Hong Kong, and Natalia has told her about rumours of the terrible conditions in the old British colony: food shortages, massacres, atrocities against women, starvation of prisoners and the rampant spread of typhoid and cholera. The misery goes on and on...

Here in Macau, things aren't much better. There are thousands of homeless beggars and this winter has been so cold. Even if the poor had any money, they wouldn't be able to buy much to eat. When did she last have any meat? Sofia can't remember. And she's fed up with fish, despite it keeping her from feeling hungry all the time.

She leaves her room and marches down the corridor to the front stairs. Leo is in the hallway. 'I'm just going to see Uncle,' she says. There's something she needs to tell him, and she'd better get on with it before he finds out from someone else.

'Give him my regards, won't you?' Leo says.

Sofia opens her mouth in surprise. Leo has never expressed anything other than disdain for Uncle in the past. Come to think of it, he hasn't been nasty to her for ages, either. 'When you get back,' Leo adds, 'I'll show you those kung fu moves you keep asking about.'

She's been dying to learn from him. She's watched him practising, kicking and punching the air as he fights imaginary enemies. She's begged Father for lessons, but he says it isn't seemly for a girl. 'You could show me now.' She can barely contain the eagerness in her voice.

Leo's brow creases. 'Later. I'll be on the front terrace at four o'clock.'

Her shoulders sag, but then she remembers her mission to visit Uncle.

The iron gate clangs shut as she steps onto the pavement. It's Natalia's afternoon off, otherwise she'd be with her like she always is. Normally, Sofia wouldn't go out on her own. There are too many desperate people on the streets. Starving people who'd rob her and throw her body into a ditch. Is she being rash? No, what she must tell Uncle is far too important to wait. The risk isn't that great, anyway. Not in broad daylight. Perhaps she should have telephoned him to say she was coming? It's too late now. She'll just have to surprise him...

She hails a passing rickshaw and jumps in. The rickshaw puller is so terribly thin. How can he stand on his own two feet, let alone pull this cart? Thankfully, she doesn't weigh much. They get to the last, steep part of the road. She climbs out, pays the man his full fare plus a generous tip, and walks on. At Uncle's door, she knocks. No answer. *Where can he be?* He's usually at home in the early afternoon and, in any case, his houseboy should have answered the door.

Sofia goes down the alleyway at the side of the house. The gate might be unlocked. She lifts the latch and lets herself in. *Rather careless of Uncle's staff not to have bolted it.* Tall bamboo shades the small patch of land. There's a smell of damp vegetation, and the path is mossy beneath her feet. *There's Uncle!* He's on the patio with two Chinese men, surrounded by boxes. Sofia stomps up to him. 'What are you doing?'

Uncle gives a start and drops a lumpy-looking package. 'How did you get in here?'

'Someone left the gate open,' she says, surprised at his tone. She points at a packet of white pills. 'Who are those for?'

'Nobody with whom you should be concerned.' Uncle takes her arm and practically drags her indoors. She glances around for his servants. 'Where is everyone?'

'Cook and amah have gone to the market.'

'But I'm here,' comes a voice from the pantry.

Sofia lets out a gasp. What's her governess doing spending her afternoon off at Uncle's? 'Why?' Sofia asks in English.

Uncle's English is heavily accented, but Natalia doesn't speak Chiu Chow and Uncle doesn't know any Russian. They continue in the language of Perfidious Albion, as Natalia likes to refer to it. 'I'll tell you why I'm here later. First of all, you've got some explaining to do. You know you're not allowed out on your own. It's far too dangerous.'

'I wanted to let Uncle know about Leo.' Sofia crosses her arms. 'But I suppose you've already told him.'

'Told me what?'

'That he's getting married to Michiko.'

There, she's said it. She plants her feet firmly apart. Uncle slams his fist down on the kitchen table, his face puce and his fat cheeks wobbling. 'Collaborating with the enemy, I'd call that.'

'Actually, I really do believe he loves her. He's been different lately.'

'How can your father agree to this?'

'You'll have to ask him that yourself. He won't say anything to me on the subject. He says I shouldn't concern myself. I'm fed up with being told I shouldn't concern myself. It's all you and Father say to me these days.' Sofia is so annoyed, she's in danger of sulking.

Uncle blows out a sigh. 'Natalia, take the child home. I'll leave it up to you to fill her in with what she needs to know. I trust your discretion, but you should have told me yourself.'

'We only found out this morning,' Natalia says quickly. 'I was about to tell you. You know I tell you everything...'

'Tell him everything?' Sofia grabs her governess's hand. 'What do you mean?'

'Come along,' Natalia says in a brusque tone. 'We'll let ourselves out.'

They walk down the hill towards the *avenida*. There's a bench underneath one of the banyan trees and Natalia sits, motioning that Sofia should do the same. 'You know your uncle is a communist, don't you? He was recruited to spread Anti-Japan and Save the Chinese Nation propaganda years ago.'

Sofia bats away a fly buzzing by her ear. 'So?'

'I met him when he visited Shanghai shortly after your mother died. I was working for the Party too, in a very minor capacity, mostly distributing leaflets when I was a freelance translator.'

'You? A communist? I thought you left Russia because of the revolution...'

'That's the story I let people believe, not the real one. I was regretting my decision to leave the mother country, thinking I could have done more at home. Then I met your uncle, who suggested I come here to keep an eye on your stepmother and her nationalist connections.'

'Then you're a spy?'

'Not really. I'm your governess first and foremost. In fact, I hardly tell your uncle anything, as there hasn't been that much to tell. I merely let him know when Siu Yin's family visits. You're my main priority these days, Sofichka.' Natalia strokes her hand. 'The Party has taken second place in my heart for years.' Natalia has called her by her pet name, and Sofia feels her governess's warmth through her fingers. But all this subterfuge? It's the stuff of espionage novels, not everyday life. And there she was, thinking Mr Kimura was a spy when all along it was Natalia. 'Who're all those boxes for?' She's fighting another attack of the sulks. How can her beloved Natalia have been deceiving her all these years?

'Your uncle is helping the anti-Japanese guerrillas smuggle medicines into the POW camps in Hong Kong. It's a wonderful thing he's doing. You should be proud of him. And you must never, ever breathe a word of this to anyone.'

'I won't.' And she definitely won't. Father would be upset. And Leo? Leo would go back to being horrible to her and that's the last thing she wants.

*　*　*

A month later, Sofia is standing at the entrance of Macau cathedral. She runs a hand down the white silk of her bridesmaid dress and clutches a posy of pink roses. Leo is waiting by the altar with Father. Michiko is due to arrive at any minute now. Sofia glances at Natalia. Her governess is standing next to her, dressed in a dark red suit. Red like her political affiliations.

Sofia remembers the story of how her parents met. Father had fallen for Uncle's favourite sister, Sofia's mother, on a visit to China, and brought her back with him to Macau. He provided Uncle with a fleet of junks in compensation. Uncle more or less sold Mother to Father, but that's the way things are done in China. For the past month, ever since she found out about her governess, Sofia has wondered if Mother was the intended spy in Father's household, substituted by Natalia after Mother's untimely death. Then she's told herself not to be silly. Uncle wouldn't have used his own sister like that.

Leo is standing tall and handsome, his thick black hair styled like Cary Grant's, her favourite film star. Will Leo stop teaching her martial arts after he's married? There's still so much she wants to learn. Leo has been patient with her, just like he used to be while he taught her to swim. The old Leo back again. It was Siu Yin who poisoned him against her. Her stepmother was furious when Father decided to give Sofia equal status to his legitimate son, despite the fact he never married Mother. Sofia can feel eyes burning a hole in the back of her neck. Siu Yin is glaring at her, hatred in her expression.

A limousine pulls up in front of the church. Sofia grips her flowers and goes to help the bride. Father insisted the Japanese girl converted to Catholicism. He likes to be seen as a good Catholic and benefactor of the various religious orders in Macau. Sofia has been brought up in the faith, but for her it's more a tradition than a conviction. What does Michiko make of the sudden change in her life? Sofia studies the girl and she's reminded of one of the pawns on her chessboard. She pushes the thought away.

Michiko is wearing a traditional white gown, on Siu Yin's insistence. It's the way all Catholic women get married in Macau. The Japanese girl resembles one of those figures on top of a wedding cake. She places her hand on her father's arm, and Sofia falls in behind them. They progress down the aisle. Mr Kimura looks from left to right and smiles at the congregation. His daughter keeps her eyes downcast.

At the altar, the Japanese man bows to Leo, and Leo returns the bow. Hysteria bubbles up inside Sofia. She claps a hand to her mouth; she must keep quiet. Her eyes water with the effort, her shoulders shake, and a muffled giggle escapes. Why is she laughing? She should be crying. She'll have a Japanese sister-in-law and Japan is the enemy. Leo, towering over his future father-in-law, shoots her a thunderous look. She's really ruined things now.

11

CHARLES

Charles is staring at a plate of cold rice and turnips, practically all he's been given to eat for the past six months. The American air-raid last October raised such false hopes of freedom. Conditions in the camp are worsening by the day. The pets people brought in with them have all disappeared; the dogs and cats have either died from starvation, or they've finished up in someone's cooking pot. Another thing, and it's odd, but he doesn't hear the croaking of frogs any more.

He thinks about Kate. She's not the giggly, sparkly Kate of before. Will he ever hear her laugh again? As a form of self-preservation, he's become almost immune to the awfulness of everything and, by the dull look in her eyes every time he sees her, numbness has seeped into her soul as well. Her mother's death has crushed her.

Charles glances at Pa, sitting opposite him and so thin his rib bones jut out over his concave stomach. Pa fiddles in the back of his mouth and pulls out a piece of molar. 'Blast! I've broken a tooth. Must have been a bit of gravel left in the rice. Bugger! I thought I'd rinsed it all out before we cooked it. And here's a black too.' He gingerly picks up a piece of cockroach dung. 'What a pong!' Pa opens his mouth.

Charles staggers to his feet. 'Don't eat it!'

'Might as well.' Almost jauntily, Pa crunches on the offending morsel. 'It's the only protein I'm likely to get.'

Half-digested rice rises in Charles's gullet. He rushes out of the room and onto the balcony. Although he's starving, he can't make himself eat such things. His guts twist. Last week, Pa caught a rat behind their quarters. Ma cut it up and pan-fried it for their supper. She lied to him and Ruth, saying it was chicken.

Chicken, ha! Charles found out later. A long, grey tail was left at the bottom of the rubbish bucket and he'd rushed out of the room then too.

A shout echoes, and he eyes the path below. Bob is waving at him, and Charles waves back. 'Just a minute. I'll come down,' he calls out, glad of the distraction.

'Japs are looking for someone ta' repair their radio in the prison.' Bob's voice is barely above a whisper. 'I remember you saying you're a radio ham. Do you think you can manage it?'

Charles built his set himself. Of course he can manage it, but does he want to? He's been in that prison once before and doesn't fancy setting foot in the place again.

'Might be useful to have a contact,' Bob says. 'Someone neutral like you who can speak the lingo.'

'I'm not sure I'm the right person for the job. Why should we help the Japs?'

'The men who escaped and were captured last summer are from the police. We need ta' find out how they are.'

'The problem is I've already had a run-in with the guards.'

'When was that?'

'Over a year ago.'

'The guards in the prison are a new lot.'

Charles thinks for a moment. *Might as well.* It would distract him from constantly fretting over his next meal and worrying about Kate. 'I'll do it.'

* * *

The following morning, Charles presents himself at the prison gates. A bandy-legged sentry looks at him with a narrowed gaze. Charles explains the purpose of his visit, and the guard takes him to an office at the side of the main building. He introduces him to a Chinese man, Fung, an electrician, who is tinkering with the radio.

'You show him how to repair set,' the guard barks, turning on his heel and striding out of the door.

Fung has a box of spare valves and Charles explains how to replace the faulty one. He chats with Fung in Cantonese. Fung is probably in his mid-thirties, balding, and has a mole on his cheek with a long hair growing out of it. He keeps referring to the Japanese as *Law Pak Tau*, and says he's allowed out of the prison every Friday morning to go into town and visit his wife. He also tells Charles he's seen the police officer prisoners; they're so emaciated they're probably dying.

The guard comes back and escorts Charles to the prison gate.

Bob is waiting at the top of the main road. 'Alreet?'

'I got on well with the electrician,' Charles says, then explains about Fung's weekly visits into town.

'I wonder if he'll agree ta' smuggle some food in for us.'

'I could wait for him on the main road the next time he comes out and ask him.'

* * *

On Friday, Charles spends the whole morning meandering up and down the road, on the off chance he'll bump into Fung. One of Bob's contacts has written a note in Chinese, which Charles will pass to Fung. It's highly dangerous, as Fung might well be a Japanese spy, but a feeling in his gut tells Charles that Fung is anti-Japanese.

At about eleven, Fung comes out of the prison gates. Charles walks up to him and deliberately stumbles. Fung bends down and helps Charles up, his mole hair quivering. Charles quickly slips him the note.

The following week, Charles bumps into him again, praying the Japanese on the hill are looking the other way. It might be considered one stumble too many. Fung passes Charles a slip of paper.

Bob is waiting for him on the village green and Charles gives him the message. Although he speaks fluent Cantonese, he can't read or write it. But one of Bob's fellow policemen can.

'Fung agreed,' Bob says the next day in the supper queue. 'He'll hang a towel out of his window in the prison just before he leaves on Fridays. You'll be able ta' see it from your balcony and get down ta' the main road in time ta' meet him.'

'Right.'

'I've managed ta' arrange chocolate fortified with vitamins sent in from outside. It'll be packed in small flat tins you can easily give ta' Fung.'

* * *

For three months, every Friday, Charles casually passes Fung on the main road. He pulls a couple of tins from his pocket and drops them into a bucket carried by the Chinese man. Clammy sweat breaks out over Charles's body. But, at the same time, he finds himself becoming increasingly addicted to the adrenalin rush.

In late July, Fung announces that he's leaving for Macau. Will his replacement carry on with the ruse? The new electrician, a man called Lai, meets Charles the following Friday. 'How much money you give me?' the man asks.

'Sorry?' There's something fishy about Lai. Fung never asked for payment. Charles shoves his hands into his pockets and shakes his head. 'No money.'

'Then no can do,' Lai says, skulking off.

Charles shrugs. *Good riddance, but what about those poor policemen?*

* * *

Charles's summer task is to help with the gardening. Fortunately, they're now able to grow their own vegetables; otherwise all they would eat would be rice, rice and more rice.

Last winter, Pa cleared a small patch in the scrub on the other side of the pathway from the Indian Quarters and planted tomatoes, lettuces, carrots, peas, and even celery. Others in the camp have done the same and these days everyone participates in a thriving seeds trade. The adults exchange them for food and cigarettes and give the rest to friends. Pa grew his first crops from the pips saved from early fruit and vegetable rations.

Now the plants produce their own seeds, and Charles spends the evenings with Ruth helping sort them into old envelopes. Instead of proper gardening equipment, they use sticks and improvise hoes and rakes by hammering what nails they can find into them.

'The tomatoes are nearly ready for picking,' Pa says.

Charles collects a rake. 'I don't need to queue for any fertilizer, do I?' Whenever the septic tanks are cleaned out, long lines form of people wanting the excrement for their allotments. Those who are first get the best bits – the ones that are firmest.

'No, son. We don't need any at present.'

Pulling up the weeds, Charles grumbles to himself. Sweat runs down the back of his neck and he's dizzy with tiredness; he should be taking a nap like Ma and Ruth.

He lets out a heavy, pent-up breath. He hardly sees Kate now that school has broken up for the summer. And in the autumn he won't be going back to class, as Professor Morris said he's taught him everything he can. Soon he'll have to join one of the working parties with the other men in order to earn more rations for his family. He'll never get the chance to spend time with Kate then.

I'll miss her.

She's become important to him. If a day goes by without seeing her, the relentless drudgery of the camp becomes a hundred times more unbearable.

Footsteps sound on the stony path as Bob arrives, perspiration running down his face.

'I had to send Lai packing,' Charles whispers. 'He wanted money. I hope he doesn't spill the beans.'

'That would implicate him as well. I'll let you in on a secret. I've been in touch with the BAAG on me radio. They might be able ta' help me mates in the prison.'

'What's the BAAG?'

'The British Army Aid Group. They smuggle medicines and other supplies in and out of the camps and gather intelligence for the Allied Forces. They're in cahoots with the anti-Japanese guer-rillas and even manage ta' get escapees from the POW camps into Free China.' Bob glances around and lowers his voice even further. 'Have ta' be careful, though. There're spies in our midst.'

'Right.'

'I'm telling you because you've helped us out. And you never know when the information might come in handy.'

Charles puts a finger to his lips.

* * *

It's rollcall, and Charles is standing next to Kate, surrounded by the sullen faces of their fellow prisoners. 'Come on, Japs have finished registering us.' He takes hold of her hand. 'Let's get away from here!'

'Shouldn't we wait for Ruth?'

'I'd rather it was just the two of us.'

People mill around and he leads her away. Where to take her but the hill above the cemetery? Even though her mother is buried below a rough-hewn headstone, there's nowhere else they can be alone. He leads Kate past the graves, and she keeps her eyes fixed on the path ahead.

He finds a patch of dry grass under an orchid tree and gently pulls her down. Kate leans back on her arms and looks at him. He averts his gaze from the hip bones jutting through the thin material of her shorts and focuses his attention on two men sculling their sampans across the bay. A tanker has lain half-sunken in the water for as long as they've been in the camp, and its dark hulk floats like a surfaced whale. The tide is out and the reek of seaweed fills the air. 'God, I can't wait for this war to end,' he groans. 'I'm fed up with being hungry all the time.'

'Me too. I sometimes think it will never end. We've been here forever. No one cares about us. No one has come to rescue us. The whole world has forgotten us.'

Her hand is close to his; he could move his little finger and touch it if he let himself. He looks at her profile; she has the prettiest nose: narrow and just the right length for her face. The corners of her bow-shaped mouth, which always used to be upturned as if she was about to explode into one of her irrepressible giggles, are now turned downwards. *How to cheer her up?*

'The Japs are suffering a real hiding at the moment.'

Kate tucks a curl behind her ear. 'What makes you say that?'

'I've got a radio hidden in the wall of our room.'

'Charles!' She frowns. 'That's terribly risky.'

'Pa and I listen to the overseas news when we can manage it. We're very careful. No one else knows.'

'Even so. I think you should get rid of it.'

'But how else would we know what's going on in the outside world? *The Hong Kong News* is full of lies.' He takes a breath. 'I found out that the Allies have practically defeated the Japs in New Guinea.'

'That's miles away from us.'

'I expect they'll go from island to island until they eventually get here.'

'It could take years. In the meantime, if the guards catch you with that radio, they'll put you in the prison.' She blinks. 'Or worse.'

'Bob has a transmitter. He receives messages in Morse from people who've escaped to China.'

'Gosh! What he's doing is even more dangerous. We must tell him to stop.'

'Don't worry!' Kate's amber eyes fix on his, the golden lights in them distracting him. *Best change the subject.* 'What are your plans for when we get out of here?' he asks.

'Boarding school, I suppose. My father would like to go to Australia. He thinks it's a better place than England to recover his health. What about you?'

'We'll probably end up in London. An uncle on Pa's side of the family will take us in. A letter came from him via the Red Cross. I fancy studying law.'

'I think you'll make a wonderful lawyer. You're good with people and you're terribly clever.'

'Not true. I didn't realise you'd be going to Australia. Somehow, I imagined you'd end up in England like me. I'll miss you.'

'And I'll miss you too.'

He moves closer to her, lifts his hand, and strokes her cheek. He can't help himself; it's so warm and lovely. Then he leans in and kisses her gently on the mouth. She pulls back, clearly surprised.

'Sorry,' he murmurs, appalled at himself.

'It was nice.'

'Nice?'

'I mean, wonderful.'

He takes her hand. 'Shall we do it again?'

'Please.'

He inclines his head towards hers and meets her lips. So soft and sweet. But a rustling sound startles him and he pulls back as Ruth skips towards them. 'There you are,' he says with false enthusiasm. 'We couldn't find you earlier.'

12

KATE

I'm sitting on a rock next to the path leading around the headland. It's a week after Charles kissed me. I've only seen him briefly at rollcall or in the supper queue since, and we've exchanged shy smiles but haven't managed to be alone together. Stanley is over-crowded; even married couples have few private moments. I wish we could be together more; I'm torn between wanting to shout my feelings to the world and the need to find out if Charles feels the same.

Dejection washes through me. The Japanese have just broken the promise they made a few weeks ago when they said they'd repatriate all the women, children, old people and those who are ill as an act of goodwill. Instead, they only repatriated the Canadians, and those lucky people left yesterday. Papa explained repatriation meant you had to have an exchange of prisoners. The only Japanese available to be exchanged with the British are some pearl fishermen caught in Australia, and the Aussies have turned their noses up at a bunch of half-starved, malaria-ridden people from Hong Kong in exchange. Someone said it was because the fishermen are familiar with the Australian coastline and they don't want them reporting back to Japan. Hopefully, that's the real reason. And I bet the internment camp in Australia is nicer than Stanley...

I hug my knees and stroke the cool stone of my jade bangle. Nearly a week ago, the American bombers returned and now they come back every day to bombard the harbour. I was filled with hope, thinking the war was about to end and I'd be able to go home. Yet the days have worn on and now I feel even lower than before.

I've tried to keep cheerful. The adults hold regular concerts and perform plays, but the good times are few and far between. Sometimes, I take a pin and push it into the back of my leg to keep the guilt for Mama's death at bay. If I'd realised how ill she was, I wouldn't have resented having to do all the washing and cleaning. I would have been nicer to her and not have answered back all the time.

Shutting my eyes, I think about that terrible night when I held Mama's hand and said goodbye to her. The pain of the loss is as strong as if it had happened yesterday. I can't bear to remember Mama's face, so still and white. I can't bear to visit her grave. I can't bear to think of my mother's body rotting in the earth.

Getting up from the rock, I dust down my shorts then traipse towards the Indian Quarters. There's Charles, standing in the middle of the village green, surrounded by a group of children, Ruth's friends, playing cowboys and Indians. I wave at him. 'Shall we go for a walk?'

Charles spreads his arms out wide. 'Sorry. Later maybe. Why don't you give me a hand?'

I glance at the kids. Generally, they run around playing games and I don't have much to do with them except when they dive-bomb me and shout 'Ratatatata!' Charles has become a sort of stand-in uncle and seems to enjoy supervising them, but I prefer to stay detached as I have no experience with young children.

Once, I spied Ruth doing her business behind a bush. It was revolting – worms wiggled among the stools. 'Make sure she washes her hands before eating,' I said to Charles. Then I told myself off for sounding like a prig.

I smile at him now; it would be rude to refuse. And anyway, I would do anything for him. 'All right.'

'We've captured Charles and we're about to scalp him,' Ruth shouts; she turns to her brother. 'Surrender, paleface!'

Charles gives me a helpless glance. 'Rescue me, please!'

I march towards him, children hanging on to me. By the time I reach him, I've started to laugh. I've been wading through a sea of infants and he looks so out of place stranded in the middle, his hands tied behind his back, his face anxious.

Collapsing on the ground, I clutch my belly as the giggles escape. 'I have you in my power. Yield!'

'All right, I give up.' Charles grins and shakes his head.

I want to push back the hair flopping across his forehead and kiss him right here in front of everyone. I untie him and our eyes meet. But the children pile on top of us in a scrum and spoil the moment. 'Come on! We can go for that walk now,' I chuckle.

On the path leading up from the Indian Quarters, I wrap my arms around his waist and breathe in his musky citrus smell. I lift my head and his mouth covers mine. I kiss him until the numbness goes. I drink him in, love for him flooding through me.

A new sensation takes hold. His hand moves slowly down my body. My heart hammers, but I don't stop him. I want his touch.

Footsteps echo. 'Hello, you two,' Jessica Chambers says brightly. 'That's a shamefaced look if ever I saw one.' Laughing, she makes her way towards the blocks of flats.

I give her back a withering look. 'Let's go to the cemetery, Charles. We can find a spot where no one will see us.'

Under the orchid tree, well away from Mama's grave, he gathers me to him. Gently, his hands explore the hollows of my back. Our kisses become more urgent and our breathing deepens.

A sudden cry comes from below. 'Kate, your father wants you to go home straight away,' Jessica shrills. 'He's been coughing blood.'

'Oh, my God!' I leap up and run down the hill.

* * *

'Have you been with that Eurasian boy?' Papa asks.

I nod.

'You're spending far too much time with him. It can't continue. People will talk.'

'Never mind about that. I've been begging you to see a doctor about that cough, but you've been too stubborn to do anything about it.'

'You know how much I hate quacks. Ever since my TB.'

'I hope it hasn't come back. The TB, I mean. What am I going to do with you?'

I wipe my sweaty hands on my shorts. There're other cases of TB in the camp, and the patients are isolated in a makeshift sanatorium behind the hospital. What if the doctors put Papa in there? How will he survive?

Papa coughs and sponges his moustache with his threadbare handkerchief, leaving a tell-tail trail of pink sputum. 'It might not be TB.'

'Well, you'll have to see the doctors. I'll take you to the hospital tomorrow.'

'Getting back to that boy you've got involved with.' Papa clears his throat. 'I can't have you making a spectacle of yourself. It won't do your reputation any good, dear girl. You're growing up and you'll be seventeen soon.'

'Charles is just a friend. There's nothing going on between us.'

'Are you sure?'

I cross my fingers behind my back. 'Absolutely. Don't worry!'

* * *

The doctors have put Papa in a side ward and they keep him under observation. I'm free to spend as much time with Charles as our lack of privacy allows. Today, I'm sitting with him under the orchid tree, his arm around me. There's movement down on the beach. The Camp Commandant's Assistant is swinging a baseball bat and shouting at a gang of European men unloading a consignment of supplies from a boat. I nudge Charles and point.

'He goes around slapping people's faces and laying into them with that paddle if they don't toe the line,' he says, taking my hand.

'Did you hear about his theories on eating grass?'

'He's been telling people they should live on it like Japanese soldiers hundreds of years ago.'

'Mr Chambers and Professor Morris have started making grass stews.'

'That can't be good for their stomachs. Human beings can't digest the stuff. We're not cows,' Charles groans. 'The war has got to end one of these days, you know. And all this will just be a memory.'

'A bad one, I'm afraid.'

'All bad?' He smiles.

'Not you, of course. You make it bearable.'

I run my fingers through my tangled curls and push them

back from my face. 'The Japanese are losing the war, though, aren't they?'

'Of course they are, bit by bit. We have to be patient.'

'But what if we all die of starvation before the Allies can get here?'

'We won't.' Charles puts his arms around me again.

I relax and snuggle against him. 'I love you.' The words spill out of my mouth before I've even thought about them. I hold my breath and wait for his response.

'I love you too. I want us to be together for always.' His mouth comes down on mine and I melt into him.

A sudden shout echoes from lower down the hill. 'Kate,' Jessica calls out. 'Time to queue for supper...'

I wish she would leave us alone.

* * *

'Your father asked me to keep an eye on you,' Jessica says as we walk down the hill. 'He doesn't approve of your friendship with that young man.'

'Why? I don't understand.'

'Charles Pearce is neither one thing nor the other. He's not Chinese and he's not English.'

'Well, I think he's very lucky to have two cultures.'

'That's the problem, don't you see? The Chinese and the expatriates don't mix. We respect each other, of course, and we work together quite happily, but our backgrounds are too different. If the races inter-marry they become part of the Eurasian community, which isn't accepted by either side.'

'I don't see why we have to take sides. I really love my amah, and her son is like a brother to me.'

'That's because they lived in your house and there were barriers, only you were just too young to notice them.'

'There aren't any barriers here in Stanley.'

'We won't be here much longer.'

'I hope not. Yet sometimes I think we will be, and we should live for now as we don't know what the future will bring.'

Jessica stands back and studies me with stern eyes. 'You have an old head on young shoulders, my dear. Just be careful!'

'What do you mean?'

'Have you started your periods yet?'

'Of course. But they stopped a few months after we got here. Mama said it was due to lack of food.'

'Don't let that boy take advantage of you, Kate. You're still very innocent and your mother isn't here to warn you.'

'I don't understand.'

Jessica looks away. 'Take care not to lose your heart completely, that's all. We don't want you getting hurt.'

'I won't.'

Charles would never hurt me. We talk about anything and everything, and with him it's as if I've found the other part of myself, the part I didn't know existed. I can guess what Jessica was going on about, but Charles is a gentleman and would never do anything I didn't want him to do. Trouble is, whenever he touches me I don't ever want him to stop...

13

KATE

Japanese voices jangle from just outside the door. I'm perched opposite Papa at the piled-up suitcases we use as a low table, sipping tepid water and nibbling from a bowl of cold rice. I'm wearing a cotton slip, but the summer air is so wet it drips down my skin and collects in the bends of my arms and behind my knees. I wipe my hands and get to my feet.

I widen my eyes. Two officers are standing on the threshold, swords hanging from their waists. Three more men in white suits and Panama hats come up from behind them. My breath catches. *Kempeitai.*

Papa raises himself slowly from his mattress and bows. He's still weak; he was only discharged from the hospital yesterday. The blood he coughed up wasn't TB in the end. Just a severe case of bronchitis.

'You got radio?' a short, tubby man asks.

'No,' Papa says firmly.

'We do search.'

There isn't enough room for Papa and me, let alone for the contingent of Japanese. The officer gives a cursory glance around then mutters something incomprehensible. The rest of the Japanese laugh and back out of the door, still laughing.

Papa sits down heavily and I go to the window. The Japanese are heading off towards the Police Block. It's too late to warn Bob. But I must find Charles.

Within minutes I'm running up the stairs to his room. It's empty except for Ruth, who is sitting on a camp bed, scooping congee from the bottom of her breakfast bowl. 'What's the matter?' she asks.

'The Japanese are prowling around looking for radios.'

'Well, they won't find any here.'

Legs shaking, I collapse on the bed. 'Are you sure?'

Ruth gives me a puzzled glance. 'Why?'

'No reason, kiddo.'

'I think my parents and Charles have gone to the canteen. Let's go and catch up with them.'

I link arms with Ruth and we walk up the main road. If only I could share my concern with her, but Charles told me Ruth doesn't know about the radio. Up ahead, I spot Derek Higgins approaching from the opposite direction.

'Guess what?' he says. 'They've arrested a top government chap, the number two in the police, and lots of other people.'

'Don't sound so pleased.' I push Ruth behind me.

Derek smirks. 'Isn't it about time we had some excitement in this boring place?'

'You're heartless and horrible.'

The echo of screams comes from the Commandant's house at the top of the hill, and I flinch.

Derek folds his arms. 'Do you know about Japanese water torture?'

I want to back away from him, but my legs have frozen.

'They tie the victims face-down on a board and pump liquid through their nose and mouth,' he says.

'H... h... how do they breathe?'

'They open their mouths even more, but the Japs fill them up with more water.'

'You're fibbing!'

Derek licks his lips. 'When the victims look like the swollen corpses of drowned people, the Japs jump on the poor buggers' stomachs.' He sniggers. 'Jets of water shoot out of their mouths, noses and even eyes.'

'You're such a sadist. I bet it's not true.'

"Tis so!'

Ruth comes out from behind me and stamps her foot. 'I hate you. Leave us alone!'

I put my arm around her. 'Come on, kiddo! I'll take you home. We can wait for your parents and brother there.'

Back in the Married Quarters, we find Charles and his father sitting on their camp beds.

'Ma's furious,' Charles whispers. 'She found us with the radio and has gone to bury it.'

'I was so worried about you.' I grab his hand. 'Thank God you're all right. And what about your mother? I hope she won't be caught.'

'She won't be. We smashed the radio into little pieces. Japs won't suspect a woman. She'll pretend to be planting something in our vegetable patch.'

I squeeze his fingers and kiss him right in front of his father and sister.

* * *

I hurry back to the Indian Quarters, but something's wrong. The village green is empty except for four men. My heart almost beats out of my chest. Bob is stumbling between two *Kempeitai* officers and a Chinese supervisor. They're marching him to the end of the blocks of flats. Then the officer makes him dig in the soft earth until he pulls out a small grey box.

Tears start gushing down my face. Papa arrives and takes me by the arm. 'Come inside this instant! It's far too dangerous out here.'

I sniff and wipe my nose. 'What have you heard?'

'It's spreading around the camp like wildfire. Japs have discovered a fortune in banknotes hidden under the bandages of a chap sent to town for an X-ray. They've arrested the top man in the Hong Kong and Shanghai Bank and some of his underlings, the fellow in charge of Medical Services, and quite a few locals. Accused them of collaborating with the BAAG and forming a resistance.'

'Derek Higgins told me about the arrests.'

'They nabbed two of the Cable and Wireless staff, as well as our friend Bob, and said they were operating secret radios.'

'How did they find out they had radios?'

'Japs have discovered some spare parts smuggled in with our supplies.'

'Who told on them?'

'Some people would sell their own grandmothers for favours or for food.'

* * *

I lie awake all night; I can't stop thinking about Bob. In the morning I rush to the hot water queue to tell Charles. Where is he? I spin on my heel and dash to the Married Quarters.

Ruth and her mother are sitting next to each other, crying. Mr Pearce hovers over them, clutching at his hands. 'It's too terrible,' he says. 'They came for him last night and said that, because he repaired their radio, he must have known about the others in the camp.'

My legs buckle and Charles's father gently helps me to a seat.

'We were kept up all night by the Japs,' Mrs Pearce sobs. 'They had a drunken party in the prison. We saw everything from our balcony.'

'One so-and-so, probably sozzled on *saké*, ran into the yard and began firing his revolver into the air,' Mr Pearce says. 'All the Japs dived for cover, then an officer came out and shot him in the shoulder. They hauled the man away, and in the end everything quietened down.'

'What do you think will happen to Charles?' Numbness fills me, the frozen sensation only he can melt.

'I don't know,' Mr Pearce says. 'No one will tell us anything.'

'They'll let him out soon, though, won't they?' I wait for Mr Pearce to reassure me, but he remains silent.

* * *

The weeks pass and Charles is still being held in the gaol, along with the others who were arrested. Early one afternoon at the end of October, I'm lingering on the hillside above the cemetery with Ruth. I spend as much time as I can with Charles's sister. It started as a way of getting news of him; now I've become more and more fond of her and enjoy our moments together.

I'm thinking about Charles. Hopefully, his arrest was a huge mistake and he'll soon be released. The Japanese said that, as Charles was over sixteen, he came under their authority and not that of the camp tribunal. He'll be tried and sentenced like everyone else. I hope it won't come to that. Mr Pearce said not to worry, as there was no proof that Charles had a radio or that he's been involved in anything untoward.

'I was with my friends by the main road this morning,' Ruth says, picking up a fallen pinecone. 'A van drove out of the prison and a hand waved through the window. Someone called out, "Goodbye".'

I look down at the shore. There's a stretch of sand near the jetty. It's usually deserted, but not today. Guards have appeared and someone has dug channels above the high-water mark.

Ruth points. 'What are those trenches for?'

'I don't know, kiddo. We'd better set off for school or we'll be late for our lessons.' I stare at the beach again. Three trucks have driven up and the guards are opening the doors. 'Wait!'

The guards line up about thirty men and one woman, roped together in groups of three with their hands tied behind their backs. They wave their rifles and push the people down to sit on the sand, then they put blindfolds on them. There's Bob in the first trio! A guard leads him forward to kneel by a trench. Then a large man, his head close-shaven, unsheathes a sword and swings it in the air.

Down comes the blade, glinting in the sun. A streak of silver. Shining. Silent. Deadly. I yelp as Bob's body topples. Leaping to my feet, I grab Ruth's hand, and we run. We run, our legs pounding the dry earth to get away from the scene of horror, our mouths open to let out our screams.

Ruth runs back to her family and I career full tilt into Papa on the pathway leading down to the Indian Quarters.

'Steady, dear girl. What on earth's the matter?'

In gasping breaths, I tell him.

He pulls me close and I sob against his chest. 'What a callous act! There's no excuse for it,' he says.

'They were laughing and j... j... joking. How can they be so cruel?'

Back in the Indian Quarters, Papa fetches a cloth and sponges vomit from my chin. I can't remember having been sick. He holds me as I weep. I spend the afternoon sitting listlessly on my mattress and go to bed early. Then I wake up screaming from a nightmare of Charles's instead of Bob's disconnected head rolling along the ground, blood spurting from his severed neck.

Papa sits down on the mattress next to me and pats my shoulder. 'There, there.'

I feel numb and empty of emotion; it's as if I've died too.

14

SOFIA

Sofia bends her fingers forward at a 90-degree angle to create a dragon claw. She must maintain the tension. It's a year since Leo's wedding, and she's practising her kung fu moves with him.

Her sister-in-law, Michiko, spends her time either in Leo's suite of rooms here at Father's, or at her family home. Michiko's mother is ill – some female problem no one will explain to Sofia – and needs Michiko to nurse her. She's there this afternoon, which is why Sofia has Leo's full attention.

Today, Sofia is the attacker and Leo is the defender. Sometimes they switch roles, but not often. Leo is still too strong for her and his attacks too rapid. One day she'll be good enough to resist him, hopefully.

They face each other and bow with their palms together. Sofia opens her arms wide and lets out a loud '*Hai!*' She flies at Leo, hands flailing, flicking her wrist for extra force so that she can dig her fingers into his arm muscles. He blocks her move and she falls back. Up on her feet, she attacks. He throws out a kick and rolls away. She goes in for the assault again. Leo's superior technique pushes her across the terrace and she must concede defeat.

'One more go,' she begs. This time she'll get him. She's determined. She goes at him like a whirling dervish, arms and legs flying out at the same time.

He aims a kick at her; she leaps up in the air and it misses its mark. Finally, she has the upper hand. She can feel victory within her grasp. She aims a zigzag motion kick at the top of Leo's foot, then grabs his leg and pushes him down. She's won.

'Well done, little sister. But you wouldn't have been able to do that if I'd used force on your pressure points.' He laughs.

'When will you teach me how to do that?'

'It's too dangerous. I could kill you and, judging by how much progress you've made recently, you could even end up killing me. Come on, let's go indoors and get ourselves something to drink. I'm parched.'

They sit in companionable silence at the large rosewood dining table, sipping iced jasmine tea. Sofia lets out a sigh of contentment. Despite the Japanese practically controlling Macau, and the destitution of people on the streets, happiness bubbles up within her. She shouldn't feel happy. Not with all the wretchedness around her, but she can't help herself.

She remembers that, after Japanese troops seized the British steamer *Sian* in the harbour, killing about twenty guards, the Japanese demanded the installation of their own advisors as an alternative to military occupation. Mr Kimura, it turned out, was what is known as a sleeper, and now advises the Portuguese administration on civilian defence. He's not actually a spy, Uncle said, just waiting until the moment comes to show his true colours...

A knock sounds at the door, and Sofia looks up. Father's houseman, Ah Chong, slinks into the room, his face pale. '*Aiyah!* Big fire. Master Leo, you go quick. Missy Michiko in hospital.'

Sofia lets out a gasp as Leo runs from the room.

She perches next to Father in his study, waiting for news. She only saw Michiko this morning at breakfast. They talked about how they both missed going to the cinema, her brother's wife opening up to her at last.

'Michiko will be all right, won't she?' Sofia touches her hand to Father's.

'I hope so,' he says.

Sofia meets his eye. 'Why didn't you object to Leo marrying a Japanese woman?' It's a question she's posed many times. Maybe today he'll finally tell her.

'I felt guilty for not giving him the love he craved from me. Michiko adores him, don't you know? I watched them together and couldn't refuse.'

'Oh,' Sofia says, frowning. She thinks back to the year between Leo's first meeting then marrying the girl. They must have seen each other in secret because she can't remember him courting her openly. She squeezes her father's fingers. 'Why couldn't you love Leo?'

'He reminds me too much of my own father, who only saw things in absolutes. There wasn't room for any compromises in his character. He could only see black or white, never the shades of grey. I'm sad to admit I disliked him, and, although I don't actually dislike Leo, I can't find it in myself to truly love him either. Not like I love you, my daughter.'

She's suspected this for years, but it's still a shock to have it confirmed. Another reason for Leo's jealousy. And an explanation for the change in him since he met Michiko, who seems to love him unreservedly.

I hope she's all right.

'What about Mr Kimura? Did you suspect he was a sleeper?'

'Absolutely not! He told me he wasn't in the military because he was colour-blind. I took it on good faith. I just wanted to get a cheap price for the pearls I'd promised Siu Yin. How was I to know Leo would start wooing the girl?'

Not long after the dinner party when Leo had first met Michiko, Siu Yin appeared with a long string of even bigger pearls than Mrs Kimura's. Why Father has to pander to her stepmother's every whim is something Sofia will never understand. Natalia has told her what she calls 'the facts of life', of course. Could it be something to do with sex? Sofia can feel a blush creep up her neck just thinking about her father having sex with Siu Yin. 'I see,' she says, although she really doesn't.

The minutes stretch into an hour, then two hours. Ah Chong brings them a tray of supper. Cold bean curd. Sofia picks at it with her chopsticks. She doesn't feel like eating. Something's wrong. Otherwise Leo would be back by now.

She can't wait any longer. She'll telephone Uncle. He'll know what's going on. 'I'll be back in a minute,' she says.

Natalia is in the front hall, standing straight-backed at the foot of the stairs. 'I've been waiting for you. Come up to your room, darlink. There's something I have to tell you.'

With a sinking sensation in her chest, Sofia follows her governess up to the first floor and into her bedroom. Natalia sits on the bed and pats the space next to her. 'I'm so sorry,' Natalia says softly. 'The whole Kimura family is dead.'

'No!' A chill feeling creeps into Sofia's bones. 'How?' Her voice trembles.

'It wasn't supposed to be this way.'

'What do you mean?'

'Leo has been collaborating with the Japanese military. Your uncle found out he's been acting as an intermediary between Mr Kimura and a group of nationalists, who've been pretending to fight Japan when all they do is block the communist guerrillas.'

'How did Uncle find this out?'

'Because I've been following Mr Kimura. And the worst thing is, he saw me this morning when I tailed him to the harbour. I'd managed to creep up and hide behind an upturned sampan on the beach, where I listened to him conspiring with those traitors and heard them giving him details of guerrilla movements. Nationalists turning against their fellow-Chinese. Unspeakable!'

'How did he see you?'

'I was attacked by seagulls. Can you believe it? Even the seagulls are starving, and they must have thought my hat was edible. I sat there as they dive-bombed me, trying to brazen it out, but one of the men came to investigate and I ran off.' Natalia pauses. 'Leo will put two and two together. He'll think I had something to do with the arson attack on Michiko's family.'

'Why should he think that?'

'Firstly, because I was following Mr Kimura. Secondly, because only the guerrillas would have carried out the assault. They're the only people who dare to resist the Japanese around here.'

'You said it wasn't supposed to be this way.'

'Some young hotheads in the brigade took it on themselves to teach Mr Kimura a lesson. They didn't mean to kill anyone. Just to frighten him. Unfortunately, with the dry weather we've had recently, the house went up like a tinderbox. There were sacks of rice blocking the back door and the family was overcome by smoke inhalation.'

Sofia starts to sob. Her shoulders heave and snot runs from her nose. She grabs hold of her governess. 'What will you do now?'

'I can't stay here. I've just come to collect my things and say goodbye, my Sofichka. You're fifteen years old now, too grown-up to need a governess. When the war is over, your father should send you to school or employ the best tutors for you to finish your education. Make sure that he does!'

Sofia goes with Natalia to her room and watches her pack. How to make Natalia change her mind? That would be foolish, though. Natalia's right: she has to leave. And soon. Sofia glances at her watch. Leo will be home any minute now. 'Hurry up!' she pleads.

* * *

'Where is she? Where's that Russian bitch?' Leo shouts, coming through the door. He marches up to Sofia and her father. 'I know all about Natalia's shenanigans this morning. She's a spy. The police have found rags soaked in kerosene dropped on the road outside the house. The fire was started deliberately. If I discover you had anything to do with this, Sofia, I'll never forgive you.'

'Now, now, Leo.' Father gets up from his chair. 'Calm down! How can you accuse your sister of something so terrible? She's only a child, for heaven's sake. And what proof do you have that Natalia is a spy?' He turns to Sofia. 'Where is she, by the way?'

'She's gone.'

'Gone?' Father repeats, a frown crinkling his brow.

'She said to tell you both that she's very sorry. She didn't mean for this to happen.'

Father sits back down. He opens his mouth then shuts it again. He takes a handkerchief from his pocket and blows his nose. 'Did you know she'd been spying on us?'

Sofia has never lied to her father and she's not going to lie to him now. 'I knew she was a communist. I found out last year.'

'See!' Leo points at Sofia. 'My bastard stepsister is in cahoots with the Russian bitch.'

'I don't want to hear language like that in my house,' Father says, shaking his finger at Leo. 'Apologise to Sofia!'

'Never! She must have known about Natalia. They've always

been thick as thieves. I'm sure there weren't any secrets between them.'

'I know I should have told you, Father, I realise that now. I thought she was harmless.' Should she tell him this is all Leo's fault for collaborating with the Japanese? She isn't a tell-tale-tit.

'Harmless?' Father's voice shakes with anger. 'How can deception ever be harmless? Go to your room, Sofia! I'll come up and talk to you when I've had a few words with Leo.'

'All right,' she says, her mouth trembling. Tears prickle, but she won't cry. Not in front of Leo.

* * *

The counterpane is cold beneath her fingers, like the icy feeling inside her. She runs her hands up and down the smooth silk. How will she cope without Natalia? She'll just have to and that's that. This war won't go on forever. When it's over, she'll start a new life. Maybe go to Hong Kong. She's always loved it there.

A knock raps at the door. 'I've been trying to talk some sense into the boy,' Father says, lowering himself onto the chair by the window. 'He won't listen. It's grief, I suppose. I can't help feeling responsible. I should never have allowed the marriage. It was bound to end in tears.'

'You weren't to know. I'm sorry for not telling you about Natalia. And I'm devastated for Leo about Michiko. Really, I am. And her family. It's so, so sad.'

'I don't understand why Leo thinks Natalia is responsible for this tragedy. He says Siu Yin's cousin caught her following him. He won't tell me anything else. Can you shed any light on this?'

What to do? She doesn't want to lie to Father. But if she says anything, Leo will find out and that'll make things even worse.

Then, there's Uncle. No one must know he's been helping the guerrillas. She made a promise she can't break. That's it. A prior promise cancels out a future lie. She gets to her feet and makes eye contact with her father. 'I don't know anything.'

15

KATE

The Pearces' balcony directly overlooks the prison exercise yard. Every evening, from five to six, I'm there, watching Charles pace up and down with the rest of the prisoners, my heart going out to him with every step he takes. I've practically haunted the place in the eighteen months since his arrest.

Ruth tugs at my sleeve. 'Can you test me on my spellings?'

'Of course, kiddo.' How resilient Ruth is! Just like the rest of the children, she's full of joy at life, even in this terrible place. I, on the other hand, have been trying hard to keep positive, telling myself the war is bound to end soon and that Charles will survive. Easier said than done, though...

Minutes later, after I've given Ruth full marks for her spellings, my heartbeat quickens. Charles has come into view. I can see him clearly. He turns his head in my direction and waves furtively. Like everyone else in the camp, he's deathly thin. At least he's still walking tall and doesn't look ill. Oh, how I long to take him in my arms...

Charles's family have been kind and welcoming. If they didn't know I loved their son before, they know it now. Papa wouldn't have been like them if it had been me who'd been imprisoned. He would have told Charles he didn't think him worthy. One day, I'll confront Papa about his prejudice, but only when liberation comes and I can love Charles openly.

I point to the flower from the orchid tree I've tucked behind my ear. If Charles can see it, he'll understand...

* * *

On 15 January, air-raid sirens blare above Stanley. I rush to the window. American planes are flying overhead. They come often now to bomb the harbour, as well as targets on Hong Kong Island and Kowloon. Papa stands next to me. 'We haven't got any white crosses on the rooftops. How will they know we're an internment camp?'

Throughout the day, I count the aircraft: over three hundred of them, the biggest raid yet. The next morning, the alarm sounds again. 'Look! They're back.' I go to the balcony. 'Thousands of them.'

'Not quite thousands,' Papa says. 'I've heard the Japs have put guns on top of the prison buildings. That's certain to attract attention.'

Japanese soldiers dash onto the village green, firing revolvers and rifles at planes miles high. 'They're running around like headless chickens.' I laugh, keeping my worry about Charles to myself. He'll be a sitting target in the prison...

A sudden rumble reverberates and four planes drop from the sky. They're heading straight for the Indian Quarters! Three American aircraft pass overhead, chasing a Japanese plane, their machine guns roaring.

'Quick! Get down!' Papa shouts.

A huge explosion rocks the building. I flinch and peer over the parapet. The Americans have gunned down the Japanese plane, which has crashed into the hillside to our right – just above the bathing beach. A plume of smoke rises and there are tell-tale signs of more planes shot down: towers of smoke come from the outlying islands, from behind the hill on the other side of Stanley Bay, and from the cove itself.

The day wears on and the air-raids continue. I curl up on my mattress, holding my breath during the attacks, and letting it in and out while waiting for the next one. Papa sits next to me, grumbling and muttering about the lack of a proper shelter.

Late in the afternoon there's a massive bang. I stumble to the back of the flat, my legs shaking so much I can hardly move. A heavy cloud is lifting from behind the cemetery and I grab Papa's arm. 'They must have hit one of the buildings at St Stephen's.'

* * *

Derek Higgins walks up to me the following morning in the water queue. 'Guess what?' he says with his habitual smirk. 'The Americans must have thought that rusty old wreck of a tanker in Stanley Bay had some strategic importance. A couple of aircraft turned to attack it, but their wings touched.'

I gasp. 'What happened to them?'

'The pilots had to jump out when the planes crashed into the hillside. One of them didn't make it and his parachute tangled up in the propellers. The other pilot got out and the Japanese shot him just as he landed.'

Tears spring to my eyes. 'Oh no! What about St Stephen's?'

'Bungalow C scored a direct hit. When the all-clear sounded, ten bodies were lying on the grass. Someone said they looked like they were asleep as they didn't have a scratch on them.'

I shake my head. 'How do you know all this?'

'Because I went up there for a look.'

'Were they all right?'

'Of course not. They were dead. Six people were taken to the infirmary. One woman died on the way there. Three more bodies were found in the wreckage. The funeral's later today and they'll be buried in a mass grave.'

'Another mass grave,' I murmur dejectedly.

Heavy-footed, I make my way back to the Indian Quarters, my chest aching. Of course they'll be buried in a mass grave. There's only one coffin in the camp. The base has been removed and it's used again and again for the many funerals, just like it was for Mama's. A picture comes into my mind of standing in the rain under a paper umbrella, and of strangers shovelling clods of earth onto my mother's shrouded body. I swallow the knot of sorrow in my throat and grip my bucket.

Papa is waiting for me. 'You haven't heard the worst.'

'What can be worse?'

'Some people didn't wait till the all-clear and looted the bungalow even before the bodies were removed.' He runs a hand through his hair. 'I often think we're interned with a bunch of animals.'

'Are you sure it was one of us? Isn't it something the Japanese would have done?'

Even as I ask the question, I remember Derek's description of the bodies and my stomach clenches.

'Japs mounted a guard as soon as they found out what happened then presented arms above the wreckage.'

'Such strange people...'

'They seem to think it's honourable to die in war, but equal to losing your soul if you're taken prisoner.'

'That explains a lot of things, but not their treatment of us.'

I stretch out on my mattress and stare at the wall. Last October

I turned eighteen. I've been in the camp for over three years and it's hard to imagine my life when peace eventually comes. What will it be like to no longer be hungry? To have proper clothes? To be able to go out and about? To be with Charles again?

And what will happen if peace doesn't come?

* * *

A week after the air-raids, I'm on the Pearces' balcony, waiting to catch sight of Charles. Tailorbirds chirp in the bushes below and a kite soars above, gliding in circles among the thermals and giving an occasional long drawn-out squealing call. I look down at the exercise yard. It's getting late. Where is he?

A chill comes over me and the hairs on my arms stand up. There's a sudden shift in the atmosphere. Anxiety radiates from Ruth and Mr and Mrs Pearce. An unexpected terror. Everyone leaps to their feet. Charles isn't among the prisoners!

'I'll go and find out what's happened,' Mr Pearce says, making his way to the door.

Mrs Pearce seizes his arm. 'Be careful, dearest!'

The next hour drags. I bite what's left of my fingernails, which stopped growing ages ago for lack of nutrients. I pace up and down the balcony, then I sit on a camp bed, then stand, then sit again, twirling my jade bangle round and round.

Mr Pearce returns and slumps down on a camp bed, his face grey. 'Charles has been drafted to a labour camp in Japan along with some of the POWs from Shamshuipo camp.'

I let out a muffled cry. Charles has been weakened by years of semi-starvation. How will he survive? I can see in Mrs Pearce's eyes the same thoughts that I've been thinking. Ruth sobs, and I put my arm around her.

'Don't worry, kiddo! Charles will be fine. You'll see!'

* * *

Time passes. Winter releases its hold, the orchid tree finishes its flowering season, and a muggy spring turns into a fierce summer. There has been no news of Charles.

I line up on the village green for a bowing lesson, heat and humidity enveloping me. The Camp Commandant is obsessed with military etiquette and seems convinced the prisoners aren't getting it right. I go through the movements, my mind elsewhere.

'How can the Japanese expect us to take this bowing seriously?' I whisper to Papa. In May, *The Hong Kong News* announced Germany's surrender. Soon afterwards, the Japanese said, 'No more newspapers,' and they became another item for black market traders. 'It's obvious they're losing the war.'

'They're doing it out of spite, I reckon.' Papa laughs, yet his eyes, staring blankly, give the lie to his apparent mirth. 'A guard said they've been tunnelling shelters and foxholes into the hills. Japs seem to think they can fight for Hong Kong. How desperate and pathetic...'

'Whenever I hear a guard coming, I run and hide or I give them my best bow.' I shrug. 'Everyone does. Don't they realise we're too weak for all this?'

To my left, Jessica Chambers is staring straight ahead. On the other side of the parade ground, a group of young men from the Hong Kong Police are grinning mockingly and making little effort to bow. I study the outline of Papa's ribs poking through his bare chest. Sweat pouring from his face, he stands to attention in the hot sunshine; I take his hand and it's like holding a bunch of twigs.

I glance at the Pearce family. Physically, they're surviving. Mentally, though, they've become listless and resigned to their circumstances, just like everyone else. They no longer mention

Charles; they probably think talking about him will jeopardise his chances. So I try to do the same and carry on as if everything will turn out for the best. And I cling to that hope; it nestles next to the numbness that has seeped back into my soul.

The Commandant struts in front of us. 'Captain Ito show you.'

The Japanese officer stands on a table. He inclines at the waist, holding his body at a forty-five-degree angle. We try to imitate him, struggling with the exertion, weak with exhaustion.

The new Formosan guards have come to stand on the sidelines, their faces unreadable. The Commandant has put them through field training over the past couple of weeks, leading them around the camp, wielding a bamboo stick. He has no chance! The Formosans don't give a damn about fighting to keep Hong Kong in Japanese hands. The Japs treat them like dogs, unaware they participate in a thriving black market with the prisoners, keeping us informed about events in the outside world. Manila has already been liberated. Surely it won't be long before it's Hong Kong's turn? My hands shake. If freedom doesn't come soon, we'll all starve to death. The situation has become that serious.

And poor Charles stuck in Japan...

* * *

The days go by in the same monotonous pattern: get up, queue for food, lie around too weak to do anything, queue again, sleep. Finally, a copy of *The Hong Kong News* is smuggled into the camp with the information we've all been longing for. Japan has surrendered. I hear about it in the supper queue and join in as everyone hugs and kisses each other. Even though I've no energy, my step quickens. 'It's over,' I say to Papa back in our room. 'The war is over.'

He stares at me. 'I can't believe it. Far too sudden.' Then he breaks into a smile and hugs me as hard as his lack of strength allows.

The next day, a notice pinned to the canteen wall informs us officially that hostilities have ceased. The Representative of Internees, one-time Colonial Secretary, has accepted responsibility for the maintenance of discipline. I read the report slowly. Then I read it again so I can relay all the facts to Papa. I let out a sigh and close my eyes. I won't have to worry about survival any more. From now on, I won't have to live behind barbed wire. Then I stare into the distance, as if by doing so I can see Charles.

Where is he? How is he?

I walk up the road and the camp is quiet. All the guards have disappeared and the Japanese are marching shamefaced to their headquarters. I make my way to the canteen. Passing the godowns, I spot a group of European policemen in uniform, patrolling the area. At least I don't have to bow any more...

* * *

It seems liberation will never come. An American aeroplane flies over and drops pamphlets saying the internees should remain calm and not leave the camp until the Allied forces arrive. Time moves on slowly as we wait for the Royal Navy. The local Red Cross representative makes a speech, promising that the authorities will increase rations and provide buses to bring visitors from Victoria City and the Kowloon camps.

One afternoon, I'm reading to Ruth in her quarters. She looks up. Charles's Auntie Julie and Uncle Phillip come into the room. Phillip Noble, a tall man with silver hair, is a Portuguese Chinese who married Mrs Pearce's sister ten years ago. They've spent the war in Macau.

'Conditions weren't much better than in Hong Kong,' Mrs

Noble says. She looks so like Mrs Pearce they could be twins. 'We didn't have much food, but at least we didn't starve.' She hugs Mrs Pearce and stares at Ruth with a sympathetic expression. 'My poor dears! You're nothing but skin and bone. The sooner we get you out of here the better. And we'll do everything we can to find out about Charles.' She goes on to explain that the Pearces' old home was destroyed in the bombing. 'And the Japanese turned our place in Kowloon into an officers' club. Before they left, they did their business in the corners of every room. Such barbarity! The whole place needs disinfecting and a fresh coat of paint.'

I shake hands with Charles's aunt. Should I beg her to get information about him quickly? That would be inappropriate, though. I'll just have to wait, and hope, and believe he'll soon be home.

* * *

Food rations in the camp improve when the Red Cross send in beans and the Japanese manage to provide more vegetables and daily meat. For years I've dreamt of filling my stomach, and now I can't digest the unaccustomed protein.

The Colonial Secretary takes the oath as Officer Administrating the Government. Papa explains it's an important move, establishing British civilian authority over the colony.

A week later, I spot a familiar figure stepping off an open-topped lorry that has drawn up next to the canteen. A slight Chinese woman with thin black hair scraped into a bun turns and flashes a gold-toothed smile at me. 'Ah Ho!' I fling myself into her arms, then lead her to the Indian Quarters. Papa stares at her in evident amazement.

'You got any washing?' she asks.

Ah Ho tells us she set off for the colony as soon as she learned about the surrender, leaving Jimmy behind. She explains that he's joined up with the communists, but Ah Ho is glad to be back with Papa and me. She didn't like bunking down in the same room as the family's pigs and chickens in China.

Ah Ho sleeps on a mat in the passageway at the rear of the flat and works alongside the other internees' amahs who've turned up in recent days, helping them prepare food in the communal kitchens. Her loyalty makes me feel humble.

A few days later, I go with Papa to visit our old home. We catch a lift in one of the buses laid on to bring visitors to the camp. It's strange leaving Stanley after more than three and a half years. In town, I stare at the devastation, the bombed buildings, the craters in the roads, the piles of debris. On the Peak, the house has been stripped of its wooden flooring and black roof tiles. And the Japanese have sunk a well in the garden. Papa puts his hand to his forehead. 'It's right where Ah Woo and I buried our valuables.'

He finds an abandoned spade and digs. Before exhaustion claims him, he strikes something and bends down to reach for one of my silver riding cups. I study the object, won with such pride in my old life.

What was all the fuss about?

* * *

At the end of August, the British fleet finally reach Hong Kong. The day before they arrive, planes fly over the camp and drop medicines and food that flutter down on green, red and white parachutes. I'm on the parade ground in front of the Married Quarters with Papa and we eagerly take a package each, nearly making ourselves sick gorging on chocolate. I grab one of the 'chutes; I've heard the rayon is perfect for making underwear.

I barely sleep I'm so excited and, when morning comes, the

drone of planes sends me dashing onto the balcony; they sweep low in formations of two, three, four or eight. I wave, cheer and cry tears of happiness at being free at last. But how can I be happy when I don't know what's happened to Charles?

On the afternoon of the official flag raising ceremony, Papa opens a suitcase and presents me with one of Mama's dresses. It's light blue cotton with a fitted waist and puffed sleeves. I rummage in the case and find a pair of leather high-heeled shoes. After parting my hair at the centre, I pin it into a Victory roll. If only I had a mirror to see my reflection...

Papa puts on a shirt and tie then escorts me to the parade ground, where we take our places with the hundreds of internees.

A strange-looking vehicle pulls up. Papa says it's called a jeep. Out of it steps the commander of the fleet, Rear Admiral Cecil Harcourt. A bugle plays the attention and the Union Jack is unfurled, followed by the flags of all the different nationalities that have been interned in the camp. Banners at half-mast, the Last Post is sounded, and planes fly overhead. Everyone sings 'Oh God, Our Help in Ages Past'.

A light wind blows in from the bay, cooling my father and me in the August heat, and lifting the notes of the bugle. The flags unfurl and fly over the colony once more.

Our hope for years to come, I sing, and the expectation I'll see Charles soon swells my heart.

* * *

A fortnight later, I'm standing at the railings of a small aircraft carrier converted from a merchant ship that will take Papa and me to Sydney, Australia. The vessel picked us up at Stanley and now we're heading out of Hong Kong waters. Chinese white dolphins frolic in the ship's bow-waves, escorting us towards the open sea. I said goodbye to Ah Ho yesterday. My amah is returning to China with the promise of a job as soon as Papa gets back from his extended leave. He's given her some of the silver dug up from the garden to help with expenses.

A blast from the ship's funnel sends vibrations through the railings. I run my hands down the cold metal then put my fingers to my mouth, tasting the salt. It reminds me of the tears I shed only hours ago.

I went to say goodbye to the Pearces straight after breakfast. They were sitting on their beds, their faces puffed from crying.

'Oh, Kate,' Mrs Pearce said, getting to her feet and putting her arms around me. 'My sister visited last night. We've had the most dreadful news.' She pointed to a cushion. 'You'd better sit down.' She took both hands and made eye contact with me. 'Be prepared for a shock, my dear. The ship…'

Mrs Pearce controlled her breathing, let a full breath stutter out, and took another.

'The ship taking Charles… Charles and the other prisoners, to Japan…' She had to stop again. The blood rushed from my head and my feet began to swim away from me.

'The ship was bombed and sunk by the Americans,' Mr Pearce said quietly, his teeth clenching shut immediately the words were out. 'Charles isn't listed… among the survivors.'

I sobbed and pleaded with his family that it couldn't be true, but they said Phillip Noble had telegraphed Shanghai, where the survivors had been taken, and Charles's name wasn't recorded among them.

I went completely silent then, shutting out the horror. I didn't look at anyone, because if I had done so it would have become real. I stared out the window and kept my body as still as I could. Ruth ran to fetch help, and there was a commotion when Papa came with Tony Chambers. They half carried me back to the

Indian Quarters. I hadn't even managed to get the Pearces' address in London.

* * *

The ship heads towards the horizon now and I turn my gaze to the back of the Peak, swathed in fog. Up there, in the swirling mists, is my home. Hong Kong recedes in the distance, and the image of Charles's face comes into my mind: high cheekbones, warm eyes and dark brown hair that flops across his forehead. I step away from the railings and glance at the back of my left hand. It's bleeding. The blood has caked under my newly grown fingernails.

PART II

1948–1949

16

JAMES

James Stevens stood next to Tony Chambers on the armour-plated bridge of the Customs Preventive ship. He glanced at the sky. *Nearly daybreak. Shouldn't be long now.* Catching smugglers would make a welcome change from surveying.

He steadied himself and rolled with the swell, breathing in the scents of China carried by the wind: the musk of wood smoke, the bitter stench of the communal latrines and the fragrance of myriad joss sticks. So different to the smell of coal fires and the rotten-egg pong of the Thames in London.

Stubbing out his cigarette, he heard his father's words as if they were being spoken right next to him: 'Join the Navy and see the world, son.'

James was a man now, twenty-five, and he'd taken his demob two years ago. He touched his inside pocket where that final letter from home nestled with his cigarettes. Hot tears welled up. No need to read it, he knew it by heart. Mother had written:

Last night one of those German doodlebugs flew over. We held our breaths as the terrible rasping, grating noise cut out and the

rocket came crashing down on the newsagents up the road. I
can't tell you how terrified we were.

James's vision blurred. A week after the letter had arrived, he'd received a telegram informing him his parents had died in a raid from another deadly flying bomb. At first, he hadn't believed it. How could they both have been carted lifeless from under a pile of debris? Mother had always tried to make the best of herself by sleeping with her chestnut-coloured hair in rag curlers every night and putting on fresh lipstick every morning. Dad never left the house unshaven. Mother would have been taken from the wreckage with pale lips and her hair still in rags. Dad's chin would have been covered in stubble.

James had gone home on leave shortly afterwards, and then he'd finally accepted the truth. A heavy sensation in his stomach, he'd stumbled over the rubble until he'd reached the two-up-two-down house where he'd grown up. The wallpaper he'd helped hang flapped in the wind; the picture of a battleship was still pinned to his bedroom wall, but the side of the building had been opened to the world. Broken glass crunched as he'd dragged his feet from room to room and, in the air, lingered the sour smell of plaster made wet by the rain.

James dried his eyes. There was no reason for him to return to London, or even England. His family was dead and the letter was the one thing he had left of them. If only he could tell Mother and Dad he'd got a job in the Far East. They would have been so proud of him... They'd never been farther than Brighton.

Now, timbers creaked in the distance and sails flapped. Bouncing on his toes, James gave the command, 'Full ahead!'

Sirens screamed as the ship surged forward. Phosphorescence from plankton glowed in the moonlight, lighting up the bow-wave. They were closing in on a large fishing junk.

He glanced at his Chief Officer. Tony wiped spray from his grey-flecked beard. 'Get ready to shoot!' he barked.

James switched on the searchlight and supervised the loading of the Vickers three-pounder. He sighted the three masts and fish-fin sails of the vessel, ploughing through the waves about three hundred yards away. A shot across the bow should do the trick. He would board the junk, order the halyards sliced, and tow it back to Hong Kong. The smugglers would have to find their own way home. 'One round ahead!' he yelled.

Third Officer Wang aimed to the side and with enough range to drop the shell in front of the junk. But it had changed tack and was going flat out to disappear around the back of a large island silhouetted against the stars.

'Bugger!' What were they playing at? It was a fair cop and they should give themselves up.

The Customs ship followed, propellers thumping, searchlight at full beam. The junk had entered a narrow inlet. James hadn't surveyed this area yet. He turned to Coxswain, a sinewy Chinese man. 'Can we get up there?' he asked.

'Sometime can. Sometime no can.'

'Cut the engines!' James then took a sounding by lowering a lead line. 'No go.'

'We'll follow them in the motorboat,' Tony said, handing James a pistol.

They lowered the runner, winching it down from its position on deck. The boat hit the water with a splash. Barely keeping his footing, James followed Tony, Wang and three sailors armed with rifles down a rope ladder that flapped in the breeze.

The sky began to lighten as James steered the boat up the creek, carefully avoiding the dark rocks looming below the surface. They rounded a bend. The junk had run ashore and the crew were scuttling like ants around a dead cockroach, carrying what looked like cans of kerosene from the flat-bottomed vessel.

The motorboat beached and James jumped out behind Tony, his boots squelching in the sludge. Exhilaration coursed through him. The sun had risen fully now; night turned into day quickly in these parts. The gang had vanished into the mangroves, but a slim youth wearing a bobble hat pulled down to his eyes, in a tunic and baggy black trousers, was struggling on the mud flats.

Tony pointed at the boy and gave the order, 'Grab him!'

James made a move in the direction of the youth, but Wang had got there before him. With deft movements, the Third Officer yanked the boy's hands behind his back and tied them.

'How dare you do this to me?' the prisoner called out in a shrill voice.

'Lash him to that iron ring at the bottom of the junk,' Tony yelled to Wang. 'The tide has turned. With any luck it'll cover him before too long.'

James stared at his Chief Officer; he couldn't believe what he was hearing. 'Is this a joke?'

'They won't let him drown. Someone will come before we have to set the lad free. And it'll save us the trouble of flushing the smugglers out of the undergrowth.'

'What makes you so sure?'

'Experience. You'll see.'

James shrugged. An ex-Royal Navy Lieutenant Commander, Tony had been in the Chinese Maritime Customs since before the war. He was in his early fifties now, twice James's age. He bowed to Tony's superior knowledge and turned away.

Wang marched the boy across the shingle, through the waist-high water, and up to the junk, where he tied him to the ring. James lowered himself down on a smooth rock, took out his cigarette case, and gave a Player's to Tony. He leaned forward. His Chief Officer pulled a lighter from his pocket and held it out.

James inhaled until his head buzzed. He turned and peered at the hostage. They were in a typical tidal creek that dried to a muddy channel at low tide, but would be flooded quickly when the tide came in. The sea had already risen as far as the boy's chest. He must be freezing; water temperatures in winter were a far cry from the tepid seas of summer. James tapped his index finger against his mouth, doubt twisting his gut. 'Are you sure this is going to work?'

'Trust me!'

James shook his head slowly. Tony must have known what he was doing. Everything was under control. He gazed at the top of the beach. In the pale sunlight, the roots of the mangrove opened out like giant fingers; they would be flooded soon. The bottom of the junk would be submerged in no time, and the boy with it. The smugglers were probably watching from behind the scrub and they might be armed. James's hand hovered over his gun.

A scream reverberated across the waves. Water was lapping at the prisoner's chin. *Enough!* James leapt to his feet. 'If you don't untie him, I will,' he said to Tony.

'Calm down!' Tony grabbed his arm. 'Someone's coming.'

A portly Chinese man was waddling towards them from the edge of the mangroves. 'Let go my niece!'

Niece? James stared at the man. The smuggler hawked phlegm from his throat and spat it onto the sand.

'Before we untie anybody,' Tony said, 'hand over the goods!'

The man wagged a finger. 'You let go my niece first!'

'The goods first,' Tony repeated.

Another scream resounded from the junk. 'Uncle!'

The smuggler barked orders to his men, and they reappeared from the mangroves with the cans.

'Go to it,' Tony said, handing James a knife.

James gave his pistol to Wang, kicked off his shoes, shrugged off his shirt, and waded into the sea. He swam hard, making frantic strokes for the final couple of yards. Then he dived underwater. In the murk he searched around for the ropes, then sliced into them.

Hands freed, the prisoner slid from his grip and swam towards the beach. James followed, but a wave came from nowhere and knocked his head against the side of the junk. He gulped salt water, his heartbeat echoing in his ears. His arms flailed and his eyes lost focus. He clutched at his throat, gasping for breath.

Someone grabbed his waistband and pulled him upwards. A hand cupped his chin; he was being hauled back to the shore.

James dragged himself to his feet, staring at the person who'd rescued him. Hat removed, wet hair fell dark and long over the slight shoulders of a young woman. *Bloody hell!*

'I thought you were supposed to be rescuing me,' she said, jutting out her chin. She shivered and rubbed her wrists where the rope had left red marks.

James coughed, and a searing pain slashed through his lungs. 'So did I,' he said, taking an agonising breath. He retched, and vomited brine. The girl studied him, her arms folded.

Wang and the smuggler came up. Teeth chattering, James took his shirt from the Third Officer. Where was Tony? James gazed around. His Chief Officer was busy seizing the goods and loading them into the motorboat. They would have to make several journeys to ferry them to the ship. James took one step forward, but his knees gave way and he grabbed hold of Wang.

Wang lifted him into the boat and James's legs scraped the rails. Tony's face came into view. 'What the hell happened to you?'

'Nearly drowned.' James coughed.

'We'd better get you to a hospital.'

He lay on the deck. Tony had gone off somewhere. Was that him in a huddle with the smugglers? James couldn't be sure. Bizarrely, the mangroves behind the beach had turned into a dragon, like the one the locals danced with at Chinese New Year. A niggle prickled at the back of his mind. Why hadn't Tony given the order to seize the junk? James coughed again; he could hardly breathe.

17

SOFIA

Sofia marched up the plank to the prow of the junk. She stared at the departing Englishmen. Her so-called rescuer's cropped curls had reminded her of the burnished copper coins she'd collected as a child. Interesting, but he was a *gwailo* foreigner and a Customs' man; she doubted she'd see him again.

'Why didn't you send someone to free me sooner?' she asked her uncle. 'I was frightened.'

'You? Afraid? What about all that kung fu?' He laughed. 'In any case, you shouldn't have stowed away on my junk.'

Uncle was right; she shouldn't have. He often took her with him now the war was over. After he'd refused this time she'd wanted to find out why. Once he'd discovered her hiding among the kerosene cans, he'd told her about his plan. His ingenious plan. Uncle was so clever.

Movement came from the edge of the swamp, and Uncle's assistant, Derek Higgins, approached, blond hair plastered to his damp forehead and a knapsack hanging from his shoulder. He negotiated the gangplank and opened his bag. With a satisfied grin, he let two gold bars drop onto the deck.

Sofia laughed. The Customs' men had fallen for the ruse. Half-drowning hadn't been part of the plan, but she was safe and so was the gold. She went down to her cabin and took off her peasant outfit. The padded tunic had been warm at first, and the binding with which she'd swathed her breasts had made it easier to run. Such a pity her shoes had got stuck...

Adrenaline had kept her going through the night, yet now her legs wobbled so much she could barely stand. She towel-dried her hair, pulled back the blanket, and climbed into her bunk. Closing her eyes, she hugged herself to stop the tremors. Uncle was wrong. For a few moments she'd been terrified nobody would cut those ropes in time.

* * *

The next evening, Sofia sat with Father drinking tea. 'It's time for my opium,' he said. 'Will you prepare my pipe?'

She followed his stooped frame to the large front room divided by a black lacquered antique Chinese screen. Despite seeing it practically every day of her life, she still loved the beauty of the Sung Dynasty city depicted in gold, the river spanned by a bridge crowded with ordinary people and aristocrats in their sedan chairs.

When she was little, she used to imagine all sorts of stories about the screen, the workers on foot carrying their goods up the path to the teahouses, the farmers tending their crops and live-stock, the boats on the river lining up to dock. An idyllic scene. It was a shame real life wasn't like that...

Father grunted. She gazed at his ravaged face. Until a year ago, he'd been handsome, but now the strains of illness had robbed him of his looks. His mouth, once full, was a thin scar; his cheeks had hollowed and his eyes seemed sunken. Tears stung Sofia's eyes and she went to open the drawer.

The stem of the pipe was fashioned out of carved ivory that had yellowed with age. She smeared a pinch of thick, sticky black resin over a pinhole in the spherical bowl at the base, lit a lamp, and held the bowl over the flame. The opium vaporised. With trembling hands, she handed the pipe to him.

Tonight, she prepared one for herself as well. It would help her cope. She sucked the rich, sweet-tasting vapour into her lungs and exhaled through her nostrils. Almost immediately, it was as if her mind had been freed. Her body relaxed. Although it wasn't customary to chat while smoking opium, there was something she needed to know. 'Father,' she said, stroking his fingers. 'Uncle told me you haven't much time left. Please say it isn't true.'

'I'm sorry, *querida*.' Father lifted his bony shoulders in a sigh. 'The cancer has spread. Don't worry, you'll be well looked after. Your brother will make sure of it. Promise me you'll be nice to him!'

Eyes half-closed, Sofia caught the sharp note in his voice. She wasn't a regular user and the rare times she smoked with him, she fell into dreams before he did.

'Promise me!'

His voice seemed to come from far away. She wanted to answer, but the opium had taken hold and she drifted off.

* * *

Sofia packed away her books in Father's study. She'd just had her last lesson with Senhor Pereira. Officially, her education was over. Father had done what Natalia had wished for her; he'd employed the best tutors. Sofia's chest squeezed. She still missed her governess so much. News had come via Uncle when the war had ended that Natalia had gone back to Russia, where she'd become a teacher. *I hope she's happy.*

As for herself, Sofia still had a lot to learn, and she couldn't wait to go out into the world and learn it. Tomorrow she would start her job with Uncle, helping him set up a cotton-spinning factory in Hong Kong. She would continue taking her turn nursing Father, of course, but she couldn't wait to learn about business. That was the future for her. She'd begged Father to let her work for him in the Consortium; he'd said it was Leo's domain now and, given their animosity towards each other, he couldn't allow it.

How to be nice to Leo? Leo no longer taught her martial arts. Leo no longer smiled at her. Leo no longer even talked to her if he could help it. Nearly five years had gone by since Michiko and her family had died. A deed for which he blamed Natalia, and, by association, Sofia. At first, each time she saw him, she'd pleaded with him that she'd known nothing about Natalia's subterfuge. Father had been right about Leo's character... He only saw things in black and white. And his jealousy had returned. It wasn't the jealousy of a boy; it was the jealousy of a grown man, insidious and so much worse.

The study door swung open, and there he was. Wasn't there a saying that you shouldn't think of the devil or you'll conjure him up? *Ha!* Except, Leo wasn't a devil; he was just flawed.

'I've come from your uncle's. He's let me down. I won't be using him for any of my shipments in future.'

'Oh?'

'You're welcome to him. I wouldn't trust him farther than I could throw him.' He spun on his heel and left the room.

A ridiculous urge to stick out her tongue came over her, but she wouldn't do it. She was too old for such nonsense. Sofia picked up her last English grammar book and shoved it into the box by her feet. The servants would deal with it later. She needed to check on Father before her martial arts teacher arrived for her weekly lesson.

18

JAMES

At the stern of his launch in Macau's Inner Harbour, James eyed the sampans and junks clustered along the foreshore. It was his first day back at work after two days in hospital and a week on leave. His lungs were back to normal, thank God, but he still hadn't tackled Tony about his failure to seize the junk. Scratching his head, James looked down at the muddy water. A sampan, deftly sculled by an old Chinese woman, had come alongside.

A lanky blond man, sat at the prow, shaded his eyes with a hand. 'Are you Lieutenant James Stevens?'

'I am.'

'Then Mr K C Leung would like you to have dinner in the Bela Vista Hotel at eight o'clock.'

'I'm sorry.' *Who the hell is K C Leung?* 'I don't accept invitations from people I don't know.'

'Mr Leung is the uncle of the girl you freed a couple of weeks ago. I'm Derek Higgins, by the way.'

James laughed. 'You already know who I am.'

'My employer makes it his business to know everything that

goes on in Macau. And he knows you've been surveying the coastline.'

'It's a heck of a task. Hasn't been updated since before the war.'

'Haven't you bitten off a bit more than you can chew?'

James straightened his back. 'Not at all.'

Higgins smirked. 'I'll see you at eight?'

'I apologise again. But I can't have dinner with a smuggler.'

'Mr Leung doesn't wish to compromise you. He merely wishes to discuss a proposal. Who knows? He might even be able to help you in your anti-smuggling operation.'

Curiouser and curiouser. Maybe Leung will shed some light on Tony's recent activities?

'The Bela Vista, you say? Why not? I've heard the food is excellent.'

Up on the bridge, James took out the charts he'd prepared from his last visit here. The shifting tides, sandbanks and mud from the Pearl River were making completion of his survey more difficult than he cared to admit. He rolled up his papers and gave his six-man crew the order to leave.

James spent the rest of the day crisscrossing the narrow straits separating Macau from China, taking soundings of the depths and recording information to be drawn up into charts. From the corner of his eye, he could see a distant junk keeping pace with his launch. He rubbed his chin. One junk looked much like another, but it was definitely the same junk, unmistakable for the rectangular patch in one of its sails.

* * *

Later, the setting sun pinking the sky, he climbed down to his dinghy. He'd put on the white full-dress uniform with gold epaulettes, kept on board for meeting local dignitaries. Not that

Leung could be considered a dignitary. James had a feeling he'd need to put on a show tonight, however, even if he had no jurisdiction in Portuguese Macau. Why had Leung invited him to dinner?

James's boatswain rowed him towards the pier. At the top of the barnacle-covered steps, James signalled for a rickshaw. A middle-aged man, with teeth that were just blackened stumps, stopped chewing a stick of sugarcane and grinned at James. His calf muscles bulging, the man loped between the shafts of the chariot, pulling him at a steady pace down a narrow street.

The aroma of sizzling pork from the pavement kitchens mingled with the swampy stench of old drains. James took in the scene around him. Zigzagging between bicycles, rickshaws and cars, a coolie in a straw hat was carrying a bamboo pole bent over his shoulder, bow-shaped from the weight of his load.

A woman with a baby in a sling on her back had stepped right into the path of the rickshaw. With a swerve, the woman turned and pushed her way between the stalls and into the open doorway of a jewellery shop. From the upstairs windows the clack of mah-jong tiles clashed with the hubbub of music and voices shouting in Macanese.

One day soon James would spend longer in Macau, maybe even his next leave, he promised himself. He'd love to explore the cobbled streets of the old town and immerse himself in the exotic atmosphere.

After loping along an avenue lined with banyan trees and up a small hill, the rickshaw arrived at the Bela Vista. Higgins was leaning against the door frame of the elegant nineteenth-century mansion. 'At last,' he said, holding a cigarette between his thumb and forefinger and flicking ash.

James settled his fare. It was only five minutes past eight; he wasn't late. He lengthened his stride and followed Higgins through the foyer, up a staircase to a mezzanine floor, then past a reception desk and bar.

In the restaurant, the smuggler got up from his seat and pulled out the chair next to him. 'Let me introduce myself properly,' he said in heavily accented English. 'I am K C Leung.'

'How do you do?' James shook hands. He sat down and glanced at the woman sitting opposite Leung. Not the dishevelled girl he'd 'rescued', but one so striking he had to look away in order not to be thought rude for staring.

'This is Miss Sofia Rodrigues,' Higgins said from the other side of the table. 'I believe you swam together but haven't met formally.'

James leaned forward and extended his hand, briefly glancing at her tight-fitting cheongsam dress, her small breasts outlined against the silk.

Sofia's warm fingers pressed his. He sat back and contemplated his surroundings. Potted palms were standing like sentinels in the corners of the room. A Latin crooner, accompanied by a pianist, was singing 'I've Got You Under My Skin'. Wooden ceiling fans stirred the air, although the heat and humidity of summer had passed.

The Bela Vista was everything he'd imagined: starched linen, silverware and candlesticks on the tables, waiters jumping to light his cigarette.

Shame you're almost certainly not here for the pleasure of your company.

Leung confirmed his order of the most expensive choices on the menu: shark's fin soup, abalone and fried shrimp.

'I hope you're fully recovered,' Sofia said, smiling at James.

'No after-effects. What about you?'

'None whatsoever.' She paused. 'Do you like Macau?'

'Very much.'

'My niece would prefer live in Hong Kong.' Leung gestured towards the girl. 'She think Macau dull. Anyway, she grew up here. Macau neutral and safer place during last war. But people starving. I got a friend who drank soup. Found human finger floating in it.'

'How disgusting.' James had heard the story before and doubted it was true.

'I was in Hong Kong during the war,' Higgins butted in. 'The Japs locked me up in the internment camp at Stanley.'

'My Chief Officer was there too,' James said. 'Commander Tony Chambers. Perhaps you remember him?'

Higgins tugged at his collar. 'The name doesn't ring a bell.'

'Are you based in Macau?' James asked.

'Here and in Hong Kong. I look after Mr Leung's business interests there. But I have a fireworks factory here.'

'Fascinating.' James smiled at Leung. 'Might I ask what those interests are?'

'This and that. This and that.'

Sofia leaned across the table. 'Our food is arriving,' she said to her uncle. 'Remember it is impolite to chat too much while eating. Let's save our energy for digestion!'

They ate in relative silence, making small talk about the dishes and toasting them with *Mao-tai* wine.

After dinner, James shot a glance at Sofia. She was regarding him in a thoughtful way. 'Derek and I will leave you now.' She stood up. 'Uncle wishes to talk to you alone.'

'You have interesting job, Lieutenant Stevens,' Leung said, fishing an ivory toothpick from his pocket and slipping it into his mouth when Sofia and Higgins had left.

James took a sip of water, watching Leung move the toothpick with his tongue.

'You found out if ships can navigate the straits?'

James rubbed his chin. 'That will depend on the tides.'

Leung removed the toothpick and put it back in his pocket. 'I think even at high tide it will be impossible.'

'Why?'

'Because mud from river always clogging up the estuary.'

'Not true. There are channels deep enough.'

'I have fleet of junks that trade between Macau and China.' Leung gave him a cold, hard stare. 'We know these waters.'

'The charts will be published.' James put his glass down. 'And, at high tide, it'll be perfectly possible for ships to navigate.'

'Maybe you make error in one of your measurements? The sea will be too shallow for ocean-going vessels.'

'I haven't made any mistakes.'

Leung laughed and slapped his thighs, great guffaws escaping from his throat. 'I give you ten thousand dollars, help you make a mistake.'

James blinked. Ten thousand dollars was more cash than he could save in years. But he wasn't open to bribes. 'I'm sorry. I can't do it.'

Leung's eyes narrowed; his mouth became a straight line. His cheeks flushed red and anger blazed in his dark irises. Then his expression changed, as if a blackboard rubber had wiped the frown off his face, and he laughed again. 'I admire your integrity, Lieutenant Stevens. You think I smuggle for my own profit? You are wrong. I am helping my country be great again. China is sleeping dragon that will wake as soon as we get rid of Kuomintang.'

'The Customs is a Chinese government organisation. I work for your country.'

'Unfortunately, you work for wrong side. What will happen to your job when communists win?'

'I'll find something else if push comes to shove.'

'Not if, but when,' Leung said.

'Well, thank you for an interesting evening and a delicious dinner.' James got to his feet. 'It's late and I need to return to my launch. Please give my compliments to your niece.'

Leung lit a cigar and waved James off. He strode past the bar. Sofia and Higgins were deep in conversation. Envy stabbed James at the thought of Higgins with the girl. She was off-limits to him, however; he'd be drummed out of the Customs if he were seen with the niece of a smuggler. God, she was beautiful, though. And exotic, with those dark-grey eyes. She spoke English with an intriguing accent, too. How did she come by that?

Back on his launch, the cool night air was a gentle caress. He lit a cigarette and stared at gas lights on the seawall reflecting in the harbour. A full moon had launched a glimmer of silver across the swell of the waves.

He gazed at the silent sea shining in the moonlight. The fishing fleet had already sailed out, the sampans like dozens of fireflies hovering on the horizon. He hoped Leung was wrong about the outcome of the civil war in China, but only a few months ago the Nationalist Government had instructed the Customs to transfer their gold reserves to Taiwan.

Not a good sign.

A rumble, like the sound of a London bus straining uphill, made James spin around. A motorised cargo junk was heading straight for his launch!

'Weigh anchor!' he yelled to his crew.

Heart pounding, he hauled himself up the steps to the bridge. The bows of the heavily built junk were curving towards him. His launch would become driftwood! Cold sweat dripped down the back of his neck.

He braced himself, ready for the collision. Then, at the last moment, the junk veered and shaved the launch's starboard quarter. Wash splashed the foredecks and the boat rocked from side to side.

Knuckles white, James gripped the railing as the junk disappeared into the darkness. An accident? Or deliberate? Could this have something to do with Leung? James wiped his forehead. He had to find out more about the smuggler and his connections...

* * *

The following evening, James found himself stepping onto a sampan back in Hong Kong at North Point. A diminutive woman then sculled him across the harbour towards small, rocky Kellett Island, the Royal Hong Kong Yacht Club headquarters.

They passed through a cluster of fishing boats, and the chatter of conversations floated across the water. James breathed in the aroma of salty spices and his mouth watered. A family was squatting at their low table on the deck of their junk, dipping chopsticks into the communal dishes. A chow dog barked as James's sampan passed the stern of a large trawler, and a bare-bottomed boy peed into the sea, sending an arc of urine into the air.

At the island's landing stage, James paid the boatwoman and clambered ashore. Steps led to a dining room overlooking the harbour.

He gave a start. There were Tony and Jessica Chambers, sitting at a table by the window! He went up to them.

'James, darling,' Jessica said, pecking him on the cheek. She bore an uncanny resemblance to Rita Hayworth. 'How lovely to see you. We must introduce you to Hong Kong society.' She tilted her head. 'Can't have you eating on your own like this.' Jessica took a black Russian cigarette with a gold foil filter from her silver cigarette case and offered him one.

James declined and held out his lighter.

Jessica inhaled deeply, her red hair catching the candlelight as she blew smoke towards him. 'There aren't many suitable ladies around.' She laughed. 'But a good-looking chap like you shouldn't have any trouble...'

'Just don't get involved with a Chinese or Eurasian woman,' Tony chipped in. 'It's not considered appropriate.'

James tensed; he'd see whomever he liked. To hell with the snobbery and prejudice that flourished in the colony. But he had to make his way in this place, he realised, where colonial attitudes governed society. From what he'd seen, and he hadn't needed to see much to form an opinion, the expatriate population was determined to keep up appearances and live as if they were in one of those glitzy 1930s films. It was unlike anything he'd ever experienced, and he'd almost had to reinvent himself here, so far from his roots.

* * *

'Can I ask you something?' James said to Tony in the office the following morning. 'With all the time off I've had recently, I haven't had the chance until now. Why didn't we seize that junk?'

'What junk?'

'You know. When I nearly drowned.'

'Ah, yes. I'll tell you in a few weeks' time.'

'But...'

Tony put a finger to the side of his nose. 'Trust me and be patient.'

James picked up a stone seal with his Chinese name, Shen Je-man, on it. He dipped it into a flat bowl of red ink and stamped his chart of the Pearl River estuary.

Bloody Tony. What is he up to? Could he be taking kickbacks from Leung? Surely not. There must be another explanation...

19

KATE

I sat next to Lieutenant James Stevens in the Customs motorboat, spots of blood seeping through my cotton gloves, the breeze blowing my hair away from my face. Even at this time of day, the port was busy: barges clustered around ships at anchor; beetle-shaped ferries plied their way towards the mainland; neon advertising signs lit up the tenements on the waterfront. It was just as I remembered, and my nerves tingled in anticipation.

Despite everything that had happened, I was glad to be back. When I'd arrived in Sydney I'd lived with Papa, who'd taken extended leave to recover from internment. Our rented house in Pymble was near the Ladies' College where I'd repeated my final year of school. The appalling conditions in Stanley towards the end had meant that I hadn't been able to concentrate on my studies.

After that first Christmas in Australia, I became a weekly boarder. Papa was soon his old self; he'd joined a golf club where he spent the days putting about on the greens or socialising in the bar, knocking back the whisky sodas and smoking his pipe as much as before the war.

To begin with, I found the unaccustomed freedom and abundance of food strange. At school the girls were pleasant enough, but they'd already formed their cliques. I made friends, but not close ones. Having lost touch with my pre-war chum, Mary, and pining for Charles, I'd found it difficult to form any attachments.

A year later, Papa returned to Hong Kong as *Taipan* of Wellspring Trading, the company he'd overseen before the war, and I started at Teacher Training College in Sydney. It was a fast-track course, only two years, to meet a shortage. And now, here I was... back in Hong Kong.

Engines grumbling, the boat was approaching its destination. Ahead, bobbing sampans lined the shore. Elegant arcaded colonial buildings took up virtually every inch of space alongside the strip of flat land, and green slopes lifted sharply behind them to the Peak. I'd lived a pampered life there in those untroubled days before the Japanese invaded; I knew everything would be different now.

We arrived at a pier with a roof pitched like a Chinese temple and there was Papa, standing in the shade next to his chauffeur-driven Daimler. I jumped off the boat and propelled myself into his arms. 'I thought we'd never get you home in time for Christmas,' he said, hugging me. 'Was that cargo ship all right?'

'Quite comfortable, actually.' I kissed him and his moustache brushed my cheek, the sensation as familiar as the aroma of tobacco radiating from him. 'You look well,' I said. He was much too thin, though... almost as thin as me.

'Thank you for meeting my daughter,' Papa said to Lieutenant Stevens. 'I really should get my own boat one day.' He let out a self-deprecating laugh. 'Why don't I organise a dinner one evening when Tony and Jessica are free, and you can join us?'

Lieutenant Stevens shook hands with Papa. 'I'd be delighted,' he said, smiling directly at me. I thanked him and followed Papa to the car, where porters had already stowed my suitcases.

In the back of the Daimler, I sank into the soft leather, my gloved hand tucked under me. I looked out at the buildings I'd known my whole life: the hundred-year-old St John's Cathedral with its gothic bell tower, the sloping roof of the Peak Tram station and its large clock face. I glanced at the back of the driver's head and my smile wavered. 'What happened to Ah Fong?'

'He died while we were in Stanley,' Papa whispered, patting my arm. 'Starvation, apparently. Dreadfully sad. This is George. Lots of locals are using European first names these days.'

Twirling my jade bangle, I thought about Jimmy. He'd changed his name as soon as he'd learnt to speak English. Did he still call himself Jimmy? Or had he gone back to his Chinese name? I frowned, trying to remember. Chun? Chun, Chun... Oh, Ming, like the vase. A tease from over a decade ago tickled my mouth. His name had been Chun Ming, or Ah Chun to his family and friends.

Gravel crunched under the Daimler's tyres. I rolled down the window. The house was nothing like the shell I'd last seen. The windows were intact again, the outside walls gleaming white, the black roof tiles all in position. Potted poinsettias lined the driveway like they'd done every December of my childhood.

The door opened, and Ah Ho stepped out. Gold teeth catching the sunlight, my old amah seemed just the same. I clambered from the car, flung my arms out wide, and ran forward. 'How are you?' I caught the scent of Chinese herbs and gripped Ah Ho's bony frame.

'Wah! You very beautiful now!'

I laughed. 'How's Jimmy?'

'He in China. He teacher like you.'

Papa gave a tolerant smile. 'Don't stand out here on the

doorstep, dear girl! You can catch up with Ah Ho later.' He made his way into the hall. 'Time for a drink before lunch.'

My heels clicking on the parquet floor, I followed him into the sitting room. Papa sat in an armchair, and dear Ah Woo, our old houseman, arrived with a whisky soda on a tray. I greeted him and was rewarded with a grin practically as wide as his face.

Later, I let myself out through the veranda doors and took a seat on the patio. My gaze was immediately drawn to the spot where, before we'd left for internment, I'd watched Papa and Ah Woo bury the family silver. The heady scent of the Bauhinia flowers wafted towards me. *Such memories!* I peeled off my blood-soaked glove and stared at the scabs on my hand. Tears welled up.

A shout came from Papa. 'Kate, where have you got to? Lunch is nearly ready!'

I dried my eyes and stared at the place where Papa and Ah Woo had dug that grave-like trench. I stuffed my gloves into my pocket. I should bury the past and everything that had happened... just like I'd buried the silver photograph all those years ago. I wouldn't harm myself any more; I would put it all behind me. Straightening my shoulders, I turned and headed back into the house.

* * *

A month after my return to the colony, I was standing on the veranda overlooking the harbour, waiting for Papa's guests to arrive. Light radiated from myriad buildings boasting neon signs below me. On the dark water, ships shimmered in the evening glow. Ferries festooned with fairy lights made their way to and from Kowloon, a giant pool of illuminations watched over by the shadowy shape of the encircling hills. All the years I'd been away,

I'd dreamed of this view, and I'd looked at it every night since I'd returned, never tiring of it.

The grumble of a car engine reverberated from the driveway, and I went indoors.

Tony and Jessica Chambers, followed by Lieutenant James Stevens, were coming through from the entrance hall. 'Jessica, how glamorous you're looking tonight,' Papa said, getting up from his armchair. He held out his hand to James. 'Welcome. What would you like to drink?'

'A gin gimlet, please.'

Papa summoned Ah Woo by ringing the small brass bell from the sideboard. 'Where has Kate got to? Oh, there she is!'

I hesitated in the doorway and then walked forward, the gold silk of my gown swishing. 'Hello, everyone!'

'Kate, darling!' Jessica aimed a kiss at my cheek. 'My goodness. You're all grown up. And so pretty. Not that you weren't before, but that ghastly camp made us all look like ghouls by the end.'

Tony strode across the room and enveloped me in a hug. I pushed down the panic spreading through me. I should have realised seeing Tony and Jessica again would crack the thin veneer with which I'd sealed the past.

At dinner, talk soon turned to the civil war in China. 'Looks as if the communists are getting the upper hand,' Tony said.

'Humph. I heard Peking has fallen without a fight,' Papa muttered.

I swallowed a lump of apprehension. 'The communists aren't going to want Hong Kong, are they?'

'They have to respect the treaties,' Jessica said. 'Don't we have a lease on the New Territories until 1997?'

Tony helped himself to a slice of beef Wellington from the dish held out by Ah Woo. 'I doubt the colony will be able to hold out against the People's Liberation Army any better than against the Japanese. Not unless we reinforce the garrison.'

'But I've only just come home,' I said, my mouth dry.

Papa reached across the table and patted my hand. 'Don't worry! China is in a complete mess. She's not going to risk the wrath of the world by attempting to invade us.'

'Good thing too,' James said. 'I've had enough war to last a lifetime.'

'What do you think of Hong Kong?' I asked him.

'Very friendly. It's a bit like a village. I mean, the European population is small so it's easy to get to know people.'

'You're right, I suppose. I just wish we had more Chinese friends. That's something I hope will change. It must be interesting for you to work for the Customs and spend so much time in China.'

'Actually, I'm planning to hand in my notice and find a shore job. The Chinese won't employ Europeans for much longer, not with the communists taking over. Tony's managed to get himself appointed General Manager of Holden's Wharf. He wants me to be his deputy as soon as he can wangle it.'

'Good luck!' I smiled.

'Thanks. Are you working?'

'I met the Director of Education last week. He said there was a shortage of teachers and, as I've just qualified, he offered me a job at my old primary school. I start on Monday.'

James lifted his glass. 'Congratulations!'

'Thank you.'

The evening ended with coffee, liqueurs and dancing to a Bing Crosby gramophone record. 'You must've been a beautiful baby,' Crosby crooned as James whispered the lyrics in my ear.

'Don't!' I stiffened. 'You're embarrassing me.'

A wry smile curved his mouth. 'I apologise for that, but I've never spoken truer words, Miss Wolseley.'

'Please, call me Kate.'

'Only if you stop referring to me as Lieutenant Stevens. I'm James.'

'James. It's a nice name.'

'And I rather like Kate.'

'Well, at least we agree on something,' I said, my lips twitching. 'I wonder if we'll agree on anything else...'

'Only one way to find out.'

'Oh?'

'We could have dinner together.'

'Let's see,' I said, regarding him sideways. *How to let him down?* 'I'm terribly booked up, you know. Perhaps you'll telephone me in a day or two?'

'Can't you tell me now?'

'I'm sorry. I really am. For some reason, I'm invited out almost every night to parties, dinner and dances. I think it's because there aren't many young women for people to invite.'

'Certainly none as lovely as you,' he said, his tone sincere. 'Shall I ring you tomorrow when you've consulted your diary?'

'Now you're making me sound pretentious. Come onto the veranda and I'll show you the view!'

I linked my arm with his and led him outside.

'It's fabulous,' he said.

'Did you know that the Chinese believe the earth is a living entity and its breath is *chi*, dragon vapour?' I pointed. 'Those hills are actually dragons that have rolled themselves south across China. In Kowloon, *gau lung* means "nine dragons". Except there're only eight of them as the emperor himself was considered a dragon, the ninth one.'

'Fascinating.'

'Hong Kong is a real dragon's lair. When I was little, I used to fantasise about the creatures coming to life while I slept. They'd be protecting the territory and keeping us safe in this haven. Pity they took a break from their duties and let the Japanese invade,' I said, gripping my arms so hard I felt a sharp pain.

Stop! I mustn't think about it; I'd resolved to leave the past buried, hadn't I? I hadn't harmed myself since I'd got back, and I wouldn't start again now. That had been part of my previous life, the lonely time in Australia when all I had were my memories.

I led James back inside and went to sit next to Jessica on the sofa, letting her prattle on about the best shops where one could buy silk. *How to get out of having dinner with James Stevens? I mused.* He was charming, admittedly. Easy to talk to and good-looking. But there was only one person who could melt the ice within me. One person who could light my inner flame. One person whom I could love...

20

JAMES

James picked his way along the quayside. *Heung Kong* – Fragrant Harbour. He let out a wry laugh. *Not very fragrant today.* Such a stench: bilge, sewage, seaweed, dead fish and a rotting pig's carcass, the flotsam of a busy port, borne on the muggy April air.

A crane was lifting a crate from the hold of a vessel. He stepped aside and stared at the Holden's Wharf godowns, lined up like army barracks, an office block in the centre. It was here that Tony was waiting for him to start his new job.

A new challenge. I can't wait.

James thought about his duties. He'd have to help oversee the unloading of European imports destined for the colony from the company's Red Funnel ships. They'd be loaded with Hong Kong re-exports, mainly of goods from China, on the return journey to England. All he needed, apparently, were good organisational skills and a degree of honesty. The last deputy had left under a black cloud, something to do with demanding too many kick-backs from the stevedores. James's administration skills were excellent. And he prided himself on his honesty; he'd proved his integrity by not accepting that bribe from Leung, hadn't he?

The lift boy slammed the doors shut and the old machine clanked up to the second floor. Eagerly, James stepped into the office. Fans whirred on the ceiling, stirring the heat and humidity of early summer. *Urgh!* Spring was practically non-existent in Hong Kong; the season had changed from cool and damp to hot and wet overnight. For the next six months he'd be scraping mould from his shoes and books and taking salt tablets to replenish the minerals he'd lose sweating. But not to worry, it was a small price to pay for getting out of war-torn Britain.

'There's your desk, old chap.' Tony pointed towards the centre of the room. 'The blackboard behind you is to keep track of all the ships unloading from the wharves and loading from junks in the harbour. There's a stack of paperwork from the godowns for you to tackle as well.'

'I'll get cracking then.' James didn't mind being Tony's work-horse; it wouldn't be forever. His salary was even better than it had been with the customs, but as soon as he found someone to back him, he wanted to start an import-export business. There was money to be made in Hong Kong, and he'd be one of those who made it.

Work kept him busy all morning, and at lunchtime he was enjoying bacon and tomato sandwiches with Tony at the USRC, the United Services Recreation Club, in the heart of Kowloon. They sat sipping coffee in the members' lounge and leafing through the newspapers.

'Bloody hell! My old ship the *Amethyst* has been caught up in the communist advance.' James put down *The South China Morning Post*. 'Apparently, she ran aground on the Yangtze, came under heavy fire, and there were a huge number of casualties.'

'That's a bit of a poor show.' Tony sat back in his armchair. 'We haven't taken sides in their civil war. What the hell was *Amethyst* doing up there anyway?'

'She was supposed to relieve *Consort* and evacuate British and Commonwealth citizens from Nanking.'

'Thank God we left the Customs when we did. I wouldn't like to be in China with all this malarkey going on.'

'You're damn right. I only hope they leave us in peace here.'

'We can't defend the colony. If it comes to that, we'll just have to hand it back. But I don't think it'll come to that, old boy.'

'I bloody hope not.' It would be just his luck if the Chinese came over the border and fucked everything up. 'Hong Kong seems to be full of nationalist Kuomintang supporters. Don't know which group is worse. The communists or the nationalists.'

'As far as I'm concerned,' Tony said, 'they're each as bad as the other. Our friend K C Leung, for instance.'

James shuffled forward in his seat. Finally, Tony had mentioned the smuggler. 'Can you tell me now why we didn't seize his junk?'

'Been meaning to fill you in but have only just got the go-ahead from Special Branch.'

'Go-ahead? Special Branch?' James's jaw dropped.

'I helped them out when I was in the Customs. Found out Leung has been smuggling goods into China. He's involved with the same guerrillas who helped some of our POWs escape during the war.'

'So that's why you let him go...'

'That and his links, or rather his niece's links, with the Macau Consortium.'

'Macau Consortium?'

'A gold trading monopoly backed by the corrupt Portuguese administration. They fly the gold into Macau from Hong Kong on seaplanes.'

'I thought gold trading was regulated by international agreements.'

'Portugal didn't sign up to them. They decided to play the open market. The China price for gold is higher than anywhere else. It isn't supposed to leave Macau, and officially it never does.'

'But unofficially...?'

'Special Branch has heard that Sofia's half-brother is smuggling the gold back into Hong Kong. They suspect local banks are buying some of it. They want to find out which ones.'

James leaned in closer, intrigued. 'And...?'

'Special Branch needs someone to keep an eye on Leo Rodrigues, and I'm no longer up to it. Also, they want someone to get the confidence of Leung's niece. She's the daughter of Paulo Rodrigues, who runs the Consortium.'

'What are you asking, exactly?'

'The Head of Special Branch, Gerry Watkins, knows Leung invited you to dinner the last time you were in Macau.'

'And?'

'Gerry wants you to go back there. Pretend to be a tourist. Contact Leung's niece. Perfectly legitimate thing to do. After all, she's quite a beauty.'

James sat back and thought for a moment. 'Do you need my answer straight away?'

Tony lit a cigarette. 'Mull it over for a couple of days then let me know. You'll be richly rewarded if you do decide to accept. Well, that's enough talk for now. We'd better get a taxi back to the office.'

At his desk, James checked bills of lading. He was finding his new job just as easy as his previous one; it hardly required any intelligence at all, and he prided himself on his intelligence. Despite his inadequate schooling, he'd pulled himself up by his own efforts to be the match of anyone he came across. He read voraciously and was addicted to a wide range of fact and fiction. Only last night, he'd had his nose buried in *The Naked and the*

Dead, one of the best war stories ever written. It was thanks to his officer training in the Navy that he'd received an education of sorts, but he'd kept on learning ever since. One thing he did lack, though, was wealth. And a place in society. He'd get both before too long. He'd bloody better...

He glanced at his watch. Time to call it a day. He'd go for a bath and a massage before catching the ferry over to the Hong Kong Island side of the harbour. It would be the ideal place to think about Tony's proposition.

* * *

In the bath house cubicle, he undressed and locked away his things in a drawer beside the bed. A uniformed attendant in soft-soled slippers wrapped him in a towel. He'd been here several times and no longer felt any shame at standing naked before another man. In fact, the whole experience had become quite impersonal. He sipped a San Miguel and relaxed.

The attendant returned and indicated that he should follow him to a room, which bore a surprising resemblance to his bathroom back at the small hotel where he'd been staying since he'd arrived in the colony: white enamel bath, wooden soap-and-sponge tray, brass taps. The attendant prepared the water, stirring it to make sure the temperature was right and adding pine-scented salts.

James immersed himself. Should he get involved with Special Branch? The sum Tony had mentioned on the way back to the office meant he'd be able to afford that Dragon yacht he was hankering after, not to mention have a bit of cash to fall back on.

I'm very tempted...

A bath boy opened the door. The slim young man with a

shaven head was stark naked. Having the bath boys work nude was probably a way of saving on drying their clothes.

'Can do?'

'Yes. Can do.' James closed his eyes and prepared to be ministered to like a baby. The boy lifted each of his limbs out of the warm soapy water. The sense of relaxation was so complete, James began to drift off. But the youth stopped washing between his toes, prodded him, and made motions with his hands that he should stand up.

After placing two boards on top of the bath at right angles to form a T, the boy signalled that James should stretch out on the stem. The young man wrapped a hot, dry towel around his forearm and rubbed him with it, rubbing and rubbing until he sloughed off the top layer of James's skin. It came away in filthy black sheets. How could there be so much dirt? He was meticulous about cleanliness and showered morning and night.

Back in the cubicle, he lay on the bed. The uniformed attendant returned and covered him with a towel, through which he massaged his arms and chest. James let his thoughts drift again. Sofia Rodrigues intrigued him. Could she be involved with the disreputable side of her family's business?

I'll have to tread carefully...

The attendant stopped pummelling and pinching and asked him to roll over. He climbed onto James's back and walked up and down his spine, kneading him with his feet. It was impossible to concentrate and James gave himself up to the massage. The attendant bent his legs up towards the back of his neck. 'Ouch!'

'*Finishy... Tippu?*' The masseur held out his trousers.

James dressed and tipped the boy. Out on the street, the heat hit him like a punch in the guts, and soon he was sweating again, moisture prickling his armpits and hairline.

He walked past shops selling embroidered linen, carved ivory statuettes, jade jewellery and other curios. Better go back to his hotel, he thought. He needed to get ready. After repeated requests, at long last, he was taking Kate Wolseley out to dinner.

21

KATE

A fan on my dressing table stirred the warm evening air as I sat marking a set of exercise books. Despite the memories, I was glad I'd come back to Hong Kong. I loved teaching at the Peak School; my job filled my days and the loneliness of Australia was fast becoming just a memory.

Sometimes, in Sydney, I used to go out to the pictures and dancing in the evenings with casual male acquaintances in order not to feel so alone. None of them could take Charles's place in my heart, though.

I shut my eyes and remembered the feel of his smooth skin against mine. One day, I'd go to the area where that ship had been sunk and lay a wreath of orchid tree flowers over his watery grave. Heart aching, I covered my face with my hands, lost in the memories of my only love.

A knock sounded, and Papa peered around the door. 'Aren't you having dinner with Lieutenant Stevens?'

I rubbed my eyes. 'Yes. With James.'

'He's a very nice young man. Entirely suitable.'

I put my pen down. 'What do you mean?'

'I think he could be right for you.'

'I'm only going out for dinner with him.' I gritted my teeth. 'Nothing more.'

'You should consider your options. I'll be retiring next year and you need to find yourself a husband if you want to stay on in Hong Kong. Someone who can keep you in the style to which you've become accustomed, as they say.'

Papa shut the door. I picked up my pen and scratched it across a spare sheet of paper. Papa treated me like a child, and no wonder... I was still living at home. I'd looked for a flat, but accommodation was at a premium because of all the war-damage. I'd just have to put up with him babying me for now. As soon as the right place became available, or I found a flatmate, I'd move.

I scrunched up the paper and threw it into the wastepaper basket. I had no intention of getting involved with James Stevens. I had no intention of getting involved with anyone. I'd only agreed to have dinner with him when he'd asked me so many times it was impolite to refuse.

I went to my wardrobe. What should I wear? *Something not too alluring.* I flicked through my dresses and found a yellow taffeta frock with a V neckline and fitted waist.

After taking a bath, I dressed, left the house, and strolled to the Peak Tram station. The bell rang and the funicular started its descent. From my seat at the front of the car, I looked out at the thick sub-tropical jungle dropping steeply down to the city below. Once, I'd glimpsed a cobra curled in the shadows; I'd seen it raise its head and spread its hood as the tram rattled by. But today there were no reptiles lurking in the undergrowth, and soon we arrived at the terminus. Stepping onto the pavement, I found a rickshaw to take me to Jimmy's Kitchen, the oldest European restaurant in Hong Kong.

James was waiting at the bar, gin gimlet in one hand and a cigarette in the other.

I took the stool next to him. 'Am I late?'

'Not at all. You're looking beautiful. That colour really suits you. What would you like to drink?'

'A brandy soda, please.' Glancing up, I was startled by the intensity of his gaze, and felt a flush up the side of my neck. 'How's the job at Holden's Wharf?' Best keep him talking about himself. That way he wouldn't be able to ask too many personal questions. Even if his deep blue eyes smiled attractively in that fine English face...

'The work is hardly exciting, but the best thing is, the company's building some flats in Kowloon.' James signalled the waiter. 'So I'll be able to move out of my hotel.' He fixed me in his gaze. 'Have you always lived on the Peak?'

'Yes. The servants love living at number eight.'

'Oh. Why?'

'The Chinese consider eight an excellent number.' A safe topic of conversation, not intimate at all. 'The word for eight sounds the same as prosperous and is also the "yinnest" of the yin numbers from one to nine.'

'Yin numbers?'

'Like everything else in nature, numbers have yin and yang qualities.' Our waiter placed my drink on the table, and I took a sip. 'Odd numbers are considered yang and even numbers are considered yin.'

'Shall we order?' James picked up the menu and handed it to me. 'Then you can tell me all about it.'

'The Mulligatawny soup is a speciality.' I pointed. 'As it says here: lightly spiced and delicious.'

'Sounds perfect. What about the beef stroganoff to follow?'

'You go ahead, James. My stomach can't digest much, so I'll just have a salad.'

'Are you sure?'

'Absolutely. It's nice to be back here, though. I used to come with my parents before the war. It was a bare-boned type of place then, with scrubbed table-tops and naked light bulbs, but the food was always excellent.'

James ordered then turned to me. 'What's the difference between yin and yang?'

'It's a very ancient concept. How do I explain without boring you?'

'I won't be bored. It's fascinating.'

I didn't care if I was boring him to death. It would stop him from inviting me out again, and I wouldn't need to put up with the intense way he looked at me. 'Yin represents femininity, darkness and passivity. I don't agree females are necessarily passive, though.'

'I see your point. What about yang then?'

'It's the opposite: masculine, bright and active. Everything has an opposite, but never absolute.'

'What do you mean?'

'No one thing is completely yin or totally yang. For example, "night", which is yin, can turn into "day", which is yang. If there's an imbalance, an excess or deficiency of one or the other, that's relative as well. A surplus of yang makes the yin become more intense.'

'Seems complex. How do you know so much about all this?'

The waiter interrupted my answer as he led us to a table in the corner, where I told James about my childhood friendship with Jimmy.

'How unusual to have a Chinese lad for a companion. As far as

I'm aware, the British and the Chinese seem to lead a sort of parallel existence in Hong Kong.'

'It's different with the servants. They're almost part of the family and we get to know them. Even so, we must be careful not to make them lose face.'

'Yes, I understand a bit about face. I used to feel as if I was treading on eggshells in the Customs.'

We finished eating, and James suggested we go on to a night club. I yawned, covering my mouth with my fingers. 'I'm sorry to be a wet blanket, but I've got to be up early for school tomorrow. Would you mind dreadfully if we didn't?'

'Not if you promise we can do this again.' He reached across the table and took my hand. 'I'm serious about my intentions towards you, Kate. Dare I hope you might feel the same way?'

I gave a start. This wasn't supposed to happen. I pulled away from him and made the excuse that I needed the loo. In the powder room, I stared at my reflection. Had I been sending the wrong signals? What the hell was I supposed to do now?

Back at our table, James was swirling a brandy. 'I'm sorry for rushing you, Kate. Please forgive me.'

I smiled at him. 'Of course.'

Outside the restaurant, he hailed a taxi. 'Shall I come with you as far as the Peak? The driver can take me to my hotel afterwards.'

'I'll be fine, thanks.'

I waved through the back window of the cab. I couldn't help liking James. He was good-looking and charming. I'd enjoy seeing him again, but I didn't want him to get the wrong idea. I would never love anyone but Charles.

22

SOFIA

By the open grave in St Michael's cemetery, Sofia picked up a handful of earth and threw it onto Father's coffin. The smell of the soil rose in the air: musty, sweet and clinging.

Father had died three days ago in his sleep; for the first and last time in his life, Paulo Rodrigues had lost a fight and the cancer had finally defeated him.

She stared at the wooden casket. He lay inside, dressed in his finest suit. Her chin wobbled and she breathed in gently; she mustn't lose control. Father had brought her up to be strong; he would have expected her to show that strength now.

How could she leave him here in this dismal depressing place, though, crammed with Victorian marble tombs and smelling of rot? Sorrow surged through her, but she couldn't let herself break down in front of all these people. She turned to go.

'Not so fast,' Leo said. 'We have to greet everyone first.'

Sofia went to stand next to him. A queue of dark-suited men had formed. They bowed and shook Leo's hand, then shuffled past and ignored her. Leo had probably orchestrated this charade to humiliate her. The last mourner presented himself. Uncle. 'I'm so sorry,' he said in Chiu Chow, taking a handkerchief from his pocket. 'I hope your father was in no pain at the end.' He dabbed eyes that were almost in danger of disappearing into his fat cheeks.

'The opium took care of that.' Sofia's voice trembled with sadness. 'He spent his last days dreaming.'

'For the best, I expect.' Uncle walked with her to the waiting car. 'What are your plans now?'

'Father has left me half his shares in the Consortium. I want to sell them to Leo and move into your house.'

Uncle patted her hand. 'Yes. It is better you come and live with me. Your mother was my dearest sister, and she would have wanted it.' He sighed. 'Why don't you have dinner with me tonight?'

'Not tonight. I'm too miserable. Can we make it tomorrow at the usual place?' Despite being in mourning, she had to eat. She also had to get out of Father's house. She kept expecting to bump into him around every corner and, when she didn't, the sense of loss was so terribly overwhelming.

* * *

In her bedroom, she changed out of her black funeral dress and put on the baggy kung fu trousers and grey tunic she usually wore at home. She went into the bathroom and splashed cold water onto her cheeks. Her face was pinched with grief and dark circles spoiled the skin under her eyes. She left the room, marched down the corridor, and knocked at Leo's door. 'We need to talk.'

'I'll meet you in Father's study. Just give me ten minutes.'

She looked him up and down. The only thing different about him since Father's death was that the arrogance, once simmering beneath the surface, now rose from him like steam from fresh horse dung.

At Father's antique desk, she pulled out a chair and waited. She didn't need to wait long. Leo crossed the room and took the seat opposite; his newly acquired Boxer dog, Balthazar, lay at his feet.

She pushed back her sleeves. 'I want to sell you my shares in the Consortium. And I'm planning to live at my uncle's.'

'That traitor!' Leo leaned down and fondled Balthazar's ears. 'He's not as clever as he thinks he is. When he was so careless with my shipment, I had him investigated. And it's not over yet.'

'What do you mean?'

'You'll find out soon enough. The terms of Father's will state that I am your legal guardian until you turn twenty-one.'

'My birthday's in October. You might as well let me go now, as you won't be able to stop me then.'

'You can go.' He slammed his hand down and sent a sheaf of papers cascading to the floor. Balthazar barked twice. 'But your shares in the Consortium will remain under my control until October.'

She clenched her fists so hard her arms shook. 'You bastard!'

'It's not me who's the bastard.' Leo's lips twisted into a smirk. 'You're an educated young woman. Think about your prospects and don't be too hasty! There are huge changes taking place in China, and the Consortium is rightly placed to take advantage.'

'I don't want to get involved with your cronies.'

'They're just members of an anti-communist action group, but Mao is gaining ground so they've fled here.'

'And now they're in Macau to make their living by pimping and extortion. I think it's revolting.'

'Your ideals will get you nowhere, Sofia. Life isn't as simple as you seem to believe.'

'There's no point in discussing it any further.' She got to her feet. Of course, she knew it wasn't that simple. She wasn't an idiot. Leo's associates must have found it hard to leave everything behind in China. She wouldn't have liked to have been forced to give up her life. She'd give it up voluntarily when the time was right.

She strode out of the room and across the hall to the staircase. As she passed the front door, the bell rang and she opened it. Derek Higgins was standing on the doorstep.

'Derek! What are you doing here?'

'I've come to give my condolences to you and your brother. I couldn't make it to the funeral.'

'Thank you. I'll call the houseman and he'll take you through to Leo.'

Sofia stared at Derek's back as he followed the servant down the corridor. What was he up to?

* * *

Sofia put down her menu and glanced around the Solmar. She'd told Uncle all about her conversation with Leo. She'd tried to persuade him to intervene on her behalf, but he'd told her she'd be better off biding her time. Five months were nothing, he'd said; they would pass quickly.

Should she tell Uncle that she'd seen Derek at the house? No. She had nothing to go on. All she could do was keep an eye on him. And what about Leo's ambiguous remark? She looked up again and put a hand to her mouth. That Englishman, James Stevens, had just walked into the restaurant.

'Good evening,' he said, coming up to the table and beaming a smile.

'Why don't you join us?' She turned to her uncle. 'That would be all right by you, wouldn't it?'

Uncle grunted his agreement, and James pulled out a chair. 'This restaurant was recommended to me,' James said. 'I'm here for a bit of sight-seeing, and I was going to give my sympathy to you tomorrow. So sorry to hear about your father.'

'He's at peace now.' Best to change the topic of conversation. Talking about Father made her too sad. 'The Solmar is famous for Macau cuisine,' she said.

'Oh?'

'Portuguese traders brought spices from Africa, India and Malaya hundreds of years ago and blended them with native vegetables and seafood. You won't find food like this anywhere else in the world.'

James shuffled his chair closer. 'Fascinating.'

'The most popular dish is *bacalhau*.'

'What's that?'

'It's salted, dried codfish imported from Portugal. Before cooking, the fish slices are soaked in water for hours and hours to get rid of the salt.'

'I don't fancy eating a fish that has come halfway across the world, even if it was in a dried state.' James laughed. 'My boss said I should try the sole.'

'You can order *Linguado Macau* if you want to play it safe. As it says on the menu,' she read, 'fresh and tender Macau soles fried and served with green salad together with cheese, shrimps and seafood.'

'Sounds superb, but I think I'll be daring and try the *bacalhau* after all.'

Ha! He rises well to a challenge. Good to know. 'Portuguese wines are excellent.' She glanced at her uncle. 'Why don't we order a bottle?'

'The best thing to drink with Macau food,' Uncle said, snapping his fingers. 'Waiter!'

They chatted about the history of the Portuguese territory while they ate. James didn't know much about it and seemed genuinely interested.

After dinner, Uncle said, 'I was expecting Derek Higgins to meet me here. I'd better set off and find him. He has to go to Hong Kong for me tomorrow, and I need to give him my instructions.'

Uncle signed a chit then made his way out of the restaurant. This was the first time in her life Sofia had been left alone with a man, and a *gwailo* foreigner at that. Her uncle *must* be worried about Derek to have gone off like that.

She pulled a fan from her handbag and cooled the sudden glow to her cheeks. 'James, how do you fancy visiting a den of iniquity?'

His eyes widened. 'Depends on what sort of iniquity you mean.'

She giggled to cover her embarrassment. What had she said? 'Isn't Macau known as the Monte Carlo of the orient? Maybe we could try a spot of gambling?'

'You had me going there for a minute.' James laughed.

Outside, he placed his hand on the small of her back and ushered her into a taxi. At his touch, a shiver went through her and her breath quickened. She gave the address to the driver and stared out of the window, bringing her emotions under control. This wasn't right; she couldn't allow herself to be attracted to an Englishman.

In the doorway of the Municipal Gaming House, she pushed past a curtain, reeling at the stench of stale tobacco. People stood shoulder to shoulder around the gambling tables, shouting their bets. 'Let's go up these stairs here to get away from the crowds!'

She gazed across the gallery circling the mezzanine floor.

Customers were sitting on uncomfortable-looking stools, lowering their stakes in rattan baskets on string to the pit below. 'They're playing *Fan-tan*.' She grabbed a seat. 'We have to gamble on how many buttons are left when the croupier has finished dividing the piles. Or you can bet on whether there will be an odd or even number.'

She threw herself into the game, exhilaration gripping her. First, she was winning, then she was losing, then she was winning again. Her grief at losing Father still festered, but he wouldn't have wanted her to be miserable. She would think about him in her quiet moments, and live life to the full.

James squirmed on his seat. 'Let's quit while the going is good! I've got the impression this game is rigged. Why don't we go to the casino in the Central Hotel instead? I've heard they've got a cabaret and a good bar. This stool is killing me.'

Out on the Street of Eternal Felicity it was raining. A rickshaw pulled up in front of them. 'We can squeeze in together,' James said.

Sofia did as he'd suggested. She took out her fan again, making a desperate attempt to cool the heat spreading to her face. She caught the scent of James's aftershave and felt the hardness of his body against her own. This *gwailo* was doing strange things to her equilibrium.

The rickshaw stopped in front of the only skyscraper towering above the surrounding two-storey buildings. A neon sign flashed a single Chinese character, the name of the hotel and the symbol for China, China being the centre of the earth.

They found a table in the nightclub on the ground floor. An electronic noticeboard on the wall behind the small orchestra disclosed the results of play from the roulette tables next door. Hostesses in cheongsam dresses fluttered like brightly coloured butterflies around the male clientele.

'What can I get you to drink?' James asked.

'A martini, please.' Cary Grant's favourite. James would think she was so sophisticated.

On the stage, a group of young women in tail feathers were dancing to the beat of the band.

'Shall we place a bet?' James signalled one of the hostesses.

Sofia chose her numbers and their drinks arrived.

'Cheers!' The cool, dry, slightly spicy liquid slipped down her throat. She lowered her glass with a gasp and grabbed James's arm. There, at a table tucked behind a screen dislodged by a passing waitress, sat Derek Higgins and Leo, their heads bowed together.

23

JAMES

James was nursing a glass of cold San Miguel opposite Gerry Watkins of Special Branch in the bar at the United Services Recreation Club. Watkins sported one of those handlebar moustaches that only certain types of men could get away with. James told him about his visit to Macau. 'When Sofia spotted her half-brother and Higgins in the casino, it was as if she'd seen a couple of ghosts. She ducked her head below the table then made me shield her from view as we sneaked out like a pair of thieves.'

Watkins took a drag from his cigarette. 'What happened then?'

'We found a rickshaw, and I left her at her uncle's mansion. She didn't invite me in, but I got the distinct impression she was about to have it out with Leung regarding Higgins's disloyalty.'

'Any idea what Higgins could have been up to?'

'I've no proof, but I'd hazard a guess he's sold out to Leo.'

'What about maintaining your contact with the girl?'

'She told me her uncle is opening a cotton-spinning factory in Kowloon next month, and said she'd send me an invitation.'

'That's good. Try and get closer to her, if you know what I mean. There must be something she needs. Find out what it is and offer to help her. As you know, the Consortium is sitting on a pile of gold and we know a lot of it is making its way into the colony. Could be the Fourteen K Triad are some of the likely recipients.'

'Fourteen K. Who are they?'

'Kuomintang supporters. Some say the name is because there're fourteen big shots. Others reckon the fourteen comes from their original address. We're in the process of identifying them and finding out what they're up to. They're called Triads because of the symbol used.'

'What sort of symbol?'

'The Chinese character, *Hung*, encased in a triangle. Represents the union of heaven, earth and man.'

'Are all Triads criminals?'

'Not necessarily. Sun Yat Sen was the founding father of the Republic of China. Well, apparently, he was a Triad, as are many of the nationalists. There are various factions, but the Fourteen K is a much bigger organisation and much more violent than any of the others.'

'I'll do my best to get closer to Sofia,' James said, intrigued. 'I'll invite her out to dinner and take it from there.'

'Perfect. By the way, a chum of mine, Duncan Smith, District Officer in Tai Po, used to row at Cambridge. He's keen to raise a crew to compete in the dragon boat races.'

'Sounds like fun. When?'

'On the first of June. Tony's game for a laugh as well. We'll have to practise a bit first to get the hang of paddling.'

James nodded. He'd been a good oarsman in the Navy. Joining in with this lark would be a way to show he was 'one of the boys', he thought.

* * *

Dressed in a pair of shorts and nothing else, James was sitting in a fishing sampan stripped of its gear, a carved dragon's head attached to the bow, and a tail fixed to the stern. For the past month he'd been training with Gerry, Tony, and Duncan Smith... a well-muscled ginger fellow. He'd being going like the clappers up and down Tolo Harbour in the New Territories, day after day, sweating buckets and trying to get the hang of driving the blade of his paddle through the water. Now he was as ready as he'd ever be.

James and Tony were perched at the front, with Gerry Watkins and Duncan Smith behind. A Chinese man was beating a drum in the prow of the boat, synchronising the paddling. Another local was acting as coxswain at the stern and steering the vessel with a long oar.

Last week, a religious ritual had taken place to wake the dragon from its slumber... when the head and tail had been fixed onto the boat. The village elder of the Tai Po clan, who managed the affairs of the district under the eye of the colonial administration, had dotted the dragon's fierce eyes with black ink. To all intents and purposes, the dragon had come alive. James smiled at the superstition of it all. Apparently, he was a dragon himself in the Chinese zodiac. He rather liked the fact that Julius Caesar and Abraham Lincoln had been dragons, but not that Hermann Göring and Francisco Franco had also belonged to the same club.

Hot sunshine beat through clouds of humidity and the air was heavy with the stench of drying fish on the quayside, not to mention the rotting seaweed on rocks by the shore. A large crowd had gathered on the waterfront to watch the races, attracted by the spectacle of seeing a *gwailo* team of foreigners competing against seasoned locals. James prodded Tony. 'Why is everyone staring?'

'It's our hairy chests, old chap.' Tony laughed. 'We're like apes as far as they're concerned.'

Sudden gongs signalled the start. James plunged his paddle into the water on the beat of the drum. It took him and his teammates a minute or two to get going. Striking the sea fast and furiously, they started to make good headway and were catching up with the fishermen. James gasped. They were heading for a direct collision!

'Hard over,' he shouted to coxswain. The Chinese man changed the direction of his oar. The boat heeled brusquely and tipped. James and Duncan, on the outside of the turn, fell into the harbour. Tony and Gerry sat in their seats and the boat slowly filled with water. The crowd on the waterfront giggled loudly, clearly embarrassed for the Englishmen at their acute loss of face.

James stood on the seabed. He clutched his sides and laughed. Tony, Gerry and Duncan chortled with him as they waded ashore. 'Well, here's another fine mess you've got me into,' James said, removing seaweed from his hair. He fell against Tony, shoulder to shoulder, and held on to him for support, letting out more belly laughs.

'Duncan's invited us for a beer and a spot of dinner back at his house,' Tony said, chuckling.

'Sorry!' James gulped in air and collected himself. 'But I've got to get a move on. Sofia and her uncle are expecting me at the opening of their factory.'

Tony winked. 'Off you go, then. I'll make your excuses.'

* * *

James took a taxi home to his new flat in Kowloon Tong. He stood at his bedroom window and lifted his gaze over the rooftops towards Lion Rock, the tallest crag in the centre of the hills that formed a backdrop to Kowloon, its shape like one of the lions in Trafalgar Square.

His flat was on the ground floor and had a garden, which made it almost like living in a house. Kowloon Tong was developing into quite a posh residential area. Not the Peak, of course, but it would do for now. One day, he would move up the social ladder and get a place that would be worthy of Kate Wolseley.

Only last night he'd taken her to dinner at the Parisian Grill and told her about his new apartment.

'I wish I didn't have to stay with my father,' she'd said, wistfully. 'It's a bit stifling. There's a teacher at school I've become friendly with and we're thinking of getting a place together. She's in a hostel now, the Helena May. But we can't find anything.'

'I'll keep my ear to the ground. Something's bound to come up,' he'd said, trying to sound more optimistic than he felt. The colony was reaching saturation point with all the refugees pouring in from across the border.

'I wonder what will happen when the dust settles. I mean, when the civil war in China is over.'

'We live our lives in complete isolation, don't we?'

'My father says, whenever there's trouble in China, people come to Hong Kong. In the past they would go back again, but I don't know if that'll happen now.'

'You're probably right. What's going on there will change the place out of all recognition.'

'When I was growing up here, I was pampered and spoilt. It's the way we lived then, but things are different now. I want to contribute. To really be a part of this place.'

'How to you propose to do that?'

'There's an orphanage in the New Territories run by an Englishwoman. She's looking for volunteers and I'm going to offer my services on Sundays.'

'What a good idea! I'm impressed.'

They'd spent the rest of the meal talking about their respective jobs, but whenever James tried to steer the conversation towards more personal matters such as Kate's tastes in music and reading matter, she'd turned the questions round. He'd found he was talking more about himself than he was listening to her.

After dinner he'd taken her dancing and she'd let him kiss her for the first time. Somehow, though, it seemed her heart wasn't in it. Something to do with the way she'd avoided a second kiss. *The proverbial ice-maiden.*

* * *

James showered, letting the tepid water wash away the smell of seaweed. Then he changed into a pair of beige slacks and an open-necked white shirt. The weather was too hot for a jacket and tie. He sent his houseboy to flag down a taxi and knocked back a glass of beer.

Half an hour later, he stood in front of the two-storey factory watching the fireworks that trailed in a long line from the top; they erupted in a cacophony, supposedly to chase away the evil spirits. The sign above the premises, *Leung's Textiles*, showed he was in the right place. James pushed open the door.

The factory floor was crowded with looms, and a receptionist ushered him up the stairs to a large suite of offices. Sofia came forward, her uncle by her side. 'We're honoured you could be our guest.' She indicated a passing waiter. 'Do help yourself to a glass of champagne.'

James glanced at Sofia; she'd moved away and was talking animatedly to another invitee. She was dressed in a simple, elegant, red cheongsam with a split up the sides, revealing her impossibly long, slender legs. God, she was beautiful. He walked over to her, reeled in by an invisible thread. 'Thanks for inviting me. And please give your uncle my congratulations. I was wondering, though, if you're free to have dinner with me?'

'I was going to invite you to come with us. Uncle has arranged for his launch to take the three of us to Aberdeen fishing village. To a floating restaurant.'

'Sounds wonderful.'

24

SOFIA

They boarded the launch at Kowloon pier. The evening air had turned cooler, and Sofia wrapped her silk stole around herself. The vessel crossed the harbour and headed out past Green Island. She chewed her lip. Would James fall in with Uncle's plan? At Aberdeen, the boat nudged into a space at the waterfront and Sofia and James stepped ashore.

Immediately, a crowd of boat women clad in black trousers, aprons, and round woven straw hats surrounded them like a flock of vultures. Sofia had thought James might have found it more amusing to cross the short stretch of water to the restaurant by sampan. A big mistake. The women pulled at James's shirt and jabbered at him in Cantonese. Sofia looked around for Uncle's boat. Too late. It was already halfway across the bay.

She negotiated a price with the most forceful of the 'vultures'. The woman then led them down the stone landing steps to her sampan. Sofia settled herself carefully with James on low rattan chairs. She eyed him contemplating the woman; he appeared mesmerised by her as she revolved a single oar in her hand, rocking back and forth on the heel and sole of her foot.

The sea was flat and black as ink, and ahead shone the gaudy neon signs of the restaurant boat: Chinese characters a foot long and wide in red, blue, and green. The night air was balmy now and redolent with the odour of brine, mixed with the aromas of spices and rice cooking in the village. The voices of the fishing people, sitting at the prows of their junks, carried across the water.

They alighted at the restaurant, where the manager greeted them and showed them the floating pantry. Moored to the seaward side, four large wooden pens had been fastened at water level, their walls bored with holes for fresh seawater. A man rode the brine in a small shell boat.

Sofia pointed to a sleek, grey grouper. The boatman tossed the fish onto a platform floating at right angles to the restaurant. A boy caught it in another net and flung it to the first in a line of cooks. With the flat of his chopper, the cook stunned the fish on a large round board, then passed it on to a second man, who gutted the fish with one stroke of a sharp knife and handed it to a third cook squatting on a stool in front of a brazier.

The fish eventually emerged on a flowered porcelain dish, steeped in soy sauce, bamboo shoots and seasoning. 'Fascinating,' James said. 'This is marvellous.'

A shout echoed, and the boy with the net held up an enormous lobster for Sofia's inspection. It waved its claws in protest as the boy took it to the cook, who chopped it up and panfried it with green onion and ginger.

Another man showed Sofia blue and gold speckled crab and pearl-grey translucent shrimp. She nodded her approval, then led James to a round table overlooking the harbour. Uncle was already there.

Sofia watched the men feasting, until they obviously couldn't eat another morsel, and drinking rice wine until their heads must have been spinning. She took care to eat and drink little; she had to keep her wits about her. James was affecting her equilibrium again... His mere presence was making her pulse dance.

'I'll leave you and take the boat back to Kowloon,' Uncle said after dinner. 'I have business to attend to on the island.'

Uncle's so-called business was a woman he'd set up in a flat in Wanchai. The plan had always been to leave Sofia alone with James. Uncle had said the Englishman would sniff around for some information and he'd told her precisely what to divulge. How did Uncle know this? She shrugged to herself and looked out the window. Their launch had tied up to the side of the restaurant. 'Time to go, James,' she said.

There was plush seating at the stern of the boat and a table for their drinks. Sofia sat next to James, poured him a brandy, then leaned back. 'One day I'll move to Hong Kong,' she said. 'When the time is right.'

'And when will that be?'

'When I've sorted out some family matters.'

'I've been meaning to ask about your family. You never mention your mother.'

'She died giving birth to me.'

'I'm sorry.' He sounded sincere.

'Mother was Uncle's favourite sister and Father's concubine. Uncle considered it an honour. Twenty years ago he wasn't as well off as he is now, but I sometimes wonder if it was more than that. Father passed a lot of business his way over the years.'

'Your English is very good. You have a Russian accent if I'm not mistaken. How did that come about?'

'I had a Russian governess. What about you? Where did you go to school?'

He seemed to hesitate a moment. 'What if I were to tell you that I'm not exactly top drawer?'

'What do you mean?' She met his eye.

'I didn't go to the right school.'

'I've never understood why the British call that "top drawer".'

James swilled the alcohol in his glass then sipped it. 'Oh, these things matter. Cost me the job of my dreams, at least.'

'Oh?'

'I went for an interview to be a Navy pilot, along with a friend of mine. Nick. He'd been to a grammar school...' Another sip went down with a swallow. '...I'd been an apprenticed plumber. He got in, I didn't.'

Sofia shook her head slowly. Should she touch his hand? No. Too forward.

'Mind you, I took it on the chin. I got my commission eventually and became a First Lieutenant. Then the end of the war came, of course. I've done well...'

'*Joss*.'

'*Joss*?'

'Luck, or fate. We're the same, you and I. We must fight harder than anyone else. I'm a Eurasian woman and I'm not from what society considers a good family. I'm a survivor and so are you. That's what's important.'

He leant towards her. 'Tell me about the family matters you need to resolve.'

'You know the Consortium imports gold freely, because Portugal didn't sign up to the gold regulation agreement?'

'Yes.'

'My father was too ill in recent years to realise Leo was getting his employees to melt down the international gold bars. Those bars weighed around twenty-seven pounds each. His men converted them into portable nine-ounce ingots, or thin gold sheets. The smugglers preferred the lower weights as they were easier to transport.'

'What smugglers? We didn't catch anyone smuggling gold when I was in the Customs.'

'They weren't smuggling the gold into China, but to Hong Kong.'

'And your uncle was involved?'

'Uncle's junks used to run some of that gold. Do you remember the first time we met?'

'How could I forget?' he chuckled.

'It was part of a bluff. Uncle told Leo that Customs had seized the gold at the same time they confiscated the cans of kerosene. Leo was suspicious, but he accepted the story.'

'I gather he's found out the truth.'

'Yes. From Derek Higgins. And now Leo wants compensation.'

'Can't say I'm surprised about Higgins.'

'He no longer works for Uncle but has become Leo's henchman.'

'Any reason for that?'

'Derek can't resist money. He'll sell out to the highest bidder every time. Apparently, he helps his parents in England, but he's also addicted to gambling, I've heard.'

'So Higgins has a human side to him after all. Who'd have thought it?' A pause. 'Why did your uncle take the gold?'

'To give to the guerrillas in China.'

'And what sort of compensation is your brother asking for?'

'He's not my brother. Leo is my half-brother and he wants to get his hands on our factory. The amount owed is twenty-eight thousand US dollars and Uncle doesn't have the cash ready.'

'I'm sorry.'

'Leo doesn't need the factory. He's doing this out of spite. He's got his shares in the Consortium and his finger in practically every pie in Macau. Uncle has transferred almost all his interests to Hong Kong, and Leo can't abide that. I think it's also because several Shanghai industrialists are setting up factories near ours. They're nationalists, just like Leo's mother's family.'

'Can Leo legitimately force your uncle to give him the factory?'

'Not legitimately, of course, as he can't admit to the smuggling. But he also has contacts through his mother with the Triads. They're gangsters.'

'I know about the Triads.' James took another sip of brandy. 'And I know someone who would be interested in more information about Leo's associates. I can't promise anything, but they might be able to help. Leave it with me for a week or so!'

'Thank you, James.' She slipped her hand into his and squeezed it gently. She couldn't help herself. He lifted her fingers and kissed the inside of her wrist. A tingle crept up her arm and heat rose from between her legs to her neck. She glanced away from him.

'Sofia. Look at me!'

She turned back to him and placed his hand over her heart.

James's eyes were so bright they appeared to burn. He lifted her chin and kissed her on the lips. She resisted for a second, but he pulled her to him, his hand on the small of her back, and she melded against him. The hardness of his chest pressed against her breasts. The sounds of the harbour receded; all she could hear was the blood rushing through her veins. It felt so very wonderful.

James's hands entwined in her hair and she kissed him back. He reached under her dress, his touch sending currents of pleasure rushing through her. Their kisses grew deeper. This was her first time kissing a man, but she knew what to do instinctively, abandoning herself to the deliciousness of it. She broke off and looked at him, hands on his face. His eyes were heavy with longing.

'Let's go down to the cabin,' she said, not caring about the consequences.

There, the darkness was soft and enveloping; the aroma of polished wood mixed with the scent of the sea. Wrapped around each other, they stumbled onto the bunk. She couldn't see him but felt him stretched out next to her, his mouth on hers, his hands in her hair.

'Tell me to stop,' he whispered.

She shook her head.

'Oh, God...'

They were desperate. His breath came in deep gasps. The split in the side of her dress allowed her to lift one leg and drape it over his. Their kisses became more urgent.

A sharp knock rapped on the cabin door. 'We arrive Kowloon pier,' the boatswain announced.

Sofia sat up and put a hand to her mouth. It felt bruised but ripe, like a soft peach ready to be devoured. She reached for the light switch.

James blinked in the fluorescence. 'I'd say we got the timing absolutely spot-on there.' He smiled.

'We were a bit hasty, don't you think?' She giggled. 'There's plenty of time for us to get to know each other. Especially if you're going to help me save the factory.'

The launch dropped James off and Sofia returned to the cabin. She lay on the bunk, stretching like a lazy cat. She'd been about to give her virginity to a man she barely knew. Only she felt as if she didn't need to get to know him; she knew him already. A shiver of worry stroked her spine, but she ignored it. No need to fret about James feeling the same way; she would trust in *Joss*.

25

KATE

You are entering The New Territories. Please drive carefully! I smiled at the notice. Weren't you always supposed to drive carefully? But we'd left the city behind and the people who lived here weren't used to traffic, I supposed. It was good to get away on my own for once; the constant attention of James, circling around me like a moth, had started to get on my nerves.

The taxi driver suddenly slammed on his brakes. I widened my gaze. A water buffalo had got out of its field and was wandering on the narrow road. After the beast had crossed to a field, we set off again past paddy fields, walled villages, deep valleys, vegetable-plots, and fruit orchards. I smiled at the old women sitting winnowing rice in rattan baskets, their wide-brimmed straw hats bobbing up and down. I marvelled at the graves and jars of human bones dotting the steep hillsides, sited with care so yin and yang were in perfect harmony. Bare-bottomed toddlers at the side of the road waved and called out, 'Hallo, bye-bye.'

Seeing them made me think about the children in Stanley. Once, I'd lined them up for their carol service; it was our last one in the camp even though we didn't know it then. I'd gazed fondly at the Japanese man conducting. The Reverend Kiyoshi Watanabe had been our latest interpreter and a more sympathetic man than any we'd had previously.

A Lutheran minister, he'd studied at the Gettysburg Seminary in the United States, where he'd been given the name John. The children in the camp called him Uncle John. The infants had sung 'Away in a manger, no crib for a bed', and I'd joined in. Uncle John then launched into a rendition of 'Holy Night' in Japanese, his tone strong and true. Yet, in the audience, several people had talked loudly and spoilt his performance. Papa told me only the other day he'd heard that Uncle John's wife and daughter had been vaporized by the Hiroshima atomic bomb. I'd wept hot tears for the suffering...

The gates of the children's home, as it was called, rose in front of me now. A formidable-looking European woman was striding down the drive, mud-coloured hair a mass of frizz, and steel-grey eyes framed by tortoiseshell glasses.

I held out my hand to the woman I'd heard so much about: Miss Denning. A missionary sent to Hong Kong in the early 1930s, I recalled, Miss Denning had been struck by the plight of hundreds of babies abandoned as a result of poverty and superstition. With support from local missionaries, she'd started the orphanage and had managed to keep going through charitable donations. During the war, she and her helpers had suffered violence, starvation, dysentery and recurrent malaria, but they'd refused to abandon their charges. I felt a rush of admiration for them.

'You'll find we're like a family,' Miss Denning said, leading me towards the building. 'The children call me Mum and our main aim is to love them as if they're truly ours. You're a teacher, I believe?' Without waiting for a reply, Miss Denning continued.

'Excellent. You can help the children with their reading. We all speak English with them and we teach them in English. If you can promise to come every Sunday, that will be perfect. We have a team of volunteers during the week, but no one on Sundays.'

The structure had been converted from an old police station. Miss Denning showed me around the ground floor dining room, children's dormitories, and staff sitting room. Upstairs was another sitting room, a kitchen, bathroom, dispensary, sick room and a superintendent's bedroom.

Miss Denning pointed through the window to a smaller building at the back. 'That's for me and Mary Williams, my right-hand lady. Oh, and the amahs.'

Downstairs, we traipsed into the schoolroom built by the side of the block. Rows of faces looked up at us, straight black hair and cheeky grins. Most of them were girls. Girl babies were of less value in Chinese culture and therefore more likely to be abandoned. My heart swelled with sympathy for them. *If only I could adopt them all...*

Another European woman, with mousey brown hair cut in a severe bob, came forward. Miss Denning introduced her, and I shook hands with Miss Williams. Miss Denning's 'right-hand lady' promptly put me to work. I sat on a stool, surrounded by the infants, and flipped open *The Three Little Pigs*. I felt a tug at my sleeve. A girl nestled by my side: wide eyes, small mouth and pointed chin. 'Hello,' I said. 'What's your name?'

'Mei Ling,' the child whispered shyly. She clambered onto my lap and told me she was five years old. I stroked her soft round cheek and hugged her. Then I stared over Mei Ling's shoulder at the far wall and thought about Papa. He visited Mama's grave every Sunday, but I hadn't been able to face going with him. I'd managed to keep my memories of Stanley sealed away; working at the orphanage would be the perfect pretext to not return to the place that brought the sorrow back to me.

* * *

At home that evening, the telephone rang and I picked up the receiver. It would be James. He usually called me at this time on a Sunday, to suggest meeting up for dinner mid-week.

'It's Chun Ming here,' a familiar voice said.

I gave a gasp. 'Jimmy!' He'd given his Chinese name. 'What a surprise! Where are you?'

'I've just arrived and I have a job teaching English at the Chinese school in Waterloo Road.' It was one of the many communist schools the government allowed to operate, just like they turned a blind eye to the news agency, communist newspapers, and other such organisations that were springing up all over the colony.

'It's wonderful you're back. What a coincidence we've both become teachers!'

'May I please speak with my mother?' Jimmy's voice had become stiff and unfriendly, not like my Chinese brother at all. I wondered why.

I rang the hand bell on the table in front of me and sent the houseman to fetch Ah Ho. She talked at length with her son. Pretending not to listen, I picked up a magazine and flicked through the pages, my heart crumpling with every word.

'*Aiyah!*' Ah Ho put down the receiver. 'Ah Chun got married. He want me go live in his flat in Mong Kok. He say no good his mama work as amah. Say very bad face for him.'

A heavy feeling in my chest, I embraced Ah Ho. 'How are we going to manage without you?' I stepped back. 'I'm sorry. Of course you must go and be with Jimmy. I'm just being selfish.'

* * *

Jimmy came to collect his mother a week later. He arrived with his wife, Li, and they sat on the sofa, their backs straight. I poured them tea. Ah Ho, even though invited, had refused to take her place next to them.

I held out a plate of cucumber sandwiches. 'Tell me what you've been doing since I last saw you,' I said to Jimmy.

'I struggled with myself for many months when I went back to China after the British surrendered.' He paused, bit into his sandwich, chewed, then swallowed. 'I joined the guerrillas and we had to fight in secret. I'd seen the corruption of the Kuomintang. They made me sick.' He sipped his tea. 'Now the revolution has triumphed and, because of my knowledge of Hong Kong, I've been sent here to live among the running dogs of imperialism. It is a great sacrifice, but I'm willing to make it for my country.'

How zealous he sounds!

'Please allow your mother to visit often,' I said hopefully.

Jimmy smiled his crooked-teeth smile and, for a couple of seconds, I caught a glimpse of my childhood friend. 'That will be acceptable.' His brown eyes met mine.

I leant towards him. 'We want to give her a monthly pension. It's the least we can do.'

'I think she will appreciate your consideration.' Jimmy had returned to formal stiffness, and I could see no way of breaking through his self-imposed barrier.

Later, her paltry luggage loaded into the car Papa had organised to take her to Jimmy's flat, Ah Ho stood sobbing in front of the house. Earlier, she'd told me she didn't want to leave but had to do her duty to her son.

I kissed my amah's wrinkled cheek. 'I'm going to miss you and

I want you to know that, if ever you need anything, you only have to call me.'

Ah Ho waved from the back seat as the car drove out the gates. I wiped my tears. Jimmy's wife, Li, had hardly spoken a word to me; she seemed such a quiet person. If only I could have breached the blockade that appeared to have risen between me and Jimmy, but he'd seemed not to have even noticed I still wore the jade bangle he and Ah Ho had given me. I doubted he'd kept my book.

I remembered the games of hopscotch on the path to the tennis courts, the walks around the Peak, my parties when he'd always been included at my insistence. At the time of the Mid-Autumn Festival, Mama and Papa used to let me stay up late with Ah Ho and Jimmy to watch the moon and eat moon cakes. Ah Ho's English was even more limited then and she called the festival 'the Moon's Birthday'. We had lanterns and mine was always shaped like a horse and Jimmy's like a goldfish, and I would play hide and seek with him in the dark. Those days would live on in my memory, but Jimmy almost certainly never thought back to his time on the Peak. He was so wrapped up in revolutionary zeal he'd probably blocked it from his mind.

I went up to my bedroom and sat at my dressing table. I'd finally lost that gaunt look I'd had since Stanley. My cheeks had rounded out and my breasts were more distinct. Charles would hardly recognise me if he saw me again. But Charles would never see me again. Charles was dead.

I thought about Jimmy, fired with enthusiasm for his cause. I needed a cause myself. Something I could believe in. Something to lift me out of this dreadful despondency and give me a reason to get on with my life.

26

CHARLES

Charles was pacing the forward deck of SS *Canton* in the warmth of a late summer dawn. He'd been up here for the past hour and the ship had just passed the lights of a sampan or, possibly, a junk. He was back. At last.

Feeling in his pocket, he crumpled the well-worn draft of the letter he'd sent to Kate nearly four years ago.

Groombridge Road
Hackney, London E9
1 December 1945

Dearest Kate

I miss you so much, and the past eighteen months have been such hell. Looking up and seeing you on that balcony, your beautiful face, and not being able to hold you in my arms and tell you how much I love you, then not being able to see you. Oh, how I've wanted to feel your sweet lips on mine and stroke your soft, warm cheek. There hasn't been a minute of every day when I haven't thought about you, my darling.

You must be wondering what happened to me. As you know, I was due to be drafted to Japan. After an overnight stay at a camp near the airport, the guards loaded us onto lorries that took us to Holden's Wharf, but there was an air-raid and pandemonium broke out. Bombs were flying everywhere, and the Japs ran for cover. Everyone else was frozen with fear, but I took the opportunity to make a dash for it. And thank God I did as so many died on that ship. Such a tragedy!

Did you know the communist guerrillas rescued Allied soldiers who escaped from camps? They also picked up almost all the shot-down American pilots. One of the guerrillas was shadowing our lorry and took me straight to a safe house in Sai Kung. I was scared out of my mind. They kept me there for a fortnight until I'd recovered my strength enough to carry on. I'll never forget those fisher people; they shared their meagre food with me and I can't tell you what a difference it made. When I got there, I could hardly walk, I was so weak, and all I could think of was holding you again.

One night, I was told to get ready to leave. Someone found me a Chinese peasant outfit, you know the sort of thing... baggy black cotton trousers and a black padded tunic. I expect I looked more local than ever and my Cantonese was good enough to fake it if we met any Japs. We set off by sampan under cover of darkness as if we were going fishing.

I had been entrusted to a sixteen-year-old. Can you imagine? Except he was the fiercest sixteen-year-old I've ever met. His name was Fei, and he'd left school at thirteen because there were Japs to fight. He'd been with the guerrillas for nearly a year and boasted six kills. He said they took few prisoners on either side. 'When the Japanese catch one of our men, do you know what they do?' he asked me. 'They press lighted cigarettes all over his face and kill him slowly. When we take one of them, we cut off his head immediately.' I just hope the same thing happens to those sadists who murdered Bob and the others. Ruth told me all about what you both saw. It must have been terrifying for you, my love. Makes me feel ill to think that you witnessed such horror.

We landed on the other side of Mirs Bay and I thought we'd arrived at a ghost village. It was completely silent. No dogs barking, no chickens clucking. We could see vegetable plots stretching up towards the darkness of the mountains behind. Bit by bit, figures came out from behind the bushes and soon we were surrounded by villagers and insurgents. They gave us condensed milk and biscuits before we started marching up the valley towards unoccupied China. We spent the night at a stronghold of the anti-Japanese resistance, in a village house together with the family's livestock.

After a breakfast of sweet cakes, we marched along the raised paths through the paddy fields. We stopped to catch our breath at several villages and were given tea and steamed buns by the women, whose men were all off fighting the Japanese. As in most of China, the only communication lines were the ribbon-like footways we were walking on, made up of low walls of mud running from one rice field to the next.

We were in smugglers' territory and climbed up wide steps, hidden under a canopy of overhanging trees and shrubs. The great flat stones had been worn smooth by the passage of thousands of padding feet, carrying merchandise unloaded from junks on the coast. At the top of the steps we had our last view of Hong Kong... a distant peak on the west coast of the bay. I thought about you, Kate, stuck in Stanley, and I prayed it would not be long before we could be together again.

On the fourth day we reached Waichow. Fei took me to the Seventh Day Adventist Mission, which overlooked the East

River and the mountains beyond. It was a haven of tranquillity, with lawns shaded by old trees, flower gardens and a lake. I stayed with the pastor and enjoyed the luxury of a bath and a shave, wishing with all my heart that you could have been there with me. You would have adored the place, Kate.

Having done his duty, Fei said goodbye. I was sad to see him go as I'd grown used to his cheerful company and had felt safe with someone who had six Japs under his belt. From then onwards, I was in the hands of the BAAG, the British Army Aid Group, which was the resistance movement we were in touch with while in the camp. Shortly after Chinese New Year we were evacuated upriver and, a few months later, sent farther north again, as the enemy was on the move.

When the Japs surrendered, I was able to make my way back to Hong Kong and found out I'd missed your departure by one day. One day! Can you believe that? Desperate, I went to your house on the Peak, but it was almost in ruins and there was no one around. I couldn't find anyone who knew how to get in touch with you. But I expect the house will be renovated and I just hope someone will forward this letter.

Darling Kate, if you get this, please write to the above address. I long for your news and to know you still love me as I love you.

Yours,

Charles xxx

Charles stopped pacing the deck. Why hadn't Kate answered his letters? He'd written to her every month for nearly a year. Perhaps she'd had second thoughts and had decided not to answer. No, that couldn't be. They'd been so close, so in love. He knew Kate and he knew she'd never forget him. The only explanation could be that his letters hadn't got through to her. Simple as that. She was probably still in Australia and, as soon as she returned to Hong Kong and found out he was here, she'd get in touch with him. He couldn't wait to see her dear, darling face again and to feel her in his arms.

He'd enjoyed the month-long voyage from Southampton once he'd got over the initial sea sickness and the wrench of saying goodbye to his family. His cabin was air-conditioned and his fellow passengers friendly. Especially the young, single women making their way out to the colony to stay with friends and relations and, possibly, meet someone to marry. They wouldn't consider him a suitable catch as he was half-Chinese, he knew, but that hadn't prevented them from flirting with him. He'd got used to flirting with girls, but he always kept them at arm's length. Kate was the only one for him.

At Port Said, an Egyptian, or *gully-gully man* as everyone called him, came on board and delighted people with his antics. Dressed in a long white robe and brown sandals, the man had waved his magician's wand and conjured up live baby chicks from behind the children's ears.

As a first-class passenger, Charles had to dress formally for dinner... except the first night and nights in port. He'd enjoyed the deck quoits, dancing, and a peculiar ceremony when they crossed the equator, with first-timers having to give a present to King Neptune. Luckily, he didn't qualify; he'd already gone through that on his voyage out to England.

The farther east they'd sailed, the closer he'd felt to his roots. There'd been some spectacular sunsets over the Indian Ocean. In Colombo he went ashore and bought tiny wooden carved elephants; they'd make useful presents. Singapore reminded him of a quieter, cleaner Hong Kong and he'd relished hearing Cantonese being spoken in the shops.

Now, the dull drone of the turbines and the song of the wind were in his ears. The sky was lightening, and the shadowy shape of islands came into sight. Ships, and freighters, and barges, and Hong Kong Island rose out of the gloom. Other people emerged on deck and Charles greeted them with a smile.

Tugboats guided SS *Canton* towards Holden's Wharf through the melee of watercraft thronging the harbour, and Charles could barely contain his excitement.

He stood at the railings and eyed the crowd gathered on the quay. There were Uncle Phillip and Auntie Julie! He waved frantically until they returned his greeting.

Disembarkation formalities completed, he ran down the gangway and they threw their arms around him.

Auntie kissed his cheek. 'Welcome home.'

Soon afterwards, Charles was sitting in their spacious sitting room in Kowloon. Peking carpets covered the waxed parquet flooring, and the antique lacquer chests and jade screens he remembered were in their usual places. The last time he'd been here, they were still in storage. 'It hardly seems any different,' he said.

'We've redecorated it to be the same as before the war.' Uncle Phillip rubbed his brow. 'As you know, we managed to hide our choice pieces in an out-of-the-way warehouse.'

Uncle, whose real estate business was flourishing after he'd made some wise investments, had arranged a job for Charles at Beacons law firm.

'It's very kind of you to help me,' he said, touching Uncle's shoulder.

'My pleasure.'

Auntie poured tea. 'How is your mother?'

Charles smiled at his aunt. Her resemblance to Ma was uncanny. It would be years before he'd see his family again, but he didn't regret his decision to return to Hong Kong. He'd been a stranger in England.

It had been a struggle to adapt at first, but thanks to his paternal uncle's generosity they hadn't wanted for anything. Initially they'd lived in the East End, but they'd moved to Chelsea after the war and Pa had started his own business dealing in Chinese antiques.

'Ma is well and so are Pa and Ruth,' he said to Aunt Julie. She was still childless after many years of marriage, and he knew she considered Ruth and him almost like her own children.

'You'll find Hong Kong is changing.' Uncle offered him a cigarette.

'Thanks, but I don't smoke,' Charles said. 'Please tell me about the changes.'

'Masses of people are pouring over the border because of the troubles in China. I'm a member of a *Kaifong* Association and we're doing our best to provide free education and health care.' Uncle took a puff from his Players.

'Where do all the refugees live?' Charles asked.

'Most of them are in squatter huts on the hillsides. The rest are on rooftops, in alleyways, anywhere they can find.'

Auntie wagged a finger. 'I think the government needs to wake up to its responsibilities and send them back to China.'

'These poor people must have good reason to abandon their homes, sever their family ties, and renounce their traditional allegiances to come here.' Uncle smiled indulgently. 'We have to accept them in the name of humanity.'

After lunch, Charles went to his room to unpack. But the amahs had got there before him and all his clothes had been tidied away, his books placed in neat piles on the chest of drawers. He'd have to get used to a house full of servants again and there would be many other changes he'd have to deal with. Returning to his roots had been the second goal that kept him focused while he'd been away. The first goal, of course, was that he'd see Kate again and rekindle their love.

* * *

Next morning, Charles crossed the harbour on the Ferry and walked the short distance to Alexandra House. The Star Ferry was still just the 'Ferry'; some things didn't change.

He stared at the union flag flying from the domed cupola on top of an elegant four-storey building perched on porticoed arcades up ahead. It was as familiar to him as a pair of old shoes. But the roads were even more crowded than he remembered: tramcars, buses, taxis, bicycles and rickshaws all vying for space with private cars in the rubbish-strewn streets. People were scurrying between the vehicles, and the noise was thunderous: horns hooting, trams jangling, bells ringing, people shouting. Charles inhaled the petrol fumes, the smell of wok oil and the stink of humanity living cheek by jowl and let out a happy sigh. He'd truly come home.

His office was on the fifth floor and he rode up in an antiquated bird cage lift, to be met by his secretary, Mabel, a Portuguese Eurasian, plump and middle-aged. The Cantonese office boy, a relation of one of Uncle Phillip's messengers, busied himself reading the paper and providing endless cups of tea. Charles and his secretary got on with the correspondence, the ordering of business cards and the like. His workmates seemed friendly, a mix of British, Eurasians and Chinese solicitors. The barriers had never been there when it came to business.

At lunchtime Charles strolled down Queen's Road. On his right loomed the granite-faced fortress of The Hong Kong and Shanghai Bank. A pair of polished bronze lions were guarding the door, symbolising the financial stability of the colony. He patted the lions like everyone else, for luck. He had it on good authority the building possessed excellent feng shui; the life-force of the dragon of the mountain flowed down from the Peak to the harbour via its premises, bringing wealth and prosperity to all who banked there.

He glanced across the road and caught sight of the back of a tall lady with long, wavy dark-brown hair, getting onto a tram. Could it be Kate? His heart quickened, but he was too late to catch up with her. *If it had been her.* The tram was already clanking its way towards Wanchai.

The Supreme Court rose on his left and Charles walked to the entrance. A statue of a blindfolded woman, witness to the impartiality of the law, stood with scales in her right hand. She held a sword in her left one to remind the population of the law's power of punishment. It wouldn't be long before he walked through that hallowed door, ready to work with a barrister and try a case to the bench.

He walked on and stopped in front of the Cenotaph, where he bowed his head and said a silent prayer as he remembered Bob and all the others who had died at Stanley.

The Glorious Dead
1914–1918
1939–1945

The imposing Hong Kong Club building stood before him. That was one place where he wouldn't be setting foot. Its constitution excluded the membership of shopkeepers, Chinese, Indians, women and other undesirables. Not that he fell into any of those categories, but Pa hadn't been considered when he'd applied to join before the war. It didn't take much intelligence to work out why.

Charles felt proud of his background, however, and ready to take on the establishment. He didn't need to be a member of any of their clubs. There were enough clubs he could join that would accept him. He thought about Henry Wolseley. Should he telephone him and ask about Kate? No, he'd find her himself. It had been too problematic from London, the distance too great, communication too erratic. Now he was back in Hong Kong, the difficulties would be different...

27

JAMES

On board his Dragon yacht, *Jade Princess*, moored at the Yacht Club, James was checking the lines and making sure they were separated, ready for departure. The boat had been built in the 1930s, and he'd bought it from a fellow about to retire in England.

Sofia was due to arrive from one of her uncle's trading junks, anchored nearby. Should he feel guilty about seeing her at the same time as Kate? He shook his head. It wasn't as if he and Kate were engaged to be married. They were simply meeting each other socially. Perhaps he really had reinvented himself in Hong Kong; he certainly wasn't the same man he'd been brought up to be. He'd never imagined himself as the type to take a mistress.

And such a mistress!

So beautiful and exotic. What he felt for Sofia was pure intoxication. She hadn't hinted she wanted anything more from him other than the occasional assignation. Was he pleased or annoyed at her casual approach? Just grateful their relationship had been kept secret; he didn't care for the disapproval of Hong Kong society. He was certain he would be ostracised if anyone found out. If only he didn't have to consider the social taboos of this bigoted place, he thought.

Sofia had taken to sailing as if it were in her blood. She appeared to have an instinctive feel for it and could have managed *Jade* quite well on her own if he'd let her. Today was the third time they would slip away at first light. They'd cruise out of the harbour on *Jade's* inboard engine and unfurl her powerful sails to find a deserted cove, where they would skinny-dip and make love in the shallows. He smiled to himself, remembering the first time. She'd laughed at the speed of his lovemaking and had made him lie back afterwards while she'd tantalised him, instructing him not to move as she ran her hands down his body.

She'd taught him the ancient Chinese art of love that she'd learnt from reading the books in her uncle's library. James was relieved Sofia hadn't learnt it from another man. She'd been a virgin and he could hardly believe his luck that she'd chosen him. Heat crept up his neck as he thought about their lovemaking. He'd learnt to prolong the pleasure and not to come too quickly.

The creak of the single oar being sculled on a sampan came across the water, and he reached out his hand to help her aboard. They set off and soon they anchored in Rocky Bay.

The sun had risen and the early morning sea was still as glass. At this time of day and mid-week, the beach was deserted. Sofia dived off the side of the boat. Her body was spare but shapely, and she swam with the assurance of someone who'd practically grown up in the sea, unlike him... He'd only learnt to swim in the Navy. He slipped on his bathing shorts and dived into the cool depths. Surfacing next to her, he shook the droplets from his hair.

She opened her arms to him and he kissed her deeply. Treading water, he manoeuvred her backwards until they reached the side of the yacht, then placed her between himself and the ladder, holding on to the rungs with both hands. She pulled off her swimming costume and tossed it into the boat. He did the same, then lifted her onto his erection. They moved in unison, the tepid seawater caressing them, every nerve in his body tingling. 'Now,' Sofia said at last. He came, then, losing himself in her, hot pleasure shooting through him. Intoxicating pleasure. No words spoken, just a physical need assuaged.

They climbed aboard the yacht and sipped the piping hot coffee Sofia had brewed in *Jade's* tiny galley. Overlooking the bay perched the exclusive bungalows of the wealthy expatriates, whose residents' committee kept out locals and undesirables. Last week he'd been invited to a party with Kate there, given by the taipan of one of the Hongs, as the larger trading companies were known. The taipan and his wife were friends of Kate's father, and they had a weekend retreat on a ridge overlooking the Shek-o golf course.

James had been envious of the fabulous location, although at the time he'd called it a bit remote. It had been an excellent opportunity to make the right contacts, but he'd longed to be with Sofia, and his passion had fought against the sensible voice inside his head that told him no good would come of his affair with her.

He glanced at her as she towel-dried her hair. *God, she's beautiful! What does she see in me?*

'Have you any news yet about helping us save the factory?' she asked, putting on fresh lipstick.

'My contacts are keen for me to meet with your uncle. To discuss possible cooperation.'

Maybe Sofia was seeing him to keep him soft for K C Leung? The sudden thought soured the coffee in James's mouth.

* * *

He met Leung at a restaurant in Kowloon, where K C had booked a private room. Sofia hadn't been included in the meeting, and Charles wondered why. Her uncle greeted him jovially and indicated for him to sit.

'I'll lay my cards on the table,' James said, sipping brandy and picking at the crispy seaweed platter with his chopsticks. 'I've been asked to find out about Leo Rodrigues's Triad contacts and the banks in receipt of smuggled gold. Sofia tells me you're in debt to him.'

'That's right. But I don't want to repay.' Leung thrust out his chest. 'I want trick him into thinking I repay.'

'How do you propose to do that?'

'He flies the gold into Macau regularly on Catalina seaplane. I'll arrange for robbery to take place after aircraft leaves Hong Kong. I need you be on my launch, pick up my men and the loot.' K C laughed and settled back in his chair with exaggerated casualness. 'I'll repay Leo with his own gold.'

'Who will steal the gold?' James blinked. The plan was foolhardy. No other word to describe it. 'And what will happen to the plane?'

'One of my associates trained to fly Catalina seaplane in Philippines. He and other man will board flight from Hong Kong to Macau and hold gun to pilot's head when seaplane reaches cruising height.'

James smirked. 'And you expect them to just hand over the plane?'

Leung's smiled. 'If they don't want get killed.'

'Then what?'

'My man will take over controls and land aircraft near Soko Islands, in most south-western waters of Hong Kong Territory.'

James shook his head. 'Why do you need me?'

'I will give you name of Hong Kong banks that buy gold from

Macau illegally. Also will find out where new Triads have set up. I know you work for Special Branch. You tell them keep out of my business in return for this.'

'What will happen to the gold?'

'My men will conceal plane and tie up captives. I want you to pick up my men and gold.'

'I still don't understand why you need me. Can't you get one of your men to do it?'

'If you involved, I know Hong Kong police not trick me.'

'Fair enough.' James paused to gather his thoughts. 'I'll let you know as soon as I've been given the green light.' He crossed his arms. Special Branch was unlikely to want Leung's information enough to countenance an inflight robbery. '*If* I'm given the green light, that is.'

'You will be. Or we won't be able to stop any violence between the nationalists and the communists. Big trouble coming from China. And new Triads very big troublemakers.' Leung lifted his glass and smiled. '*Yum sing!* Or "bottoms up" as you British say.' And he drained his brandy in one gulp.

They ate quickly, talking about the food (delicious) and weather (too hot and wet). They had little in common, apart from Sofia. Did her uncle know about their affair? If so, he must have sanctioned it...

James couldn't fathom the man. Because he was Chinese, he supposed, but also for his political convictions. China was an enigma to him, and the people so different to any he'd encountered before. Fascinating, though. He'd like to learn more about the culture. James was starting to feel ever more intrigued by the locals than by the stuffy expatriates with whom he socialised.

Take Henry Wolseley, a typical Colonel Blimp character, almost a stereotype; but then, most of the expatriates in Hong Kong were like that. How had he produced such a sweet daughter as Kate? *Ah, Kate!* He was fond of her and glad he wasn't exactly two-timing her. She deserved better.

Heat spread up from James's groin. God, Sofia was enticing. What if he risked everything and allowed himself to fall in love with her? Perhaps she didn't want that. After all, she'd given him no indication...

28

SOFIA

'I don't understand why you want to leave the Consortium, Sofia.' Leo lit a cigarette. 'Why give up all the power and influence we have here in Macau for the life of an ordinary person in Hong Kong?'

'I don't intend to be *ordinary*,' she said, straightening her back as she sat opposite him in Father's study. Balthazar, as usual, lay on the rug at his feet. The dog went everywhere with him; he would spoil it with titbits from the table and employed a servant solely to take it for walks.

'Hong Kong will flourish. And I intend to flourish with it,' she said.

'How's that? With a piddling factory spinning cotton?' He laughed, blowing smoke towards her. 'That's hardly going to make you a millionaire.'

'The factory is just a start. I'll invest my capital in the company. Uncle and I will develop it into a proper textiles business, manu-facturing clothing.'

'And set yourselves up to rival businesses in England?' He sneered. 'I don't think so.'

'Our labour costs will be much lower. We'll be more competitive.'

'What about quality control?'

'I'll go to Britain and learn from the experts.'

'All these plans of yours will come to nothing when I take over the factory,' he said, balancing his cigarette on the edge of the ashtray. 'I'll sell it to the highest bidder to get back my money. Many industrialists are leaving Shanghai to set up in Hong Kong. One of them will jump at the chance.'

'Uncle will pay you back. Give him time!'

'Time is at a premium, haven't you heard? Run along now, little bastard sister.' He waved her off. 'I've got a meeting to go to.'

Sofia huffed and left him to his own devices. Then she concealed herself behind the rhododendron bushes in the front garden and waited until he emerged from the house. Derek Higgins was with him. How she hated that man! He'd served Uncle like a slave and here he was kow-towing to Leo as if he were some sort of god.

She remembered that Derek needed money for his family. And he had to feed his gambling habit. Uncle had paid him a fair wage, only it wouldn't have made Derek rich. Neither would his fireworks factory, a small concern he ran on a shoestring. But it wasn't an excuse to betray Uncle.

Stealthily, Sofia set off to follow Leo and Derek, keeping out of sight as they walked towards the old Inner Harbour. There, the deep-sea junks clustered five abreast, washing hanging from a forest of bare masts. The temperature must have been in the nineties and the humidity was so high the air practically dripped moisture. But she hardly noticed she was so used to it.

She strode past the shipwrights, who were constructing their junks on cradles over a canal. Spicy aromas of food mingled with the stench of rotting rubbish. She ducked down a dark alleyway and hid behind a stall. Leo and Derek disappeared into a teahouse. Sofia crept up to the shuttered window and peered through the cracks. She stiffened. They were talking to three Chinese men. One of the men had leant back in his chair; his jacket had fallen open. She widened her eyes. There was a gun in a holster strapped to his chest!

She stared at the men for a long time and memorised their features. Then she rushed home and strode into the sitting room, where Uncle was sitting under the ceiling fan.

'If the men are returning to Hong Kong on the afternoon ferry I need to be on it too,' she said after she'd told him what she'd seen. 'Now I know what they look like, it'll be easy enough to keep an eye on them.'

'You did well.' Uncle handed her a wad of Hong Kong dollars. 'Make sure you treat yourself to something nice at Lane Crawford while you are there.'

'Thank you. I just hope I'll be able to follow those men without problems.'

'I'll telephone one of my associates to meet you as you disembark.'

* * *

Four hours later, a slight young man with a round face and crooked teeth greeted her at the pier on Hong Kong Island. 'My name is Chun Ming,' he said.

'Pleased to meet you,' she responded, falling into step with him as the three Triads climbed onto rickshaws.

Sofia and Chun Ming followed the rickshaws in a taxi to the Ferry. They managed to get onto the same boat across the harbour and stood behind the men in the queue for another taxi.

Past the airport, they stopped in front of what looked like a shanty town. There were shacks everywhere but for some crumbling old buildings in the centre. 'I feared as much,' Chun Ming said. 'Kowloon Walled City.'

'Oh?'

'It's the only part of Hong Kong that has stayed under the control of China. About six and a half acres of land, it wasn't and never has been a city.'

'Now I remember. Wasn't it a Chinese military fort when Hong Kong was ceded to Britain over a hundred years ago?'

'You mean when Britain grabbed Hong Kong in an unequal treaty. There's no point following them in there. It's full of Kuomintang supporters. No wonder the Triads have moved in...'

'Thank you for bringing me here, Chun Ming. This information will be invaluable.'

Their taxi turned around and Sofia dropped him at his flat. In Tsuen Wan, she paid the driver and went up to her office. She dialled James's number and asked if they could meet.

'I'm sorry, sweetheart. If I'd known you were going to be in town, I wouldn't have made prior arrangements. I'm having dinner with my boss and his wife at the Parisian Grill. When do you go back to Macau?'

Should she tell him not until tomorrow? *No.* 'On the evening ferry,' she lied.

* * *

At eight o'clock, Sofia was hiding behind a stall on the pavement outside the Parisian Grill. Why hadn't James invited her to meet his friends? Perhaps he wasn't ready. She wanted to see what they looked like. One day, she'd meet them properly. When James realised how much he loved her and didn't care what others thought.

A taxi pulled up. James was in the back seat. *Oh, no!* He wasn't alone. He was with a European woman, just the two of them, and no sign of anyone who could be his boss. The girl seemed much too young to be Tony Chambers's wife, and she was beautiful, willowy, with a heart-shaped face, and a fragile look that would make any man want to protect her.

Sofia chewed her thumbnail. Should she march up to them and demand an explanation? But she had no rights over James, no rights at all. Hadn't she played it cool with him up until now?

The next time she saw him she'd find out about the Englishwoman and she'd let him know how she felt, she resolved. It was time to tell him she loved him. The physical attraction she'd felt for him initially had grown into a deep love. If anyone were to ask her why that was, she'd find it difficult to explain other than the fact she wouldn't be happy if she had to live without him. He made her feel complete.

She wrapped her arms around herself. Uncle would be pleased with her spying this afternoon. Now he had something to give James in exchange for helping to save the factory. Uncle hadn't told her what his plans were, but she had her own thoughts on what was needed, and those thoughts included James, Englishwoman or no Englishwoman.

29

KATE

In the Wellspring box at the Happy Valley racecourse, I was tapping my foot and listening to Papa chat with Arnaud de Montreuil, the French consul-general. I'd much rather have spent the afternoon at home, but my father had insisted on bringing me with him, saying he had important guests and needed me to help entertain them. Also, I suspected he'd wanted me here because he'd invited James.

'Love,' Papa had said when I'd told him I hadn't forgotten Charles. 'Love comes when you make a life together.'

'Is that what happened between you and Mama?' I'd asked. 'I know the story. After you met her in Southampton at the end of the first war, you came out to Hong Kong to better your prospects. Six months later, Mama embarked on a P & O liner, leaving behind everything familiar to her. You must have loved each other right from the start.'

'Your mother and I came from the same background,' he'd said with a sigh.

I stopped tapping my foot and went to stand next to James, who was watching the race, a betting slip in his hand. An electric machine on the other side of the track showed the enormous sums of money being gambled. People were leaning over the balcony in the next box, most of them Chinese. Unlike Papa's other clubs, the Hong Kong Jockey Club approved of local members.

A tall man turned around. Seconds passed while he stared right at me. My heart thudded, and my knees began to give way. I stepped back, found a seat and undid the top button of my blouse. The walls of the box were closing in on me. Taking a few deep breaths, I got up and excused myself. 'I need some fresh air,' I murmured to no one in particular.

'You do seem rather peaky.' James glanced at me. 'Shall I come with you?'

'Don't worry! I'll be fine.'

Outside, I fought my way through the crowds towards the entrance of the Jockey Club. Across the road, there was a cemetery. *Another damn cemetery!* I walked through the pillared entrance, climbed the steep hillside, and sat on a patch of grass. I had a clear view of the clock tower in the centre of the two members' stands. On the other side of the valley was Blue Pool Road, where Papa and I used to ride every Sunday.

A lone figure came through the gates of the racetrack. He walked just like Charles used to, swinging his right arm with each step. The man crossed the road and climbed up the hill. Sudden fine drizzle fell and soaked my hat.

My heart sang. *It's Charles! He's alive!* He stood in front of me and unfurled his umbrella. His adult face had become even more finely chiselled, his shoulders had broadened and his body, under a well-tailored suit, had filled out. But his hair still flopped across his forehead in that same maddening way.

'I saw you leave and wondered where you were going with such a determined look on your face,' he said, taking off his jacket and spreading it on the grass. 'The ground is damp, let's sit on this.'

Feeling hot, I removed my cotton gloves and stuffed them into my handbag. Charles was looking away, probably to avoid meeting my eyes. As well he might, not having contacted me. Should I ask him why? *No*. He was sitting so stiffly; the years had turned him into a stranger. It wasn't the sort of question you could put to a stranger.

I pulled down my skirt. 'Did you know the Japanese kept the Jockey Club open during the war?' *Might as well fill the silence with small talk*. 'They called it the Hong Kong Race Club and changed the names of the ponies from English to Chinese.'

'Apparently, they used the ponies to pull passenger carts when the buses stopped running after the petrol ran out.'

'They even ate some of them.' I shuddered. 'How's your family?' I was aware of his gaze on my face now.

'Ruth is doing well at school. She wants to become a doctor.'

'Gosh, how clever of her!'

'I expect she'll come back to Hong Kong when she's qualified. She keeps going on and on about how much she misses this place.'

I glanced at my watch. 'I'd better be getting back before they start worrying about me.'

Charles got to his feet and held out his hand. His touch was so familiar; a mad impulse took hold of me to reach out and stroke his face. Before I could stop myself, my fingers were laced in his and I was kissing him. 'Oh God, Charles, I thought you were dead,' I said between kisses. 'Why didn't you contact me?'

'B... b... but I did. I wrote to you.'

'Well, I didn't receive your letters.'

'I wrote every month for a year.'

'How can they have all gone missing?'

'I wrote to your address on the Peak in the hopes someone would forward them.'

'I never received them,' I repeated, looking into his eyes.

'I was worried you'd had second thoughts, but then I told myself you'd never do that. I'm right, aren't I, Kate?'

I kissed him again, full on the lips, and it was like coming home after a long, long journey. I was where I should be, in Charles's arms. How could anything ever part us again?

As if he'd read my thoughts, Charles said, 'What about your father? Do you think he could have intercepted my letters?'

'No, I'm sure he wouldn't have. I expect the letters got lost in the post. Or they weren't forwarded. That's much more probable.'

Charles took my hand and kissed it. 'Your father didn't approve of us in Stanley. He's hardly likely to have changed his mind now. Perhaps we should keep our love a secret until we know where we stand with him? I don't want to cause a rift between you.'

A bubble of disappointment formed in my chest and I turned away from him. 'I don't care about that, my darling. I don't care about anything but us, and I want to tell everyone.'

'We will when the time is right,' he said, turning me towards him. He stroked my cheek. 'Oh, Kate, how I've longed to do that. I want everything to be perfect for you. No arguments with your father. And I need to prepare my family as well.'

His family? Surely there wouldn't be any problems with them? 'Why's that?'

'My uncle and aunt have become very Chinese since the war. I'm sure they'll grow to love you, but I need to give them time to get used to the idea.'

'It's all so complicated. I wish people were more open-minded.'

'Hong Kong has become a melting pot of China. A place of

refugees, and my uncle and aunt fit in better with the Chinese community than the English. There's an old saying: all rivers running into the China Sea turn salty.'

'What's that mean?'

'All ethnic groups living in China get assimilated eventually.'

'I think they're privileged to have a dual background.'

'How can they fit in with both cultures?' Charles shrugged. 'Before the war, they could be part of the Eurasian community. Where's it now? Disappeared.'

'I suppose you're talking about yourself as well.' I reached for his hand. 'What about me? Am I too English for you?'

Charles gave one of his heartbreakingly beautiful smiles. 'Oh, my sweet love. I don't think of you like that. You're Kate, the other part of me. Together we can overcome all this prejudice. I'm sure of it. We just need to take things slowly so we get what's best for us.'

'Fair enough.' I smiled. 'Only an hour ago I believed you were dead. Now I know different, my life has meaning again. I'll be satisfied with seeing you in secret for a while.' I sighed. 'How will we know when the time is right to tell everyone, though?'

'We'll know. Will you trust me?'

'I suppose so. At least come back with me to the Wellspring box and say hello. That can be the first step.'

'Of course,' he said, and we kissed again.

In the race-stand, Jessica and Tony welcomed Charles as if he were a long-lost friend. And Papa's guests seemed fascinated to meet him, the nephew of millionaire Phillip Noble no less! The French consul-general even promised a dinner invitation. But Papa stared at Charles as if he'd seen some sort of apparition.

Charles exchanged business cards with James and Arnaud. 'My uncle is expecting me,' he said. 'Nice to see you again, Kate.' His tone was false-jaunty.

'Nice to see you too.' *How long will I be able to keep up this silly pretence?*

From the other side of me, James pointed. 'You've dropped one of your gloves, Kate.'

Before I could do anything, Charles retrieved it. The message in his eyes was clear: love mixed with the fundamental decency that was essentially Charles. *My Charles.*

* * *

In the car on the way home, Papa lit his pipe. 'Did you know how Charles Pearce's uncle came to be so filthy rich?'

'Filthy rich. What a horrible expression. Please enlighten me!'

Seemingly unfazed, Papa sucked on his pipe. 'His father was an ordinary Portuguese Eurasian bank clerk. I believe Phillip Noble was educated at one of those elite schools that offered scholarships to local boys.'

'Oh?' *What was he going on about?*

'Before the war, he'd already started building his real estate empire. From the safety of Macau, he gave instructions to his contacts to buy up duress notes.'

'Duress notes?'

'Hong Kong dollars issued by local bankers under Japanese orders. Noble got them at a fraction of their face value. Of course, on liberation, the Hong Kong and Shanghai Bank honoured the notes at their full worth and he made millions.'

'That's not exactly dishonest. He gambled and won.'

'We're getting too many of these rich Chinese in the colony. Place isn't the same at all.'

I clenched my jaw. It was useless to argue with Papa and far too distressing. Didn't he realise Hong Kong was changing? I saw it all around me. More and more people were flooding in from

China. Because of all the wealth the rich immigrants were bringing with them, the shops were booming. The Chinese *taitais* went on shopping sprees all morning and played mah-jong all afternoon, just like the bored British missies did before the war. In the old days, they would only shop at Lane Crawford's and White-away's department stores. Now there was much more choice and you could buy anything... if you had the money.

It was such a contrast to the abject poverty of those who'd crossed the border with nothing. Beggars thronged the streets nowadays, and shanty towns were springing up everywhere. Papa seemed oblivious to their misery, but I couldn't ignore it. I was determined to find a way to help; I just hadn't found it yet.

I thought about Charles, and happiness fizzed through me. *Hopefully, it won't be long before we can announce our love to the world.*

30

CHARLES

Charles was one of the first guests to arrive at the consul-general's villa. He stood in the garden with a glass of chilled white wine and gazed at the enchanting view. Balanced on a rocky promontory between Repulse Bay and Deep Water Bay, the property overlooked Middle Island and the South China Sea beyond. 'Just like the Côte d'Azur,' Arnaud had said a minute ago before he went off to greet other people. And he was right.

Charles exhaled a long slow breath. He hadn't been able to stop thinking about Kate since last Saturday. Mid-week he'd called her, but her father had answered the phone and he'd made up the excuse of a wrong number. Charles gritted his teeth. Although he had no evidence, he was certain Henry Wolseley had intercepted his letters. It was a gut feeling. Charles wanted everything to be perfect for Kate, for her to have the wedding of her dreams with her father in doting attendance. But the man was a bigot, unfortunately.

Charles sipped his drink and looked around. Arnaud, a flashy character, was circulating among his guests. 'I only invite beautiful women to my parties,' Charles remembered him saying when they were introduced at the races. The Frenchman had stared pointedly at Kate. Now, as if on cue, her laughter tinkled from the other side of the lawn.

She was standing next to that Englishman, James. Charles stood in the shadows and watched her. In the camp, she'd almost been a beauty, but semi-starvation had kept her from blooming into the lovely woman she'd now become. Her bow-shaped lips parted in a half-smile, and his heart rate quickened. She was still slim, even thin, but her figure was curvy. How he wanted to hold her in his arms and kiss her.

At dinner, he sat next to Jessica Chambers. She must have been in her early thirties, and the years as well as his new position in society had shrunk the gap that used to exist between them. Jessica leant towards him. 'How do you find life in Hong Kong these days, Charles?'

'Different in some ways, yet fundamentally it's the same old place.'

'Where are you living?' She lifted her soup spoon and drank a mouthful of vichyssoise.

'I'm still at my uncle's but I'm moving into a flat in Pokfulam next week.'

'And how is work?' Jessica's bright red lipstick had smeared the wine glass she held to her lips.

Most of his cases involved petty family disputes. Bigger cases would come his way once he became better known. 'So far so good. It helps to have the right contacts, of course.'

'Of course.' Jessica swept her gaze around the room. 'Isn't this an interesting mix of people? Quite different from the stuffy parties we used to go to before the war.'

Charles studied the other tables. Kate was at Arnaud's table and James had been placed to the left of Arnaud's wife, Adèle, at the head of her own table. Two standard poodles sprawled at her feet, and she was feeding them scraps from her plate. The other guests were a varied bunch, and the ladies all beautiful.

Charles listened to the woman on his left. Statuesque, blonde, probably Danish judging by her accent, with a voluptuous bosom in danger of escaping from her low-cut dress. She was discussing a development at exclusive Shek-o with the Englishman on her right. 'I don't understand why they don't let the Chinese buy houses next to the golf club.'

Hong Kong was changing, but some changes were taking longer than others, Charles mused. He was the only Oriental at his table. He gazed around again; each table had its own token local representative. How open-minded of Arnaud...

The blonde now smiled at Charles. 'I'm delighted to meet you. I hardly meet any Chinese. Everyone here keeps to a small social circle of like-minded people, inviting each other and being invited by each other to an endless round of parties. I do think Arnaud is clever to give these mixed dos.'

'Quite,' he responded, not knowing what else to say.

After coffee, the ladies disappeared to the powder-rooms, and the men went through to the sitting room to smoke cigars and drink port. Charles lowered himself down next to Tony Chambers on a plush white sofa. Through the open doors, he stared at servants clearing the tables from the terrace. 'What happens next?' he asked.

Tony blew cigar smoke. 'Usually dancing to gramophone records.'

'Ah,' Charles said.

He took his leave and wandered into the garden, separated from the main road by a high boundary wall with Chinese roof tiles on top. He went to the place where he'd stood earlier and admired the full moon reflected in the inky blackness of the sea below. Bushes lined the bank and steps led down to the beach, where white sand glittered in the moonlight. On the horizon, the lights of the fishing sampans flickered in the September night. He wasn't surprised when Kate came up; their minds had always been in tune.

'It's glorious, isn't it?' she said.

'Absolutely.'

'Can you smell those roses?'

'I can...'

Kate's floral perfume mixed with the heady scent of the flowers. If only he could take her in his arms and crush her against him! He gripped the iron rail so hard his knuckles turned white.

Out of the blue, the Englishman appeared at his elbow. 'Ah, here you are, Kate. I've come to claim you for a dance. Good to see you again, Charles.'

'Likewise,' he said.

Kate walked to the veranda with James and they started to perform a slow waltz. Was something going on between them? Charles shoved his fists into his pockets. *No, Kate wouldn't...*

He strode across the lawn and bumped into Jessica. She grabbed his arm. 'I hope you're a good dancer.'

The music had switched to a tango, and he led Jessica in an open embrace. Out of the corner of his eye, he saw Kate standing on the side, watching him. Jessica performed a leg hook and, after what seemed like hours, the record finished.

'I'm exhausted,' Jessica said. 'Let me hand you over.'

What could he say? He was holding Kate before he could think of anything and doing the slow-slow-quick-quick of a foxtrot. 'You're a good dancer,' she whispered. 'I knew you would be.'

Charles held her gently, not too close, but she pressed her lovely body against his and he started to respond.

'I was expecting you to ring me,' she said.

'I did, but your father answered. I think it'll be better if you rang me.'

Kate leant back and regarded him in a thoughtful way. 'All right.'

Charles felt her melding into him again. *Oh God! Oh God!* He wanted her so desperately it was like a knife twisting his gut. 'Do you mind if we take a break?' He dropped his hold. 'I'll get us some refreshments. What would you like?'

'A brandy soda, please.'

Ten minutes later, he returned with their drinks. *Damn!* She was sitting on the side talking with James. Charles handed Kate her brandy and pulled up a chair, but she was giggling at something James had said and hardly seemed to notice him. *Damn again!* The Englishman had taken her hand and was patting it while laughing at himself. Charles could feel his cheeks burning. Perhaps there *was* something going on between them? No. Kate was a beautiful young woman and was bound to attract admirers. Especially as she'd thought he was dead until a few days ago. He could trust her, he knew he could. Whether he could trust James Stevens, however, was another matter...

31

KATE

I was on my way back from the orphanage. My taxi halted at traffic lights, and I stared out of the window. A man was striding up a rough track leading to a steep hillside on the far side of the crossing, swinging his arms like Charles did. I told the driver to stop and paid the fare. I had to see him again. *If it was him.* I'd spoken to him on the phone a couple of times, but it wasn't the same as being with him face to face. He'd asked me about James Stevens, and I'd told him James was just a friend. I couldn't help feeling pleased Charles loved me enough to be jealous.

I set off at a brisk pace, walking past coolies carrying heavy bundles on their shoulder-poles and rickshaws laden with packages. Then I came to a flattened area, almost a plateau at the top of the path. Built in close proximity stood thousands of huts made of thin wood, corrugated iron, and old packing cases. A whole city had risen from bare ground. People turned and stared at me.

A bare-bottomed toddler, his lower lip quivering, nose running with phlegm and tears streaming, hid behind his mother's legs. The woman, a baby slung from her back, picked up her child and ran off down a narrow alleyway. Everywhere, washing hung out to dry. Where did these poor women get the water to wash their clothes? There was a standpipe down by the main road; they must have to carry buckets all the way up here. Obviously, there were no sewerage facilities and a stench in the air reminded me of Stanley.

I looked around for Charles. He'd disappeared and I doubted it had really been him that I'd seen. I was out of place here; it was so different from my usual haunts. And I was frightened. Not of the people, who seemed more scared of me than I of them, but of the poverty. I started to trace my steps back down to Waterloo Road. Someone tapped me on the shoulder, and I turned around.

'What are you doing here?' Charles asked.

'I could ask the same thing of you,' I said, smiling.

'My uncle has built cheap blocks of flats on some land he bought. I was getting the names of people to re-house. It's a drop in the ocean, though. There are far too many refugees.'

Charles offered me a lift home, and I walked with him to where he'd parked his car in Kadoorie Avenue. I breathed in the faint citrus smell of him, intensely aware of his physical presence, his broad shoulders tapering to a slim waist. 'It's turned out to be a gorgeous afternoon,' I said, falling into the safe refuge of small talk.

Bright sunshine had cleared away the humidity that had clung to me like a blanket while I'd been at the orphanage. I pointed at two magpies, perched in an orchid tree. 'One for sorrow, two for joy.'

Charles took his keys from his pocket and led me to an MGA Coupé parked in front of his uncle's house. 'Shall we take the car hood off?'

'What fun.' I glanced back at the tree, remembering the one in Stanley. Had Charles made the same connection?

'How about a spin?' he said.

We crossed the harbour in the vehicular ferry, headed through the mid-levels, skirted Happy Valley, went over the gap and down towards the south. Charles turned right onto Island Road, the MG's engine making a purring sound, and we motored towards Aberdeen fishing village.

'This was the fragrant harbour that gave Hong Kong its name,' he said. 'In the last century the British would stop off and get fresh water from a waterfall. The fragrance came from the scent of the joss sticks traded here.'

'I always thought the name referred to Victoria Harbour, which isn't fragrant at all.'

Charles seemed to relax behind the wheel of his car, sure of himself as he drove me around the back of the island. I was so aware of him it hurt— his thigh long and lean on the other side of the gear stick, his strong, capable hands on the steering wheel.

'I've just rented a flat in Bisney Road,' he said. 'Moved in yesterday. Would you like to see it?'

'I'd love to.'

The apartment was on the second floor of a new three-storey block. There were staff quarters and three bedrooms, but so far he'd only furnished one of them. I stood at the door to his room and stared at his bed, a flush spreading through me. Turning abruptly, I collided with him.

He took me in his arms and kissed me. It felt wonderful. My body fused to his and I kissed him back, real kisses, the years of longing unravelling like a dropped stitch. He lifted his head and his eyes sought mine. 'Kate?' His voice cracked with emotion.

I nodded.

Charles steered me backwards and we toppled onto the quilt. My hand slipped under his shirt and I caressed his smooth chest. He undid the buttons of my blouse, reached behind and unclasped my bra.

His mouth explored my breasts. 'Oh, Charles...' I was losing myself to the pleasure. I couldn't think of anything but him. My one and only love. He pulled down my panties, and I unbuckled his trouser belt.

It was my first time and I'd expected discomfort. But all I wanted was to keep him inside me forever. Exquisite sensation filled my body.

Oh Charles, oh Charles, at last.

The pleasure built and built, and I was melting with it. Then something happened, something I'd read about yet never imagined could be so extraordinary, and I let out a low shuddering moan. Charles quickly withdrew. 'I love you so much,' I said, turning to smile at him.

'And I love you too, my darling.' He stroked my cheek. 'I want you here with me, you know I do, but we have to be patient. So, I think it's time I got you home to your father.'

I wanted to shake him and tell him Papa didn't matter. But something stopped me. Of course my father mattered. Hands trembling, I put on my panties, buttoned up my blouse, and picked up my handbag. 'Let's go, then.'

All the way back up to the Peak, I maintained silence. I'd made love with Charles; I should have been bubbling with happiness. Instead, though, my insides were tied up in knots.

32

CHARLES

Charles dropped Kate off at her front gate. He watched her striding away from him, and an invisible hand squeezed his heart. She'd been so quiet in the car. Too quiet. Should he run after her? He grabbed the door handle. He pushed down, then stopped himself. He had to be cautious, otherwise he'd make mistakes and he wouldn't achieve his goal. Kate meant the world to him; her happiness was paramount.

He drove back to his flat. Thankfully, his amah had been out at the market when he'd brought Kate here earlier. Tittle-tattle spread around the colony through the servants' grapevine, and God forbid Kate should be the subject of the latest gossip.

Stepping into the hallway, he called for Ah Tong and requested an early supper. His emotions drained, he collapsed on the sofa and sipped a beer, listening to his amah clattering in the kitchen. Shame he had little appetite, but he had to give Ah Tong face and do honour to the meal.

After he'd eaten the sweet and sour fish, every bite an effort, he drew a bath. Lying back in the tub, he remembered the first time he'd met Kate. She was sitting in the cemetery, unaware he was watching her twirl her plaits like a little girl. Later, he'd fallen in love with her sweet face, her amber eyes and irrepressible giggle. She'd been young for her age and he'd loved her innocence, probably the result of her sheltered upbringing. Kate was the apple of Henry Wolseley's eye; anyone could see that. And she reciprocated her father's adoration. If Charles were to cause a breach between them, it would affect Kate for the rest of her life. He couldn't do that to her.

* * *

The following evening, he drove towards the car ferry terminal through streets lined with four-storey buildings, their flimsy wooden balconies festooned with washing strung on bamboo poles. The poor of the city lived here in sub-standard housing. Most of the flats had no bathrooms, no toilets, no courtyards and only one kitchen for about twenty families. It was far worse than Stanley. The apartments were divided into eight-foot square cubicles shared by five or more people. Charles had experienced overcrowding, but this was on a much greater scale than in the internment camp.

Filthy pavements were lined with stalls selling everything from congee to cans of cola, and in between stretched the mats of the street sleepers – whole families who hadn't been able to find anywhere to live. He opened the window of his MG and reeled at the stink of human ordure, rotten fruit, decaying vegetables, and cooking oil. Strident Cantonese voices filled the air – shouted conversations interspersed with the cries of the hawkers. Rain pummelled the roof of his car and ran down the windscreen. Charles wound up the window.

On the ferry he stayed in his MG. He thought about Kate, as Kowloon emerged from the mist with its hills and teeming tenements. Perhaps they shouldn't have made love – they weren't married yet – but it had been just how he'd dreamt it would be. When they'd melted into each other, he'd pulsed with such love for her he could have died at that moment and felt fulfilled.

Except he hadn't died, of course, and hopefully, he and Kate would have a future together. He stared around him. Living here was like living in a human ant colony, he thought. People building, toiling, making, striving, and always hoping for better days to come. Everyone wanted to accumulate wealth; it was the goal of every person, from the lowly street sleeper to those who were already rich but who had every intention of getting richer. It formed part of the Chinese character, and he didn't disapprove. Hong Kong was an amalgamation of east and west, just like he was. Charles sighed. How to break through Henry Wolseley's prejudice and be accepted as a suitable match for his daughter? The ferry was docking, and Charles started the car. There had to be a way, there just had to be...

* * *

'You've got too thin,' Auntie exclaimed, greeting him at the door of the house. Charles kissed her cheek as she dragged him over the threshold. She led him to a tray of dim sum. 'You eat,' she ordered. 'I'll go check on dinner.'

Uncle came into the room, dressed casually in an open-necked shirt. 'Good to see you, Charles. How're things?'

He talked about his current case, a family dispute about a Last Will and Testament, taking care not to reveal any names. Uncle listened and cracked sunflower seeds between his teeth. 'Seems you're already doing well. Isn't it time you married? In fact, your aunt and I have been looking out for you and we think we've found you the perfect wife.'

Surely his uncle wasn't being serious? 'Thank you,' Charles mumbled, his English side taking over. 'But I'll find my own wife if you don't mind.'

Auntie returned with a tray of drinks and placed it on the coffee table. 'When do you have the time to meet the right girl? We'll invite a young lady we know, and her parents, to dinner.'

'Don't forget the Chinese are matchmakers and we're half-Chinese,' Uncle said. 'People with the same social status are expected to marry each other. If their families don't intervene, then how else can they meet?'

'Seems to me more like a business arrangement than finding a person you love.' Charles laughed.

'Love? Very romantic of you.' Uncle lit a cigarette. 'Believe me! It's much better to marry someone from the right background.'

'Actually, I've already met my future wife. Kate Wolseley.'

Uncle sat up straight and blew out a puff of smoke. He coughed. 'Who?'

'The girl we met at Stanley?' Auntie turned to Charles. 'She's not for the likes of you.'

'How can you say that? Excuse me for being blunt, but you're in a mixed marriage and so is Ma.'

'We're women. It's easier for a Chinese woman to marry a foreigner. But when I say easier, it wasn't that easy. Our family was against it.'

'The other way round is very rare,' Uncle said. 'Miss Wolseley will be shunned by her circle. You'll make her very unhappy.'

It was as he'd feared. They didn't understand. Hong Kong was changing, and he and Kate would be at the forefront of that change. 'Don't worry! I know what I'm doing.'

Uncle shrugged. 'I certainly hope so.'

'Please can I introduce her to you properly?'

'We'll invite her to dinner,' Auntie said.

Charles grinned. Kate would knock them off their feet, he knew she would.

* * *

Two days later, Charles waited with his relatives in the private room of a Kowloon restaurant. He hadn't seen Kate since they'd made love, and he longed for her so much it was as if he'd been living in a vacuum. Their waiter placed a dish of appetizers on the table. Charles breathed in the aromas of ginger, garlic and sesame oil. The food would be good here; at the entrance he'd spied tanks full of fish swimming about in happy ignorance of their destiny.

His heart rate quickened. He couldn't wait to see Kate again. How would she get on with his uncle and aunt? And, more importantly, how would they get on with her?

The door swung open and in she walked. Her eyes sought his and she gave a tentative smile. Dressed in a pale blue cotton dress, nipped in at the waist with a full skirt, she looked stunning. Charles got to his feet and squeezed her fingers. 'Uncle, Aunt, this is Kate, my soulmate.' He knew he was being corny but couldn't help himself.

Formalities over, Kate sat down next to him. She beamed at Aunt Julie. 'I do like your cheongsam, Mrs Noble. I wish I could wear one myself, only I'm not sure I have the figure for it.'

'You're very slim, so should be no problem. I'll take you to my tailor.' Aunt Julie smiled.

Charles clasped Kate's hand under the table. So far so good. Then Uncle butted in. 'What opinion does your father have about my nephew, Miss Wolseley?'

Kate blushed. 'What do you mean?'

'Uncle,' Charles said. 'Do you have to be so outspoken?'

'I'm sorry. I didn't mean to be rude. Just concerned for you both.'

'We're taking things slowly, Mr Noble,' Kate said. 'My father will come round to the idea of Charles and I being together eventually.'

'Do you really believe that? I know of no other Englishwoman involved with someone from our background.'

'Now, now, Phillip,' Aunt Julie said. 'Can't you see how in love these two are?'

Auntie was practically cooing, but Uncle's face had taken on a stern expression.

Kate smiled at him. 'Mr Noble, we're not rushing into anything.'

'I don't want Charles to get hurt.'

'Neither do I,' she said firmly.

'Good.' Uncle rang the bell for their waiter. 'We'll discuss this no further. Let's enjoy our meal.'

'Thank God,' Charles said, keeping his voice neutral. 'I was beginning to think we'd never get anything to eat.' He'd been on the point of making his excuses and leaving the restaurant with Kate. This was supposed to be a social event, not an interrogation.

* * *

The rest of the meal passed with no major hiccoughs, although it seemed that Uncle ordered specific dishes to test Kate's resilience: from braised chicken feet to noodles served with one thousand-year-old eggs. However, she did Charles proud and tried everything, all the while speaking only when she was spoken to and smiling her sweet smile. He could see she was working her magic on his uncle, charming him into compliance. She already had Aunt Julie eating out of her hand. They'd even arranged a shopping expedition to buy the right silk for a cheongsam. What would Henry Wolseley say when he saw his daughter dressed like a local? He'd probably have a fit. Charles chortled to himself, then sipped from his cup of Jasmine tea.

Dinner over, he stepped outside with his arm around Kate. A forest of neon signs lit up the night and crowds of people thronged the street, pushing past each other into the open doorways of shops selling Chinese medicines, jade, cameras, and linen. The clack-clack of abacuses totalling up sales echoed down the pavement. Most of the women shoppers were dressed in black: from their baggy cotton trousers to their high-necked jackets buttoned diagonally across their bodies. Charles knew from experience that they only dressed in bright colours on special occasions. He couldn't wait to see Kate in a cheongsam. Turning to her, he said, 'That didn't go too badly, did it?'

'Your aunt was lovely to me. But your uncle still needs convincing, I think.'

'Just his character, darling. He's always been cautious. Never does anything without giving it a lot of thought. He'll come round eventually. How could anyone not love you?'

She laughed and squeezed his arm. 'And you. We need to tell my father soon. I can't bear not seeing you every day. And I hate lying to him. He thinks I'm having dinner with James tonight.'

He kissed her. 'We'll tell him soon, I promise.' A bubble of jealousy formed in his chest. 'We can't have him thinking you're serious about James, can we?'

'You know I'm nothing of the sort,' she said, kissing him back.

Charles spotted a taxi and lifted his hand. 'Time to get you back to Hong Kong side, I suppose. I don't like the thought of parting for the night. I'd give anything to wake up with you tomorrow morning.'

'So would I,' she said with a sigh.

They settled into the back seat of the cab, and he put his arms around her. She snuggled against him then lifted her chin. His mouth came down on hers, love for her throbbing through him. Kate's lips parted and he kissed her deeply, his hands cupping her breasts. *God, how I want her.* She gave a soft moan, and he made himself pull away. 'We're behaving like a couple of adolescents not wanting their parents to find out what they're up to.' He stroked her cheek. 'One thing is certain, though. I can't go on like this much longer.'

33

SOFIA

Dressed in a halter-neck top and shorts, Sofia stepped out of the sampan and paid the boatwoman. She'd accepted James's invitation to spend the day on his yacht. A whole day! *My first time seen in public with him.* She pushed away her worries about the Englishwoman.

Laden down with her picnic basket and swimming things, she clambered aboard *Jade* to be enfolded in James's warm embrace. The yacht putt-putted out of the harbour, its inboard engine just about coping with the swell. In Junk Bay, James unfurled the sails and the yacht bucked at a list. Sofia tossed back her hair, tasting the salt of the sea on her lips and feeling the exhilaration of running with the wind.

They rounded the headland and tied up to a jetty in Joss House Bay. Here, it was calm and the air redolent with the odour of brine. She changed into her swimsuit in the miniscule cabin, then looked over the side of the boat. 'It's so clear you can see right down to the sand on the seabed,' she said.

She swam with James in the deserted cove, then climbed back onto the yacht, put on her shorts, and unpacked sandwiches while James opened two bottles of Tiger beer. 'Shall we go for a walk after lunch?' She would ask him about the Englishwoman later.

They ate in comfortable silence, rinsed their plates with seawater, and then stepped ashore. Cicadas screeched in the undergrowth as they strolled towards the temple at the base of the hill. Sofia breathed in the pungent stench of fish drying on rattan mats under the portals of the grey-walled, green-roof-tiled buildings. Mongrels sat in the shade scratching their fleas. Children gawked at them and called out, 'Hallo, bye-bye.'

In the cool of the darkened temple, an old hag, with a few strands of grey hair scraped back in a bun, was kow-towing before the altar with a statue of the goddess of the sea.

'That's Tin Hau. She protects fishermen and sailors.' Sofia pointed at the blackened face of the effigy and pulled at James's sleeve. 'We should pay our respects to her. Light joss-sticks, bow three times and she'll bring us good luck.'

James turned his head towards the Buddha-like image. 'I'd rather get out of here,' he whispered, his cheeks pale. 'This place is giving me the heebie-jeebies.'

He grabbed her hand and pulled her out into the sunshine. His fingers were ice-cold, even in this heat. 'I've got the distinct impression someone just walked over my grave,' he rasped.

Back on the yacht, she stretched out next to him. 'I'm curious,' he said after kissing her. 'What do you see in me?'

'I don't understand.'

'You're incredibly beautiful, Sofia, and I'm just an ordinary bloke.'

'I just seem exotic to you, that's all. I feel as though I've known you all my life. Maybe even in another life.'

'Do you believe in reincarnation?'

'I'm not sure... I sort of believe in the supernatural. You can't help but feel it in Hong Kong. The Chinese belief in ghosts is so strong.'

'Then you aren't a Buddhist?'

'No. My uncle is one, you could say, but he's a typical Chinese in that he is also a Taoist and follows Confucius. And he venerates his ancestors and believes in all the different deities, just to be on the safe side and despite being a communist.' She took in a deep breath. 'I was brought up a Roman Catholic, because of my father.'

'That temple gave me the creeps.' James shuddered. 'The smell of the incense made me think of nothing but death.'

'Let me rub your back,' Sofia said. 'You know how it soothes you.' *Not a good moment to ask him about the Englishwoman.*

It was two days later, and Sofia was working on the solo martial art forms she practised most afternoons in order to build up her flexibility. Her teacher had told her to train her form as if she were sparring and to spar as if it were a form. Sofia placed her hands on the carpet in her office and pushed herself to her feet. She blocked and punched the air, flowing with the movements and, as she did so, she imagined she was fighting Leo.

Uncle had finally let her in on his plan; it was a daring scheme, but it was also ingenious. Chun Ming and one of Uncle's associates would commit air piracy. Sofia couldn't wait to see Leo's face when he found out he'd been robbed. He wouldn't be able to find any proof to connect the deed with Uncle, even if he suspected it. Chun Ming would fade into obscurity, knowing he'd helped derail a nationalist, and Uncle's associate would leave for America to rally support for Mao.

It was time the Americans were told they'd backed the wrong

horse, Sofia mused. Chiang Kai Shek was a war lord and his Kuomintang party so corrupt they would bleed sleaze if you pricked them. She remembered Uncle's attempt to bribe James last December. Uncle was an old rogue and many of his business practices suspect, but he loved China and knew the only way for it to prosper was through radical change.

Sofia went down to the shop floor. She sighed. The heads of her workers bowed over the looms, the clamour of the machinery deafening. She walked alongside the rows of young women. They were here to earn a wage that might have been considered subsistence-level by some, but for these people it was a means of subsistence they wouldn't otherwise have. They deserved her respect and she should become more involved in their interests. She would put a stop to using the girls to work the looms at night, she resolved. It might halve profits, but the practice had to end. If she set up sleeping facilities and ensured her workers were adequately fed, productivity would almost certainly improve.

Back in her office, she dialled James's number. She needed to check he'd been given the go-ahead by Special Branch. And it was time she asked him about the Englishwoman.

They arranged to meet at their usual place – a quiet hotel on the road from Kowloon to the New Territories. She phoned for a taxi to pick her up, then took a shower.

James was waiting for her on the veranda skirting the back of the hotel. She gazed at the clear view stretching towards Hong Kong Island... Rivers and rivers of lights. A plane was coming in from the west, banking low before lining up for the runway at Kai Tak Airport. The warm evening air, rich with the perfume of frangipani, caressed her bare arms.

'I'd love to have dinner with you at the Parisian Grill one evening,' she said to James. 'I've heard the food is excellent.'

'I went there the other week, as a matter of fact.' He paused. 'Of course I'll take you.'

'Did you go alone?'

James glanced away, appearing to consider the question. He lifted his shoulders in a brief shrug. 'I met this girl, Kate Wolseley, who has all the right connections for me to make my way in Hong Kong.' His eyes searched hers and he gave a sheepish smile. 'I'd been hoping one of her father's friends would back me in an import-export business and I suppose I was using her. I'm ashamed of that now.'

'There is another way, you know. Import-export is too old-fashioned. The future is in manufacturing.' She thought for a moment. *Is it too soon to ask him? No.* 'I'd like to offer you a partner-ship in the factory.'

'Sofia, you don't have to do that.' He put his arms around her and nuzzled her ear, sending a wave of pleasure through her. 'I'm totally smitten with you and should have told you before now.'

'Totally smitten?'

'I mean I'm in love with you. Dare I believe you feel the same way about me?'

Her mouth too dry to speak, she wrapped her arms around his waist and hugged him. Her heart sang with happiness. *James loves me, not the Englishwoman.*

He led her to their room. They undressed and she stretched out next to him on the cool sheets, the ceiling fans stirring the air around them. She touched him, bending over him so that her hair caressed his face. She kissed his eyelids and moved her mouth down his body, burying her fingers in his chest hair. Then she pressed her lips to his flat stomach.

She took him in her hand, feeling him grow until the size of him made her smile. She wanted the whole of him, every inch.

She straddled him, and once he was fully inside her, she moved slowly up and down.

'Ah, Sofia, what are you doing to me?'

'Shush, relax,' she said, her voice throaty. She kept her movements unhurried, and concentrated hard to contain her rising desire.

'Oh, yes,' he said, moving in time with her. 'Oh, yes!'

'My love,' she said, pushing down on him, rotating her pelvis, finally allowing her pleasure to build as James thrust back at her. Hot throbbing ripples of sensation, again and again and again. She collapsed next to him, spent.

'Darling, shall we call for room service? I'm hungry,' she said, giggling.

'You little minx,' James said, laughing. 'You've had your wicked way with me and now all you can think about is food.'

'Didn't I please you?' she asked with a kiss to his chest.

'You more than pleased me,' he said, his hand cupping her chin. He traced his fingers over her mouth then down to her breasts.

With another giggle, she slapped his hand away. 'If I don't have supper soon I'll faint.' Much as she longed to repeat the lovemaking, she had to talk to him first.

They washed, dressed, and ate at a table in the corner of the room, enjoying steaming hot wonton soup, chicken with cashew nuts, and crispy noodles followed by pomelo and star fruit. Sofia sat back in her chair and watched James wipe his mouth with a linen napkin. 'Have you held your meeting with Special Branch yet?' she enquired.

'They won't commit themselves to approving an actual robbery. I didn't think they would,' he said. 'However, provided everything goes according to plan and we get the gold off the plane before the police arrive, they won't pursue the matter.'

'And in return?'

'They want the names of the banks receiving the smuggled gold, as well as the details of your half-brother's contacts.'

'Uncle knows the banks and he already has the details of Leo's associates. He bribed Derek Higgins. As you know, Derek needs money.'

'Strange fellow. Bit of an enigma, don't you think?'

'Most definitely.' She stroked James's hand. 'What shall we do now?'

'What would you like to do?' James leaned forward and kissed her lips.

'I'm serious about you becoming a partner in the factory,' she said, ignoring the heat rising between her thighs. Business first, pleasure later. 'We would make a great team.'

'But I don't know anything about cotton-spinning.'

'I'll teach you. We import raw cotton from Pakistan at the moment. You could help us secure suppliers in America and Mexico. It would mean travelling to those countries and making contacts. You'd be the right person for the job.'

'I might enjoy that. Who do you ship the yarn to?'

'Mainly Indonesia and Malaya. Uncle has family there. But markets in Asia are wide open, as much of Japan's textile industry has been bombed to smithereens. In fact, Uncle bought his looms from the Japanese. He told me it gave him a sense of satisfaction buying them from the defeated enemy.'

'Hmm.' James rubbed at his chin. 'How do you see the future of the factory?'

'Currently, we can only produce coarse yarn, because of Hong Kong's summer heat and humidity. I want to install air conditioning as soon as we can afford it and then conditions will be suitable to spin finer yarn. I'd like to move into weaving, dyeing and eventually garment manufacturing.'

'Sounds like you've got it all mapped out, sweetheart.'

Could she hope that she and James would have a future together? She sighed to herself. Only if everything went according to Uncle's plan and she could get away from Leo. *Leo.* She shuddered. *I won't think about him now.*

James carried her back to the bed. 'This time, let me do the work,' he said, sitting her down. 'Open your legs.'

Her first thought was, thank God she'd had a wash. Then, she couldn't think any more, just feel, as his tongue explored her folds. And it was wonderful, so, so wonderful. She couldn't stop coming, wave after wave, her pleasure as great as the ocean. He lifted his head and rolled her back. She parted her thighs for him, swallowing him into her until they were one. James and Sofia. The perfect partnership. She looked deep into his eyes while they rocked together. 'I love you, James.'

34

KATE

I had stepped onto the veranda to enjoy the evening view. Glancing at my watch, I realised it was time to get on with some marking and preparing tomorrow's lessons. I'd been distracting myself from my frustration at not seeing Charles by concentrating on my job. I'd even taken my pupils on a daytrip to the children's home, where they'd each given the orphans new toys donated by their parents. Every day for the past week, I'd spoken at length with Charles on the phone, but only when Papa was out. Was Charles being too cautious? He was like his uncle in that respect. Maybe I should come right out and tell Papa myself...

I lowered my gaze towards Kowloon, then stepped back in surprise. Billows of black smoke were rising from a hillside and an orange glow lit up the sky. I ran indoors. 'It looks like one of the squatter camps is on fire,' I said to Papa, my hands flailing. 'We've got to help. Come on! Those poor, poor people.'

In the kitchen, I asked Ah Woo to find some food and fill as many vacuum flasks as he could with hot tea. Murmuring under his breath and clearly thinking his young missy had gone mad, he opened a cupboard and removed a large Dundee cake which he sliced into small pieces. Then he put some old teacups into a cardboard box.

I went back to the veranda. Papa was holding a pair of binoculars to his eyes. 'You aren't seriously thinking of going over there?'

'I've got to do something.'

'What can you do? Leave it to the authorities, dear girl!'

'It's George's day off. Can you give me a lift?'

'All right. All right. Hold on!'

Papa fetched his keys. I raided the linen cupboard for blankets, bundling them up and taking them to the car. Ah Woo carried baskets of flasks and food. Papa loaded everything into the boot. All three of us got into the Daimler and set off down the Peak. 'Can't you go a bit faster?' I begged Papa.

'These hairpin bends are too dangerous for speed. Be patient!'

We took the car ferry across the harbour, then drove until we arrived at a roadblock. 'I'm a doctor,' I lied to the Chinese policeman at the barricade. 'Please let me through!'

There was nowhere to park, so Ah Woo and I left Papa with the car. Thousands of people, evacuated from the inferno, were sitting on the streets. The air was bitter with the acrid stench of burning rubber and textiles. Flakes of ash floated down; some of them still glowed red from the flames. A fire engine, its hose attached to a street hydrant, sprayed water in a high arc that hardly seemed to make any difference.

I ran backwards and forwards to the car with Ah Woo, distributing blankets, slices of cake, and tea to the shocked refugees. A young woman sat on the kerb, clutching a small child to her breast. Silent tears squeezed from her eyes. Her husband cradled their other child, a baby, and made soothing sounds. I went up to them with a thermos flask and a china cup. They took the tea from me and nodded their thanks.

I went back to Papa, Ah Woo at my heels. 'It seems as if everyone got out, thank God.'

'Good. Can we go home now? I'm missing a concert on the wireless.'

'Is that all you can think about? Haven't you got any conscience?'

'Of course I have, but I'm realistic as well. This mess isn't of our making. I've said it before, and I'll say it again. Let the authorities handle it, dear girl!'

'I can't stand by and watch. I've got to help these people. Surely there must be something I can do?'

'You could start a charity, I suppose,' Papa said, shaking his head. 'Involve Jessica! She's good at organising things. Remember the amateur dramatics in the camp?'

A vision of Mama tripping the boards flashed into my mind, and I swallowed my guilt. One day I'd visit Mama's grave. But only when I was ready. The memories were still too painful. I stared at the thin white scars on the backs of my hands and sighed.

* * *

The Ladies' Recreation Club sprawled down the side of the Peak at the mid-levels: a clubhouse, tennis courts and a couple of swimming pools. A waiter showed me to a table in the corner.

Jessica came through the door and took the chair opposite. She delved into her handbag for her cigarette case. 'I'm not late, am I?'

'No. I'm early. Shall we order straight away?'

'Definitely. I could eat a horse.'

'I hope not.' I let out a laugh. 'I'd never eat horse meat.'

'Ever since Stanley, my stomach always seems to be crying out for food.' Jessica flicked open her lighter and lit a cigarette.

'Thankfully, I've managed to keep my figure despite becoming a complete glutton.'

The waiter took our orders – steak for Jessica and fillet of sole for me. Jessica moved to sit on the edge of her chair. 'So, you want to set up a charity to help the refugees?'

'I thought we could begin by organising a ball at the Peninsula Hotel. We could sell the tickets above the odds and get people to donate prizes for a raffle. It's not much, but it would be a start.'

'And it'll be fun.' She smiled.

We chatted about setting up the charity until our food arrived, then went on to discuss my teaching job and work at the orphanage.

'And here I am, living a life of leisure,' Jessica said. 'Tony and I have been trying to start a family, but no go I'm afraid. Seems semi-starvation has buggered up my baby works.'

'I'm so sorry,' I said, shocked.

'There's a specialist in London I plan to visit next year. Now, tell me! I'm dying to know. Why aren't you seeing James any more?'

I stiffened. 'What a question!'

'Tony heard it from James himself. He was a bit concerned, as he bumped into him with the daughter of Paulo Rodrigues on the Ferry the other day. Then James told Tony he wanted to resign from Holden's Wharf and help the girl expand her cotton spinning business.'

I gripped the tablecloth. 'I wondered why he hasn't phoned recently. I thought it was because I was giving him the cold shoulder.'

'And why did you do that? As if I can't guess…'

'Charles Pearce, of course.'

'I hope you know what you're doing, Kate. Crossing over the cultural gap is a huge step.'

'That's why we're keeping it secret from Papa until the time is right.' I reached across the table for her hand. 'Promise me you won't tell him!'

'Of course not. I'm on your side, as a matter of fact. Charles is a charming young man. I sat next to him at dinner the other week, remember? And he can certainly dance. He doesn't even look terribly Chinese. If I didn't know, I'd say he was Mexican...'

Just the sort of thing Jessica would say, but it's kindly meant, I suppose.

In the taxi on the way back to the Peak, I wound down the window and let the night air blow through my hair. I slumped back in my seat. It wasn't that I wanted to be with James, but I envied him and Sofia managing to be together despite their different backgrounds. I straightened my back and set my jaw. How to resolve the problem of Papa? Jessica had said during lunch that he would be a tough nut to crack. It was true; he was set in his old-fashioned ways. What I needed was a catalyst. Something to jolt him into the twentieth century. *Perhaps I should pack my bags and leave. But where would I go?* The Helena May had a waiting list as long as a train and I'd searched for a flat but hadn't been able to find anything. I slumped back in my seat again.

35

SOFIA

Sofia lay in the cabin of her uncle's launch. The nausea had subsided, but she'd spent the two hours since they'd left Kowloon going to and from the heads and vomiting. She ran a jerky hand through her hair. What a time to catch a tummy bug, she told herself. She swung her feet slowly to the floor and went up to the bridge.

'I don't know what came over me,' she said to James. 'I'm feeling a lot better now.'

'That's good.' He put his arm around her and kissed the top of her head. 'I was worried about you. You still look a bit pale, though.'

'I'll be all right once I've eaten something.' She kissed the pulse beneath his ear. 'Come down to the lower deck for some lunch. The plane won't be here for a while yet.'

At the stern of the launch, she sipped a soda water and munched on a cream cracker. They were motoring past Siu A Chau, the northernmost of the dozen or so islands making up the Soko group south of Lan Tau – Hong Kong's largest island. She eyed crystal-white sands and lush green vegetation rising to a small hill. Supposedly there was a hamlet hidden there somewhere, but otherwise the place was uninhabited. A small shrine nestled by the shore, painted bright red, and rocks at the far end stood up like ninepins.

The Catalina seaplane would touch down between Siu A Chau and Tai A Chau, the largest of the Sokos, just within the colony's territorial waters. She glanced upwards and caught sight of Lantau Peak... a broad cone to the north.

Once they'd put masks on to conceal their identities, she and James would secure the Catalina and its prisoners with the help of Chun Ming and Uncle's pilot, Wing Yan. Then they'd pick up the gold and head back to Kowloon by way of the dumbbell-shaped island of Cheung Chau, where it had been arranged for them to leave Uncle's men in a safe house. The Marine Police would be tipped off by Special Branch as soon as the plane took off. By the time the authorities' boats arrived, Sofia and the others would be long gone.

Staring at the island across the short stretch of sea before them, she said to James, 'Have you heard the story of Cheung Potsai, the famous pirate?'

'Can't say that I have.' He shook his head.

'According to legend, he had a fleet of over one thousand war-junks equipped with cannon and over ten thousand men at his command.'

'How long ago was that?'

'The last decades of the eighteenth and beginning of the nineteenth century. Apparently, he had an English concubine and he lived with her in a sumptuously furnished cavern on Cheung Chau.'

'Strange he should meet an Englishwoman in those days.'

'She fell in love with him after he'd captured a British clipper and held her for ransom.'

'Just like I've fallen in love with you.'

'I'm not a pirate,' she said, laughing.

'Ah, but your uncle is. This whole malarkey smacks of piracy, in my opinion.'

Ignoring his remark, she pointed ahead. 'They say the Englishwoman's grave is on that island.'

* * *

After they'd eaten, she went back to the bridge with James. The rumble of an engine echoed, and she shaded her eyes. The seaplane had levelled out over Lantau, but instead of starting its descent, it was tossing from one side to the other. Sofia clapped her hands to her cheeks. It had overshot its intended landing spot. *Holy Mother of God!* The plane had gone into a nosedive.

James swung around. 'What the hell?'

In the distance, the Catalina had plunged into the sea.

'Oh no!' Sofia felt sick again.

'Bugger!' James grabbed the charts, hung on to the table, and ran a finger down the map. 'She's ditched about ten miles away, I reckon,' he said, his voice a pitch higher than usual. 'We must go there straight away.'

They approached the crash site at high speed. Within minutes, it seemed, although it probably took longer, they spotted jetsam bobbing on top of the waves. Sofia looked around for the plane. Nothing. Suitcases floated on the surface and coldness spread through her.

James caught hold of her arm. 'Look!'

She followed his gaze and there was someone, a man, clutching a piece of wreckage.

James grabbed a lifebuoy and threw it to the man. Sofia went to fetch a blanket while James and the boat-boy lifted the survivor onto the deck.

Chun Ming lay stretched out, his face white and heavily bruised; he was shaking, and his leg dangled limply, obviously badly broken. 'What happened?' Sofia wrapped the blanket around him, but he stared at her as if he had no idea who she was.

James made radio contact with Gerry Watkins. Sofia listened to the brief conversation, trembling. 'Fair enough,' James said to Watkins. 'We'll take him to Queen Mary Hospital.'

'He's washed his hands of the matter,' James said, pacing the deck. 'We're off the hook because of the deal with your uncle. But the plane has crashed, and the police are in the know, so Chun Ming will be investigated. There's no chance of recovering the gold, I'm afraid.'

Sofia cradled Chun Ming's head in her lap. She didn't care about the gold. All she could think about was the plane's final moments as it went down, taking everyone on board but Chun Ming with it.

* * *

Two days later, Sofia stood by the foot of Chun Ming's hospital bed. He was sleeping, his face serene against the white of the sheets. His pyjamas had been buttoned up wrongly and she longed to re-button them, but she didn't want to disturb him. His leg was in a pulley and covered in bandages. She sat down on the chair by his bedside.

He opened his eyes and smiled weakly.

A Chinese nurse, a wisp of black hair poking out from her cap, busied around them, arranging the red gladioli Sofia had brought. After plumping up Chun Ming's pillows and helping him take a sip of water, the nurse left the room.

Sofia took hold of Chun Ming's hand. 'How do you feel?'

His face wore a pained expression. 'I'll be all right.'

'What happened?'

'I can't remember much.'

'Do you think you can piece things together if I prompt you?'

'I'll try.' Chun Ming grimaced. 'Well, a few minutes after take-off, I think it was, Wing Yan put a gun to the pilot's head. He demanded the controls, but the pilot refused.'

'What happened next?'

'Let me think...' Chun Ming stared at the opposite wall for what seemed like an age, his forehead wrinkling. 'I remember now. I ordered the co-pilot and Derek Higgins, who was carrying the gold for your half-brother, and the other passengers to move to the side of the cabin so I could cover them with my gun.'

'And then what?'

'The plane hit a patch of turbulence and Higgins drew his own gun.'

'Did he fire it?'

'No. Higgins lunged at Wing Yan, who lost his balance. Both guns went off and a bullet hit the pilot in the back of the neck.'

Shock wheeled through Sofia. 'How terrible!' she exclaimed.

'The pilot's body fell forward onto the flight controls. The plane veered left, then right, and then nose-dived. Everyone was screaming and I managed to jump out the door just before we hit the sea.'

'There's no easy way to tell you this, Chun Ming, but you've got to know.' Sofia leant forward. 'There's a policeman outside this room. Now that you've regained consciousness, he will want to interview you.'

'Why?'

'They know about the robbery and they've recovered the pilot's body.'

'I didn't shoot him.'

'I know. But you're the only survivor.'

'I'm sorry about those who died. I never expected this outcome.'

'I'm sorry too about them all, even Derek Higgins.' She glanced down at the bed sheet.

'I agree. He was very unpleasant, but I didn't want him to die.'

'Uncle will send some money to his parents,' Sofia said, patting Chung Ming's hand. 'He has great respect for family.' *As if that will make it all right!*

'What about the factory?'

'You're not to worry about that. The main thing is you will get better. We'll find you a good lawyer. In fact, I don't think that policeman can interrogate you until you have one.'

A trolley rattled past the door and she stood up. 'I must go, but I'll be back tomorrow.'

She picked up her handbag. Two Chinese women were coming into the room. The Englishwoman, the one she'd seen with James, followed them.

'Li! Ma!' Chun Ming called out.

'Hello. I'm Kate Wolseley.' The Englishwoman smiled at Sofia. 'Chun Ming and I grew up together.'

Sofia took a step back and touched her throat. Dizziness spread through her. She grabbed hold of the side of the chair. Her legs folded beneath her and she slipped to the floor.

36

KATE

After leaving the hospital, I took a taxi to the Ferry. The cymbals and high-pitched song of Cantonese opera were playing on the radio and the cab stank of stale cigarette smoke. Outside, though, Hong Kong shimmered in shades of green and blue. The humid clouds of summer had given way to the lucidity that only happened at this time of the year, when it truly became a place of mountains, sea and sky. But the sound of pile drivers echoed in the air, disturbing the serenity. Such a shame that so many hills were being bulldozed down to fill in parts of the harbour and make room for unrelenting construction work, I thought.

Poor Sofia. I'd rushed forward to catch hold of her and help her to sit on a chair when she'd nearly fainted. Her face was greyish and perspiration had shone on her forehead. Ah Ho grabbed a glass and filled it from the water jug on Chun Ming's bedside table. But Sofia resolutely refused to see a doctor. What an incredibly beautiful woman she was, with her thick dark-brown hair and large grey oriental eyes, not to mention an almost perfect figure (perhaps her chest was a bit flat). No wonder James had fallen for her...

I was furious with him. Between them, Chun Ming and Sofia had told me the whole story. James should have persuaded K C Leung to find another way to repay Leo Rodrigues. People had died as a result of Leung's so-called ruse.

Leaning back, I shut my eyes. Charles had responded to my call from the hospital's reception desk with a swift agreement to meet me at the Peninsula Hotel. If anyone could help Jimmy, Charles would be that person. He said he had a client to see in Kowloon beforehand. That suited me fine; I'd combine meeting Charles with confirming the final details of the ball, which was due to take place the day before my twenty-third birthday.

The taxi dropped me at the Ferry and I found a seat on the top deck in the covered central section. The sides were open to the view and a sampan floated past with an old man holding a fishing line, his long grey goatee flapping in the breeze. All around us, vessels weaved and crossed, passed and turned, like a pool of carp in a feeding frenzy.

On Kowloon side, as everyone always called it, I walked for five minutes until I arrived at the Peninsula. It was here that the Governor had surrendered to the Japanese on Christmas Day, 1941. Japanese officers had occupied the hotel, which became their headquarters. Now it was 'the finest hotel east of Suez' again. A sudden sensation of loss spread through me; Mama used to bring me here and treat me to a milkshake sometimes after school.

A fountain was playing in the forecourt as usual as I climbed the steps to the entrance, glancing upwards at the horseshoe-shaped structure. Two bellboys in white uniforms opened the double doors. I crossed the marble floor to the manager's office, where I confirmed the menu for the ball and made sure all the arrangements were in place.

I thanked the manager and stepped into the lobby. A string quartet on the corner balcony was playing 'Greensleeves'. There was Charles in an armchair at a table across the room. I drank in the sight of him: his broad shoulders, lean body and long legs. He looked up and smiled his wonderful smile, making my pulse race.

Last week we'd gone to the pictures together and had seen the film *Easter Parade*, starring Judy Garland and Fred Astaire, but that had been the only time we'd managed a date since dinner with Charles' relatives. I'd loved the Irving Berlin soundtrack and had been humming 'Stepping out with My Baby' so much I'd been driving my school colleagues mad. In the cinema, Charles and I had kissed in the darkness. He'd held me in his arms and I'd felt the hardness of his chest against my breasts. How I longed to make love with him again...

The clink of cutlery mixed with the murmur of conversation as Charles pulled out a chair and gave me a peck on the cheek. 'How wonderful to see you, darling,' he said. He signalled the bow-tied waiter. 'Indian, Earl Grey or Jasmine tea?'

'Indian, please.'

Charles gave our order. Then he placed the tips of his fingers together. 'Tell me, my love, why did you want to see me so urgently? Purely business, you said. What business?'

'The Catalina seaplane.'

A frown creased his forehead. 'What's that got to do with you?'

'Not me. My old amah's son.'

I explained about my hospital visit and we both expressed surprise that Derek Higgins had also been involved in the catastrophe. 'It would mean so much if you could help,' I said. 'Not just to me. Ah Ho must be worried sick about Chun Ming.'

A bicycle bell rang, as one of the pageboys walked past us, holding a small blackboard aloft to page someone. Charles leant forward. 'Where did you say the plane went down?'

'Beyond the Soko Islands.'

'Have the police interviewed Chun Ming yet?'

'No. They'll wait until you can be there.'

'Good. I'll get my secretary to make the arrangements.'

Our waiter arrived and placed a silver tray on the table, laden with a typical English afternoon tea: wafer-thin sandwiches, sponge cake and scones. I lifted the silver teapot and poured.

Charles offered me a cucumber sandwich then took one for himself. 'Tell me more about James's involvement.'

'Sofia said he was working secretly for Special Branch. Apparently, James brokered a deal with Leung for information about local banks smuggling the Consortium's gold into Hong Kong.' I sipped my tea. 'Leung also provided details of a new group of Triads from China who are setting up here. In return, Special Branch agreed to let him get away with the robbery.'

'Right. That will make it easier. Special Branch won't want this to get out.'

I crumpled my linen napkin, stiff with starch. Charles was looking at me intensely, bathing me in the warmth of his regard. 'Jessica and I are organising a charity ball here to coincide with the Mid-Autumn Festival next week,' I said. 'Would you like to buy a ticket? It's fancy dress and the theme is China.'

'Why not?' He smiled. 'What are you wearing?'

'The cheongsam I'm having made. I'm going as Madam Chiang Kai Shek. I bought the material with your aunt yesterday.'

'So glad you two are getting on. Auntie will convince Uncle about us, you'll see. He always comes round to her way of seeing things in the end.'

We lapsed into silence while Charles ate his way through all the cake and sandwiches. Putting my napkin down, I pushed back my chair. 'Well, I'd better be off. I took an afternoon's leave of absence from school to visit Chun Ming, and my headmistress will be cross if she gets reports that I've been seen having tea at the Pen. Are you going back to Hong Kong side now?'

'Yes, my love, I'll take the Ferry with you.'

I held his hand and we walked past the bus station to the concourse. I didn't care if any of Papa's chums saw us, and Charles didn't seem to mind either. A stiff breeze was blowing and I held on to my hat with my other hand. We went through the turnstile then up the ramp to the ferry.

'Did you know a tropical cyclone is headed our way?' Charles said. 'The Royal Observatory has launched typhoon signal number one. I've heard the storm won't be here for a couple of days, but do take care, my darling.'

'I wondered why it has turned so windy. Don't worry, I'll be safe on the Peak. Papa has perfected the art of organising typhoon shutters.' A sudden thought occurred to me. 'I've just had a brilliant idea. We can tell Papa you're helping Jimmy, I mean Chun Ming. That will be a perfectly legitimate excuse for us to see each other. Then, once he gets used to you being around, we'll inform him we're in love.'

A doubtful expression crossed Charles's face. 'Something tells me it isn't going to be that simple.'

'Well, have you got a better plan?'

'No,' he said, taking my face in his hands and kissing me.

'Good. I'll tell Papa about you helping us.'

37

CHARLES

Charles dialled Kate's number. He wanted to fill her in on developments in Chun Ming's case, but her houseboy answered the phone and said she'd gone to the children's home in the New Territories. Apparently, she went every Sunday.

He put down the phone. Why hadn't Kate told him that's what she did on her day off? It was a marvellous thing for her to do. Except, it was so like her not to tell him; she wouldn't want him to think she was boasting. They'd spoken only yesterday and she'd said her father hadn't batted an eyelid when she'd explained he was helping Chun Ming. Charles was under no illusions, however. Expatriates and locals always worked well together as far as business was concerned. It was only in their personal lives that they didn't mix.

The wireless blared from the kitchen. Yesterday, typhoon signal number three had gone up and winds had strengthened throughout the day, but by early this morning it seemed the storm had turned away. Charles glanced out of the window; the trees were bending in an alarming fashion. A news flash came on and he jumped to his feet. The typhoon had turned around and was heading straight for Hong Kong!

Wendy, as the storm was known, was expected to pass near the colony late that afternoon at the same time as the predicted high tide. There were fears of a tidal wave in Tolo Harbour.

Good God! That's close to the children's home...

Charles grabbed his car keys, ran downstairs and jumped into his MG. The wind was whipping the trees by the side of the road and sending rubbish flying up into the air, buffeting his small car. He had to use all his strength to keep it on the road.

At the Ferry, a policeman stopped him. The boats had all gone to the typhoon shelters. He wouldn't be able to get across.

Charles drove frantically round to the back of the Hong Kong Club, found a space, reversed into it, and ran to the pier.

There was a man in a walla walla motorboat, his craft cresting the waves like a rollercoaster. 'You wan' go Kowloon side?'

'Yes. How much?'

'Fifty dollar!'

'Too much!'

'Fifty dollar!' the man insisted.

Charles looked around; there weren't any other boats. He climbed down the ladder and jumped into the vessel. Warm rain drenching him, he sat next to the boatman and held on for dear life as the walla walla jerked, plunged, and pitched its way across the harbour.

On Kowloon side, Charles clambered ashore, found a phone booth, and dialled the Wolseleys' number. Henry answered.

'I'm on my way to the New Territories,' Charles said. 'Have you heard from Kate?'

'I can't get through to the orphanage. The phone lines must be down. Very grateful to you if you'd check on my daughter.'

'I'll try my best.'

'Just make sure she's all right!'

Charles got into the back of the only cab prepared to take him to Sha Tin. Rain was sheeting horizontally across the road, broken glass flying in the air and shop signs swaying. The streets, normally crowded with people, were eerily empty.

Half an hour later, the taxi skirted the edge of the rising waters and pulled up outside the gates of the orphanage. Charles paid the driver. The man told him he lived locally and was heading home anyway, but that didn't stop him from charging thirty dollars.

Charles ran up the steep driveway to the front door. It was swinging on its hinges. A corridor spanned the front of the building and he went into the first room, a dining room with long tables down the centre and a smell of burnt rice. No one. Next, he strode into a sitting room boasting chintz-covered sofas and rattan armchairs. Empty. Three children's dormitories with unmade beds made up the rest of the rooms. Where was Kate? There was a door at the end of the corridor, and he pushed it open.

There she was, in a large schoolroom, mopping up rainwater that had come in through the shuttered windows. She stared at him, eyes wide. 'What are you doing here?'

'God, Kate! Why didn't you tell me this is what you do with your time?'

'Well, now you're here, you can help,' she said with a wry smile. 'Sorry I'm not more welcoming, but I'm exhausted.' She handed him the mop and waved towards a frizzy-haired European woman sitting with a group of children in the dry patch at the far end of the room. 'Miss Denning, this is my friend, Charles. Looks like he's come to give us a hand.'

'Good. You stay here with the little ones, Kate, and I'll go and find Mary. I think she's with the amahs and the older children.'

Charles gazed out through a crack in the shutters. The fields below, a short time ago sodden with water, were now completely submerged. People had moved up to the green-tiled roofs of the nearby walled village, clutching their possessions; some had even carried up pigs, chickens and dogs. The orphanage was on a hill, but it was a small one. Would the waters reach them here?

He mopped up as much as he could, then went over to where Kate was sitting with a small girl on her lap.

'Who's this?' he asked.

'Mei Ling.' Kate kissed the girl on the cheek.

He lowered himself to sit cross-legged next to her. The child regarded him suspiciously. 'I don't suppose she sees many men,' he said, unable to keep the emotion from his voice. He really admired Kate for what she was doing but couldn't find the words to say so in front of the children.

'Why don't you read Mei Ling a story? She likes *The Three Little Pigs.*'

Gradually, the child's eyes lost their mistrustful look. Charles enjoyed reading to her; it reminded him of the times he'd read to Ruth when she was Mei Ling's age. The girl's eyelids closed and she drifted off to sleep.

Outside, the wind bellowed and rattled the windows. What was happening to those poor people in the village below? He couldn't bear to think. And what would happen to them if the sea rose further?

'You didn't explain why you came here,' Kate whispered.

'I wanted to tell you that Chun Ming will be sent back to China when his leg is out of plaster. He won't stand trial in Hong Kong.'

'Good!'

'Yesterday I spoke to the senior partner in my firm and he confirmed my belief that, because the plane came down in Chinese waters, the colony won't have jurisdiction. I contacted

James Stevens, and he got in touch with Special Branch. I found out he'd done the deal this morning.'

'I wonder what will happen to Chun Ming when he's in China...'

'He'll probably receive a hero's welcome from the communists. They're poised to take Canton and he's an ardent party member. Also, he fought with them during the occupation, didn't he?'

'Of course. That should make it easier for him.'

'When I interviewed him yesterday morning, he told me he knew Fei, the fierce young man I met at the end of the war who got me through Japanese lines. I was glad to have been of help to Chun Ming, my love. I don't condone what he did, though. It was misguided to say the least.'

'What did James have to say for himself?'

'Nothing much. I got the impression he didn't want to talk about it...'

* * *

In the late afternoon, the wind died down and the rain abated. There was nothing more he and Kate could do here, as Miss Denning had returned and taken charge. They said goodbye to the children and walked down the slope towards the village. Kate cried out in dismay at the devastation: debris everywhere, people wailing and frantically digging in the wreckage as they searched for their loved ones, torn-up vegetation strewn across the road, a large fishing junk tossed up on the land. Dead animals floated on the receding waters, and the shanty town he'd seen by the main road had been reduced to splintered planks of wood. It was incredible that so much damage could have happened in such a short time. Charles put his arm around Kate and she burrowed into his shoulder, sobbing.

Sirens shrilled and three fire engines arrived, followed by five ambulances and a police car. There was little he and Kate could do to help, other than comfort the grieving. In the early evening, Charles found a taxi and took Kate to the Ferry. She was silent throughout the journey, her face pale with apparent shock and tiredness. They arrived on Hong Kong side, and he walked with her to his car.

'Thank you for getting Chun Ming off, my darling,' Kate said. 'I don't mean to sound ungrateful, but you could have waited to tell me tomorrow, couldn't you?'

'I was worried about you. Also, when I phoned your father to find out if he'd heard from you, he asked me to make sure you were all right.'

'Then please come in for a drink when we get to my place.'

* * *

A gardener was sweeping up leaves, and repositioning flowerpots at the edge of the driveway. Charles parked to the side, steering clear of a couple of amahs taking down the typhoon shutters.

'This is quite a house,' he said.

Kate led him through the front door. 'I suppose it *is* a bit big for the two of us. I'm longing to get away, but you know how difficult it is to find somewhere. You were lucky to have your uncle's contacts to get your flat, weren't you?'

She was right; he would have found it impossible if Uncle Phillip hadn't been a friend of his landlord. Waiting lists for accommodation were notoriously long.

In the sitting room, Henry Wolseley got up from his armchair and held out his hand to Charles. 'Dashed grateful to you,' he said before going up to Kate and hugging her. 'Bally typhoon. Wasn't supposed to change course like that. Are you both all right?'

'We're fine,' Kate said. 'But lots of other people aren't, I'm afraid. We could do with a drink.'

'Of course.' Henry rang a hand bell. 'Where's Ah Woo? Ah! There he is.'

Charles asked for a San Miguel and Kate a brandy soda. Their drinks arrived, and Kate led him to the veranda to admire the view. The typhoon had cleared the air and, from this height, it was possible to see the mountains of China on the distant horizon behind the Kowloon hills.

'You'll stay for supper, won't you?' she said.

'As long as your father doesn't mind.'

'Of course he won't mind. He thinks we're just friends. Friends have supper together, don't they?'

'We should be able to tell him we're more than friends soon, my darling. That's if your plan works...'

38

SOFIA

Sofia unlocked the front door of Father's villa (she'd never think of it as Leo's) and strode across the tiled hall to the sideboard. She rang for the houseboy. 'Is my brother home?'

'Yes, missy.'

'Please tell him I'm here.'

Within seconds, Balthazar at his heels, Leo stood in front of her and folded his arms. 'What can I do for you?'

'I'm very well thank you, how are you?'

'Sarcasm will get you nowhere,' Leo said, his mouth turning up at one corner. 'Why are you here?'

'I have your money.' She handed him an envelope containing a banker's draft.

'How did you manage that?' Leo slid out the cheque. 'You haven't received your inheritance yet.'

'I went to the biggest bank in Hong Kong and they were quite happy to lend me the money, secured on the factory and its machinery.' James had helped organise the loan once his partnership in the business had been confirmed.

'Fair enough. You win, little sister.' Leo smirked. 'For now.'

'Here are my house keys. I'm leaving Macau for good so I won't need them any more.'

Leo took the keys and frowned. 'Tell your uncle I know he was involved with the seaplane catastrophe. Someone has talked. Leung had better watch his back.'

'What are you talking about?'

'I think you know perfectly well.'

'I know nothing of the sort.' She folded her arms. 'And there is no way you can connect my uncle with that tragedy.'

'He was seen with a man known to have trained as a pilot in the Philippines.'

'You're just making this up, Leo.'

'The Consortium has lost nearly thirty thousand American dollars. That's a lot of money by any reckoning, over one hundred and forty thousand Hong Kong dollars in fact. Strangely enough, roughly similar in value to your bank draft.'

'Only a coincidence. I'll go upstairs now and pack the last of my things.' She left the room.

Dratted Leo. He's too clever by far. Too, too clever.

* * *

Sofia took the afternoon steamer. Whenever she left Macau for the bright lights of the British colony, it was as if she were being jolted from the nineteenth into the twentieth century. In Macau, time seemed to have stood still and nothing had changed in decades. Many of the buildings in the beautiful old terraces were crumbling into decay, and the whole place had a feeling of decadence. She was glad to be on this ship, with her trunk of clothes in the hold and her jewellery in a bag by her side. Finally, she was getting away from Leo and everything to do with him.

She thought about Derek Higgins. Apparently, he had been

able to manufacture firecrackers in Macau, whereas in Hong Kong, factory regulations would have made his methods impossible. Derek's workers had caught terrible illnesses by inhaling poisonous vapours. Some had even blown themselves up. No questions had ever been asked by the authorities. People had done the work because they'd been desperate for employment. They would find other healthier jobs now, hopefully. She wasn't sorry Derek's body hadn't been found. He'd been a shark and he'd ended up a shark's dinner, for sure.

As for Leo, no doubt he'd continue his trajectory to become the most powerful man in Macau. Almost certainly, he would be running the place in a few years' time. She was well out of it, she realised. If she'd stayed he would have involved her in no end of shady dealings; it was the way he operated.

Her future lay with the factory. She and James would develop it into a profitable, legitimate business together. She had to build security. Not just for herself, but for her child. She was pregnant; she'd found out from her doctor yesterday, although she'd suspected it since nearly fainting at the hospital. She smiled to herself. After each lovemaking session with James, she'd douched with Chinese herbs, the advice she'd read in one of Uncle's books. Not the right advice, as it had turned out...

She looked out of the porthole. The colour of the sea had changed from muddy to turquoise blue, so they must have left the Pearl River Estuary. Soon, they passed Lantau Island and entered Hong Kong's Victoria Harbour. Here was her future. Here was James, the man she loved. Here she would bring up their child.

* * *

She passed through immigration and spotted James waiting for her. She went up to him, her heartbeat quickening. How would he react when she told him about the baby? When would she tell him? He came up and took her hand luggage. 'Where's this trunk you warned me about?'

'Over there.' She pointed.

'Good thing I organised a lorry, then,' he said, laughing. 'It's enormous.'

They clambered into the front cab, and the vehicle made its way to the car ferry. Crossing the harbour, they got out and stood on the foredeck.

James hooked his arm around her waist. 'How did things go when you paid off Leo?'

'He's not stupid, you know.' She leant against him. 'He suspects Uncle set up the robbery. He can't prove it, but we need to be aware we have a dangerous enemy.'

'How far does his influence extend? Surely not to Hong Kong?'

'He's only a big fish in the small pond of Macau. But, don't forget he has connections with the Triads here.'

'I haven't forgotten. I'll make sure Special Branch keep me informed if they hear anything. What news of Chun Ming?'

'The only people who know of his involvement are us, his family, Kate Wolseley and Charles Pearce. Let's hope it stays that way. If Leo gets wind of his participation in the robbery, it'll be difficult to keep him safe. I wonder if we can get him back to China before his leg is out of plaster...'

'I'll have a word with Gerry Watkins.'

They returned to the lorry and disembarked. After twenty minutes, they arrived at their hotel, the one they always used. Only this time they'd booked a suite to tide them over until they found a flat. James had given up his lodgings in Kowloon Tong when he'd resigned from Holden's Wharf.

James took off his shoes and stretched out on the bed cover.

She sat next to him and took his hand. 'There's something I need to tell you.'

'Oh,' he said with a frown. 'Something good or something bad?'

'Something good. At least, I think it is.'

'Well, then, tell me.'

'I'm pregnant,' she said, meeting his gaze.

A smile spread across his face. 'Are you sure?'

'I saw my doctor yesterday. You'll be a father next April.'

'Sweetheart, that's wonderful. I was going to do this in a more romantic setting, but there's no time like the present, as they say.'

'What were you going to do?'

'Ask you to marry me. Will you, Sofia? You'll make me the happiest man alive.'

'Yes. Oh, yes,' she said, her heart singing.

'We can get a special licence. Do it as soon as possible to avoid any scandal. You know what this place is like.'

She laid herself next to him. 'It will be scandalous enough you marrying me without the extra gossip about when our baby was conceived.'

He held out his arms. 'I love you, Sofia Rodrigues, and I'll love you as long as I live.'

'I love you too, James. In this life and the next.'

39

KATE

I was looking for some scissors. Spread out on my desk were the pictures painted by my class of eight-year-olds; I wanted to cut them out and paste them onto a frieze. I'd searched everywhere in my bedroom; I must have left the wretched things at school. *How annoying!* I ran downstairs to Papa's study and leafed through the papers on the top of the desk. Nothing.

I checked the top drawer. No luck.

Then I tried the bottom one. Locked.

Is it worth all this bother for a pair of scissors? One last try...

I opened the top drawer again. A key was sticking out from under Papa's writing folder. I picked it up and inserted it in the bottom drawer.

Success!

I slid open the drawer and rummaged through it. *Why aren't there any damn scissors here, for heaven's sake?* I'd have to try the kitchen. As I began to shut the drawer, I caught sight of envelopes tied up in string.

Sucking in a quick breath, I picked them up and peered at the post-marks. London. I flicked through ten letters sent between

October 1945 and October 1946. Someone had scribbled out our address on the Peak and had forwarded them to Sydney.

Charles's handwriting. I'd know it anywhere.

I struggled with the knot, fingers shaking. Eventually it loosened and the letters spilled out onto the desk. I picked them up and stared at them, one by one. Hands trembling, I opened the first envelope and started to read.

Dearest Kate

I miss you so much, and the past eighteen months have been such hell...

* * *

How could Papa have kept them from me all these years? Didn't he realise how unhappy I'd been? With heavy arms, I dragged myself up the stairs and flung myself onto the bed, clutching the envelopes to my chest. The front door slammed, and I rushed downstairs. Papa had already sat in his armchair, lit his pipe, and unfurled his newspaper. 'My goodness, you look as if your feathers have been well and truly ruffled, dear girl.'

'I've found Charles's letters.' I lifted my chin. 'That was a bit remiss of you, don't you think? It would have been safer to have destroyed them.'

Papa was silent for a moment. 'Would have been against the law,' he said, sucking on his pipe and putting down *The South China Morning Post.*

'And not giving them to me wasn't?'

'I would have given them to you eventually. When you'd settled down with a proper chap.'

'And Charles Pearce isn't a "proper chap"? Is that it? How could you?' I curled my lip. 'You let me think he was dead.'

'I believed there could be no future for the two of you in Hong Kong. I didn't want my daughter excluded by society and made unhappy. Time is a huge healer. I thought you'd forget all about him.'

'What a horrible cliché! In any case, time hasn't healed anything,' I spat. 'You broke my heart and I'd be grateful if you no longer interfered in my life.'

I turned on my heel and bounded back up to my room. Determinedly ignoring Papa knocking on the door, I read through the other nine letters. Charles wrote about how he'd started a law degree at King's College. He described his course and his fellow students, his life in London and how Ruth and his parents were getting on. Each letter pleaded for a response until the final one stated he would no longer be writing; it was clearly a useless exercise.

The knocking continued. 'I'm sorry,' Papa said. 'It was wrong of me. Can you forgive me?'

'It's not just me who needs to forgive you. Charles and I are in love. If you won't accept that then I'm afraid you'll lose me. The truth is, I can't live without him.'

'Can you do up my buttons, please?' I asked Ah Ho. She'd come back to work for us after Chun Ming and his wife had left for China yesterday. My amah and I were in the room I'd taken for the night at the Peninsula Hotel, and I was putting on my dress... the cheongsam I'd had made at Aunt Julie's tailor's.

'*Aiyah!* Missy, you very beautiful,' Ah Ho said, smiling her gold-toothed smile.

I glanced down at my figure: the green silk clung to my breasts, my stomach and my hips. 'Ah Ho, what are you calling me missy for? I'm Katie.'

'Now you grown up, you missy,' Ah Ho huffed.

'I'm sorry,' I said, giving myself a mental kick for making her lose face.

I stole a glance at Ah Ho: her hair was thinning more than ever and there were new wrinkles in her cheeks. The worry about Chun Ming had aged her. Of course Ah Ho would visit her son in China, but she was probably missing him already. It must have been a huge wrench seeing him off at the train station. Everything had happened so quickly. One minute he was in the hospital and the next he was leaving, still on crutches, Li by his side. I'd got there just in time to say goodbye.

Ah Ho fastened my last button. I looked down at myself again and blushed; I should have asked the tailor not to make the slits up the side of my legs so high.

A knock came at the door. I slipped on my mask and stared at the apparition in the doorway. Jessica's face was heavily made up with white powder, thick black eyebrows and ruby red lips; a black wig covered her hair. 'What a marvellous Empress of China you make, Jessica!'

'How did you know it was me?'

'The masks only cover our eyes. It will be easy to recognise people, won't it?'

'Just a bit of fun. And we'll be taking them off before supper, won't we? Come on! Time to get the show on the road, as they say.'

I hugged my amah. 'Thank you for helping me, Ah Ho. George will take you home now.'

I picked up my evening-bag and made sure my dance card, lipstick and powder were inside. Then I followed Jessica down the corridor to the lift where Tony, dressed as the Emperor of China, was waiting.

All the way down to the mezzanine floor, I worried. What if we didn't sell enough raffle tickets? And what about Charles? Tonight I would tell him my father had hidden his letters. He'd been right all along...

* * *

The ballroom, capable of seating 800 guests, overlooked the harbour. Pillars with Corinthian capitals lined the doors onto what was called the roof terrace. (Not the top of the multi-storey building, but the roof over the hotel's entrance.) I walked across the parquet floor, glistening after its daily polish, and glanced up at the slightly domed ceiling, painted rain-washed blue. On a podium at the far end, members of the Filipino swing band I'd arranged were tuning their instruments. I checked the table numbers and verified the names of the guests at each table, making sure Charles and I were placed together with Sofia and James. I'd put Papa at the grandees' table, with Jessica and Tony, the governor, the taipans of the trading companies and their wives. Everything was ready and, within minutes, people began filing in through the double doors.

'Isn't that Charles?' Jessica pointed towards a tall man next to the bar. He was dressed as an ancient Chinese warrior, wearing knee-high boots and leather armour. My heart skipped a beat; I quickly glanced around at the other guests. There were James and Sofia, in People's Liberation Army uniforms (how on earth?), standing slightly apart from everyone else.

I went up to them. 'I'm so glad you could come,' I said, squeezing Sofia's hand. 'Let's get ourselves something to drink then we should fill in our dance cards.'

'Already done,' James said. 'I'm not having my fiancée dance with anyone else.'

I tried to stop my mouth from falling open; I didn't succeed. 'Congratulations!' I embraced them both. 'When's the happy day?'

'Pretty soon, actually.' James grinned. 'Needs must, as they say.'

I stood back and stared at him. What did he mean? Realisation dawned and I smiled. 'Then let me congratulate you again.'

'We were wondering if you and Charles would be witnesses at the civil service,' James said. 'We've managed to get a special licence.'

'I'd be delighted. But you'll have to ask Charles yourself.'

'Ask me what?' Charles said, coming up and shaking hands with James.

'We're tying the knot. Kate has said she'll be a witness. We'd be honoured if you'd agree to be one as well.'

'With great pleasure. The City Hall, I presume?'

'Ten in the morning next Saturday.' James signalled a passing waiter carrying a tray of champagne cocktails.

I took a glass and lifted it to my lips, my eyes meeting Charles's. 'Have you got any space on your dance card?' he asked.

'I've only pencilled in Tony and my father.'

'Please may I have the honour of dancing with you for all the others? That dress is far too enticing.'

'Well, my darling, I can't dance every dance, you know. I must make sure our volunteers go round and sell all the tickets for the raffles. And I have to sell some myself.'

'Then let me help you.' He smiled.

* * *

During supper, Tony performed his role as Master of Ceremonies with aplomb, making the draws for the donated prizes between each course. The meal seemed to go on forever, but money had poured in and there would be enough to begin funding a children's clinic in one of the squatter areas. It was a small start, but a good one.

Papa, dressed as a mandarin, joined Tony on the podium. 'Ladies and gentlemen,' he said. 'I would like to propose a toast to my dear daughter, Kate, whose birthday it is tomorrow, and who has organised this marvellous ball with the help of Jessica Chambers. And thank you to all who've donated prizes. You've been hugely generous and I'm sure you'll agree a splendid time has been had by everyone. Raise your glasses! To Kate and to Jessica!'

There was a resounding cheer and my cheeks burned. Charles came up. 'This is my dance, I think. The last waltz.'

He twirled me closer and closer to the double doors until we were standing on the roof terrace... alone, the two of us. Then he kissed me. I felt as if I was swimming underwater as the kiss went on and on and on: delicious, sweet, tender and utterly perfect.

'It's midnight. Happy birthday, darling Kate.'

'Thank you.' I took a deep breath. 'There's something I have to tell you.' The sound of a ship's horn reverberated in the distance, and I stared at the neon lights reflecting in the harbour. I steeled myself. 'I found your letters. My father seems to have "forgotten" to give them to me.'

'What!' Charles frowned. 'He was almost civil when I had supper with you the other night, and I'd started to think the letters had simply got lost.'

'He'll apologise to you in person. It was very wrong of him. I told him that I loved you and wanted to be with you, come what may. He blathered on about how difficult my life would be and I said I didn't care.'

'I hope I haven't caused a rift between you,' Charles said, putting his arms around me again.

'Papa always spoiled me when I was a child.' I rubbed my

cheek against the leather armour of Charles's costume. 'It was as if he had to make up for Mama being the way she was, unable to show affection.' I breathed in Charles's citrus scent. 'Papa seemed genuinely sorry about the letters. He loves me and wants me to be happy. Only now does he understand how much my happiness is tied to you.'

'And mine to you,' Charles said, kissing me again. 'And mine to you.'

I kissed him back, drowning in him, melting with love and desire for him. He cupped my breasts and a tingle went through me as my nipples hardened. Then footsteps sounded; another couple had come onto the terrace. I shook myself and took Charles's hand. 'Let's see how James and Sofia are getting on,' I said, leading him back into the ballroom. 'Everyone seems to be giving them the cold shoulder.'

40

JAMES

James woke early on his first Monday as a married man. He glanced at Sofia, sleeping peacefully next to him, her luxurious hair spread over the pillow. He wrapped a tendril around his finger and lifted it to his lips, inhaling the vanilla scent of the Shalimar perfume she used. God, he was lucky. To think he'd once been ashamed to be seen with her. All because he'd wanted to fit in. He didn't need to fit in with the expatriates. He didn't give a flying fuck about most of them. He didn't need anyone or anything but his darling wife.

Sofia stretched and yawned. 'What time is it?'

'Time to get up and go to work. It's the tenth of October, the Double Tenth, don't forget. The nationalists will be celebrating the anniversary of the end of imperial rule. We need to establish our presence at the factory.'

'Are you expecting any trouble?'

'We did have a spot of bother after Mao declared his Republic ten days ago, and our workers flew their flags with communist slogans. They upset the right-wingers next door.'

'Why didn't you tell me this before?' She creased her brow.

'I've got the situation fully under control.' He gave her a reassuring smile.

'Are you sure?'

'On Friday, one of the girls told me she'd seen a flag with the slogan 'Long Live the Chinese Republic' flying across the road. Don't worry! I promptly told the right-wingers there to take it down. The wording was too political, I said, and it would stir up trouble with those who'd been celebrating the foundation of the People's Republic. I said it was inappropriate for a British colony.'

'I hope you haven't made things worse,' Sofia said, pouring him a coffee from the tray by their bed.

'Most of the locals have no interest whatsoever in politics. Their allegiances are more a way of affirming they belong to a specific community. There's absolutely nothing to worry about, sweetheart.'

'If you say so, James,' she said. But from her expression and lack of a smile, she appeared unconvinced. Unease spread through him.

* * *

They arrived at the factory, and James made a tour of the floor. The young single women, the bulk of their labour force, were sitting in rows bent over their looms. They were paid at piece rather than time-rate, so it was in their interests to get on with their work.

He went to the office and helped Sofia with the correspondence... letters to cotton suppliers in the United States and Mexico.

The phone rang and Sofia picked up the receiver. She was speaking Chinese, her tone agitated. She put down the receiver.

'That was my uncle. There's a rumour you've told the nationalists not to celebrate.'

'Not true at all. I just didn't want them to provoke the communists.'

Another shrill came from the telephone, and Sofia picked up again. She passed the receiver to James.

It was Special Branch. 'Gerry. What can I do for you?'

'Word is the Triads are agitating the nationalists next door to your factory. The police are sending backup for you.'

Shouts echoed, and James went to the window. Below, a crowd of men and women were milling around yelling slogans. His breath caught. 'Come downstairs,' he said to Sofia. 'We'd better make sure all the doors are locked.'

They rushed to the factory entrance. But it was too late. The mob was forcing its way inside. The women who worked on the looms were cowering on the floor, their arms over their heads.

James's ears pounded. If only he'd learnt to speak Cantonese, he would tell the rabble a thing or two. 'This is outrageous,' he shouted. 'Go away! You've got no business to be here.'

Pure hatred shone on their faces. A young woman, black hair in a pigtail, bared her teeth. A burly bald man screamed his rage, spittle flying, the whites of his eyes blazing. The group pushed and shoved their way towards James. He raised his fists to fight them off. Then more people came up from behind.

Someone grabbed him and tied his hands behind his back. The mob pushed him down on the floor, and he struggled against the bindings. A skinny young man slapped him on the face, unleashing a stream of foul language; that much he understood. He fought against the cords. The youth slapped him again, harder. Blood trickled from the corner of his mouth.

More rioters burst through the doors and started hurling Molotov cocktails into the air. Explosions went off all over the factory. The looms caught fire. The first group appeared distracted by what was going on. Keeping his eye on them, James inched his way over to where Sofia had curled into a ball by the wall. He had to protect her and their child.

He threw himself over her, covering her body with his. Something struck him below his mouth. A sharp pain pierced his neck. Then he was falling, falling, falling into the darkness...

41

SOFIA

Sofia opened her eyes; there was blood everywhere. Blood covered her face, her arms and her chest.

Holy Mary, Mother of God!

James lay slumped to the side, a gurgling sound coming from him.

Sweet Jesus!

A glass shard stuck out of his neck. Blood was spurting from the wound.

Please God, let him be all right!

Hands shaking, she pulled off her blouse and clasped it around the glass to stem the flow. Her fingers were cold... so, so cold. James's eyes were closed and his face had gone white. She looked around for help.

The rioters had already run off.

Cowards!

Smoke billowed from the looms. The factory girls were still cowering with their arms over their heads. The sound of sirens came from outside, and her teeth chattered uncontrollably.

Four policemen burst through the door – a European and three Chinese. The *gwailo* came up and lifted James's wrist, then shook his head slowly. Sofia sat back and let out a keening wail.

'No, no, no!'

The policeman barked orders to his men to help the girls leave the factory. He handed Sofia his jacket, then lifted James. She glanced down; she was only wearing her bra. She quickly covered herself.

'We have to leave the building,' the policeman said. 'The fire's taking hold, but we've radioed for assistance. Where's the cotton stored? That stuff is extremely flammable.'

The policeman's words seemed to be coming from the end of a long tunnel. What was he asking her? She couldn't think...

Outside, a crowd had gathered and the policemen were setting up a safety cordon. Sofia staggered to the pavement.

Where was James?

More sirens wailed. An ambulance and two fire engines pulled up. Sofia stared around. She couldn't see James. 'Where's my husband?' she cried out, clutching at her blood-stained skirt.

A nurse draped a blanket around her shoulders, led her to the ambulance, and sat her down before going to a water boiler. She returned to Sofia with a cup of hot sweet tea. Sofia swallowed the warm liquid, and her tears, frozen until then, gushed freely. She cried for the brave man who'd died saving her and their child. She cried for a life cut short in its prime. She cried for her baby who wouldn't know its father. And she cried for herself.

The nurse spoke to her in Cantonese and patted her back. Sofia sobbed until she had no tears left. Lifting her chin, she could see the stretcher at the side of the ambulance holding a body wrapped in a sheet. *James.*

'We'll take you to Kowloon Hospital,' the nurse said. 'When the doctor has examined you, you'll need somewhere to rest and someone to look after you. Do you have anyone who can take care of you while you get over the shock?'

Sofia thought for a moment. Uncle? She would phone him from the hospital, but she wouldn't go to his flat. He'd installed his mistress there and she wouldn't be welcome. And some of this was Uncle's fault. If James hadn't got involved with him, he'd still be alive. Guilt flooded through her; James had died because he loved her, not because of Uncle.

There was only one person Sofia could call on. A most unlikely person, but something told her that person would comfort her and make her feel safe.

* * *

It was early evening by the time she rang the bell at Kate's home. She'd gone back to the hotel to change and had cried again when she'd caught sight of James's comb by the side of the basin, with a few of his hairs still in it. She'd lain on his side of the bed and had hugged his pillow, which still had the scent of Old Spice. If she'd stayed there, she'd have gone mad.

A servant opened the gate and ushered her into the Wolseleys' sitting room. Within minutes, Kate was by her side. 'I'm so relieved to see you,' Kate said, leading her to the sofa and sitting her down. 'I heard the news on the radio and I've been trying to find out how to locate you. Please stay here. My father and I rattle around in this big old place. I'm so sorry, Sofia. I can't begin to imagine what you must be going through.'

'What about your father? Won't he mind?'

'Leave him to me. He's out tonight at a dinner party, so it's just the two of us. You don't have to talk if you don't want to. Oh dear, I didn't mean to make you cry. Here, have my handkerchief.'

Sobbing, Sofia described the assault on the factory, and Kate listened quietly. Then she told Kate about the hospital. Kate asked about the baby, and she said her child wasn't in any danger. She was grateful Kate didn't question her about her plans. She needed time to think. In the meantime, she was secure in this sumptuous mansion. Leo wouldn't be able to get at her here.

* * *

Two days later, Sofia was standing in the visitation room of the funeral parlour. James was laid out in front of her. Had he known, at that last moment of consciousness, he was going to die? One life given for two saved. James wouldn't have thought twice.

Tears streaming, she shivered in the air-conditioned atmosphere. It was freezing, of course; it needed to be. No stinking corpses in this sanitary place. She took her gloves from her handbag, but they made little difference.

James was covered in a white silk sheet that had been pulled up to his ears, to hide his mortal wound and the signs of an autopsy carried out under police orders. His fine-looking face was almost unscathed, just a small cut above the left eye. The glass shard from the Molotov cocktail had shattered on his chin and had severed the jugular vein in his neck. She reached down and touched his icy cheek, kissed him on the forehead and whispered, 'Goodbye, my one and only love.'

It was hard to shake off the feeling of unreality. How could this be James lying there? He had been so full of life, so wonderful and so, so gallant. How could fate have dealt him such a blow? It wasn't fair. He was in his mid-twenties... Far too young to die.

* * *

The Wolseleys' driver took Sofia to the Victoria business district. The Daimler meandered through the usual motley collection of trams, cars and rickshaws and pulled up outside Alexandra House. She got out and rode up to the fifth floor in the lift, then strode down the hallway. The receptionist showed her to a meeting room where Charles Pearce, James's recently appointed solicitor, was waiting for her.

'It's really quite simple,' Charles said. 'James has left you his stake in Leung's Textiles and all his chattels. He has also willed you his yacht, *Jade Princess*.'

Everything was exactly as he'd said it would be when Uncle had handed over his shares in the business. Could it only have been last month? All had been done according to the book; she would have security for herself and the child.

'I've started the insurance claim,' Charles said. 'Thankfully, the fire brigade managed to save the building. It's just the looms that need replacing.'

'Thank you.'

'Did you see the newspapers this morning? The government is launching a full investigation.' He picked up the paper and read: '"It is clear that the tragedy isn't attributable primarily to the crowd excitement, which might have been engendered by the Double Tenth celebrations. The attack was clearly fomented by criminals."'

'My half-brother is linked to the Triads, you know. I strongly suspect him of being behind James's death, but I won't be able to prove it.'

'The police will find out something that can be proved, surely?'

'I wouldn't count on it. Leo is very clever. He'll have covered his tracks.'

'You know him better than anyone, of course.'

'And I hope I'll be able to live in peace from him,' she said with a sigh.

* * *

James's funeral was held the next day at St John's Cathedral; the church was almost full. Dressed in black with a veil over her face, Sofia sat next to Uncle and Kate. James's catafalque appeared, covered in white orchids, with Tony Chambers, Arnaud de Montreuil, Charles Pearce and Henry Wolseley walking alongside. Everyone got to their feet and the men placed James's coffin before the altar.

Sofia stood as straight as a reed, her head upright, keeping a tight rein on her emotions. She wouldn't let her grief show; if she did, she wouldn't be able to control herself. She could feel James's spirit watching her; he would know how she felt as he lingered between this world and the next. She wanted him to be proud of her.

It was cool in the church, the air stirred by fans attached to long poles hanging from the ceiling. Their whirring almost drowned out the sound of the traffic changing gear to climb the steep road outside. She looked up at the stained-glass windows that had replaced those removed by the Japanese during the war. The window in the east showed Christ on the cross with his mother and Mary gazing up at him, placed there as a memorial to those who had suffered during the occupation and to those who had given their lives.

Everyone got to their feet and she picked up her hymn book. "'The Lord's my shepherd, I'll not want.'" She joined in, clasping the back of the pew in front of her. The singing came to an end, and Sofia knelt and prayed. She was out of practice and could only think of the Lord's Prayer. The service continued, and she went through the mechanical responses she'd practised in her childhood; they came back to her like an often-repeated rhyme, the Anglican Service remarkably like the Roman Catholic, although the latter had usually been in Latin.

The dean said a prayer of farewell, entrusting James to God. 'We will now proceed in cortege to Happy Valley.'

An hour later, Sofia stood in front of the group of people gathered around the open grave. She'd deliberately distanced herself from Kate and Charles. This was her cross to bear and she'd do so with dignity. James's spirit was fading into the next world now; she could sense it.

The dean's cassock swayed gently in the breeze. 'We therefore commit James's body to the ground, earth to earth, ashes to ashes, dust to dust, in the sure and certain hope of the Resurrection to eternal life.'

Sofia stuffed the corner of her handkerchief into her mouth to stop herself from screaming.

* * *

The next day, she visited the factory and surveyed the destruction. Her workforce was sweeping up the mess made by the damaged looms. The girls came up and commiserated with her.

In the office, she sat in front of her desk and determination surged through her. She would build the business up again as a memorial to James. Leo would have to hand over her inheritance next week, and she would use some of it to buy a flat. She couldn't presume on the Wolseleys any longer, nor did she want to; she valued her independence.

Kate had battled her father to let her stay with them, reminding him she was James's wife and he couldn't turn his back on her. Mr Wolseley had been stiff and resistant at first, but he'd mellowed as the days had gone by, and now it seemed he couldn't do enough for her. As for Kate, Sofia had come to realise the Englishwoman had an inner strength that would help her overcome the obstacles to her happiness. It was obvious Kate and Charles belonged together, and the sooner Henry Wolseley got used to the idea the better.

42

KATE

I hugged Sofia. 'I'll miss you terribly,' I said. And I would. I'd grown extremely fond of her. 'Make sure you keep in touch.'

'I will.' Sofia got into her taxi. 'You must come and visit soon.' Through her uncle's connections, Sofia had managed to find a flat in the mid-levels. She'd told me that she would apply for a British passport as soon as possible. Her marriage to James meant that she could claim nationality. She wanted to sever all ties with her family in Macau.

As I stepped into the hall, the telephone rang and I picked up the receiver.

'How do you fancy a spin out to Stanley?' Charles said. 'It's a beautiful day.'

I still hadn't visited the cemetery; I'd told Charles at James's funeral that I hadn't been able to face it, and he'd squeezed my hand in sympathy. 'I don't know if I'm ready to go back there yet.'

'I think it's time. Come on, darling. It will do you good.'

I changed into a pair of navy slacks and a white linen blouse, then went to tell Papa where I was going. He looked up at me as I stepped into his study. 'Charles is driving me to Stanley,' I said. 'I'll take some flowers for Mama's grave.'

'Would you, my dear? The ones I put there last week will need replacing, and it will save me having to do it tomorrow. Your young man is turning out to be a pleasant surprise, I must say. A very pleasant surprise.'

'So he's a proper chap after all, is he?' I tilted my head.

Papa had the grace to look flustered. 'His handling of Jimmy's debacle and the way he brought you home after the typhoon certainly impressed me. And I apologised to him about the letters, didn't I?'

Papa had invited Charles for dinner last week, just the two of them. I wished I could have been a fly on the wall. Neither of them had told me much about what they'd said, other than the fact that Papa had agreed that I could see Charles openly.

'Thank you for that, and for making Sofia so welcome in the end. I don't know what she would have done otherwise.'

Papa cleared his throat. 'Nonsense! I like Sofia. She'll go far, mark my words!'

* * *

The nearer we drove to Stanley, the more my nerves jangled. Charles was right, though – I had to do this; I'd bottled it up too long.

'I know what you're thinking, my love,' Charles said. 'You're strong enough. Believe me.'

He parked in front of a small temple on the other side of the village.

'What are we doing here?' I asked, surprised.

Charles led me up a small flight of steps to the portal. Inside, it was cool and dark. Incense perfumed the air and, in the dull light of myriad joss sticks, a glass pane shimmered on the far wall. 'Come closer!'

'How bizarre!' Behind the glass was a tiger skin. I read the notice fixed to the left: *This tiger weighed two hundred and forty pounds and was seventy-three inches long and three feet high. It was shot by an Indian policeman in front of Stanley police station in the year of 1942.*

'I wonder why it's here...'

Charles held me close. 'Well, I think this is a fitting resting place, don't you?'

'Yes, I do.' I glanced at the blackened face of the statue of Tin Hau, in an alcove behind offerings of fruit. There were fresh flowers on an altar in the centre of the temple. It had been good to come here. The tiger had brought me closer to Charles in Stanley. And the beast was working its enchantment on me even now. 'I'm ready. Let's go to the cemetery!'

Charles drove through the village, past the police station and the school, and parked below the path leading up to the graveyard.

I reached for the bouquet of purple orchids and my rucksack on the back seat. We went up a flight of newly built steps with grassy slopes on either side. Mama's grave was at the top. The roughly hewn headstone had been replaced by a proper marble plinth.

Kneeling, I removed the dried-out chrysanthemums from the vase at the base, then filled it with water from the bottle I'd stashed in my bag. I put my hand on the cool stone and whispered, 'I'm here. I haven't forgotten you. I'm so sorry I haven't come before now.' I looked up and caught Charles watching me, love in his eyes. Getting to my feet, I dusted down my slacks. 'Let's pay our respects to Bob.'

A line of headstones with the names of those whose final

resting place was unknown had been placed here after the war. Beyond, we found Bob's grave and bowed our heads. I remembered the last time I'd seen him.

There was a question I'd been meaning to ask Charles.

'Did the Japanese torture you when you were in the prison?'

'No,' he said quietly. 'But I heard screams. Those poor policemen...'

I took his hand. 'Thank you for bringing me here, my darling. It hasn't been as bad as I thought.'

'They say we should always confront our fears, don't they? Look! There's our orchid tree. It's still here. Shall we sit for a bit?'

We sat side by side. Charles put his arms around me, and I lifted my face to receive his kiss. The rich, heady fragrance of the Bauhinia flowers filled my nostrils. I plucked a heart-shaped leaf and crushed it between my fingers.

'I love you so much, Kate,' he said, looking into my eyes. 'What happened to James has made me realise we have to take every chance of happiness we're given. Who knows how much time we have left?'

I studied the headstones and nodded. Then I gazed at his face. His hair was in his eyes. I reached up and brushed it back. 'When we're married, and only if you agree, of course, I'd like us to adopt Mei Ling. Oh, and I want Ah Ho to come and work for us.'

'Is that a proposal, Kate?'

'Yes.'

'Then, I accept.' He stroked my cheek, his fingers warm against my skin.

He kissed me again, more possessively this time, and I met his passion with my own. It had always been Charles. Since the first moment I saw him. I thought about James and Sofia. Charles was right: we had to take every chance of happiness we were given, but also pay it back tenfold. 'And Mei Ling?'

'She can be the first of our children.'

'How many shall we have?'

'That's entirely up to you. As many as you like, and of course Ah Ho can be their amah.'

The leaves of the orchid tree sighed in the breeze. I rested my head on his shoulder, twirled my jade bangle, and contemplated the sampans at anchor in the bay below.

ACKNOWLEDGEMENTS

I continue to be hugely grateful for all the support I receive from the entire team at Boldwood Books.

I would also like to thank the following people:

Ann Bennett, Tony Fyler, Safia Moore and Jo Ozkan, my talented fellow writers, for their helpful comments on early drafts.

John Hudspith for his excellent input.

My family: my late parents and grandparents, Veronica, Douglas, Doris and Vernon, whose lives inspired this novel; my brother, Diarmuid, and my sister, Clodagh, for their encouragement.

Victor, my husband, for his love and support. Our son, Paul, and his wife, Lili, for their help with technology.

Last, but not least, I thank you, dear reader, for buying this book and reading it.

AUTHOR'S NOTE

I was privileged to have grown up in Hong Kong during the post-war era, and I hope that my personal experience of a time and place which no longer exist has lent an authenticity to my writing. *Daughter of War* is, however, a work of fiction. All the characters are products of my imagination. My mother had an amah, Ah Ho, who looked after me when I was a child; I loved her dearly, but the Ah Ho of my novel is simply inspired by her.

My grandparents, Doris and Vernon Walker, were interned in Stanley. I remember my grandmother telling me Ah Ho's first words to her on liberation, which I have used in *Daughter of War*. Gran and Grandpa didn't like to talk about their harrowing time in the camp. Like Flora with Henry, Doris was caught nursing Vernon during a bout of TB when the Japanese attacked. My mother, Veronica, had been evacuated to Australia. Between the ages of fourteen and eighteen she learnt to cope without her parents, an experience which affected her for the rest of her life.

When my grandparents were finally liberated, they were so thin they resembled walking skeletons, and both died relatively young due to post-starvation-related illnesses. Their lives were similar to Henry's and Flora's, in that they lived on the Peak in a house with nine servants and shared some of the colonial attitudes of my expatriate characters; however, that's as far as the similarities go.

Family stories did inspire parts of *Daughter of War*. My father, Douglas Bland, was an officer in The Chinese Maritime Customs from 1946 to 1948, making charts and chasing smugglers up and down the South China Coast. He told me of an incident when a young man had been tied to a junk, and also about a bribery attempt. James and Sofia's story is not that of my parents, however. Dad was a businessman and a prominent Hong Kong artist.

Mum was a teacher like Kate, and shared some of her physical characteristics, but that's all. I wanted to take a girl from my mother's background and have her fall in love with a man whom my grandparents would have considered unsuitable. Hong Kong today is a different place to the old colony, and mixed marriages have become commonplace. I like to think Kate and Charles would have been at the forefront of that change.

As I said, this is not a family history; it's a romance. All the locations in my story are real, however, as are the events that took place in Stanley. I have used George Wright Nooth's involvement with smuggling chocolate fortified with vitamins into the prison as a reason for Charles to fall under the suspicion of the Japanese.

A ship, *Lisbon Maru*, taking POWs to Japan, was sunk by the Americans, but that happened in 1942, not 1945. I have also taken the liberty of bringing forward in time the violence in Tsuen Wan, caused by escalating tensions between pro-Nationalist and pro-Communist factions. There wasn't a Typhoon Wendy in Hong Kong in 1949; I have based my typhoon on the notorious Typhoon Wanda.

The children's home is inspired by Miss Dibden's Shatin Babies' Home. James's hapless dragon boat race is taken from the first competition between expatriates and locals, recounted by Denis Bray. James and Sofia's dinner on the floating restaurant was inspired by the one in *A Many Splendoured Thing*. And K C Leung's attempt to steal Leo's gold was based on the world's first air piracy, an attempted skyjack that went disastrously wrong in Hong Kong on 16 July 1948.

With respect to the spelling of Chinese names, I've used the orthography that was current in the 1940s.

The following books have provided me with inspiration and information:

Alan Birch & Martin Cole, *Captive Christmas*
Martin Booth, *Golden Boy*
Denis Bray, *Hong Kong Metamorphosis*
Christopher Briggs, *The Sea Gate*
Jean Gittins, *Stanley: Behind Barbed Wire*
Vicky Lee, *Being Eurasian*
Tim Luard, *Escape from Hong Kong*
F.D. Ommanney, *Fragrant Harbour*
Gwen Priestwood, *Through Japanese Barbed Wire*
Han Suyin, *A Many Splendoured Thing*
George Wright-Nooth, *Prisoner of the Turnip Heads*

ABOUT THE AUTHOR

Siobhan Daiko writes powerful and sweeping historical fiction set in Italy during the second World War, with strong women at its heart. She now lives near Venice, having been a teacher in Wales for many years.

Sign up to Siobhan Daiko's mailing list for news, competitions and updates on future books.

Visit Siobhan's website: www.siobhandaiko.org

Follow Siobhan on social media here:

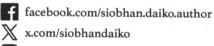

facebook.com/siobhan.daiko.author

x.com/siobhandaiko

instagram.com/siobhandaiko_books

ALSO BY SIOBHAN DAIKO

The Girl from Venice

The Girl from Portofino

The Girl from Bologna

The Tuscan Orphan

Daughters of Tuscany

Daughter of War

Daughter of Hong Kong